The Pickup

NIKKI ASH

Dedication

To Brittany—for telling me my book sucked, making me cry, and convincing me to rewrite the entire story! (Okay, maybe not the entire story...) You might be an asshole, but you're my asshole. <3

Prologue

NICK

Twenty years old

I've just gotten back to my dorm, and I'm fucking exhausted. I'm ready to take a hot shower then go see my girlfriend, Samantha. I throw my gym bag on the bed and grab a change of clothes and a towel. Stripping out of my sweatpants and shirt, I turn the water on as hot as it can go and wait for it to heat up. Once I can see the fog filling the bathroom, I get in. Standing with my back toward the hot water, I let it rain down on my sore muscles. Between sitting on a crowded, uncomfortable-as-fuck bus for the ten-hour trip to and from D.C. for our first football game of the season, the lumpy king-size bed I had to share in the hotel with my teammate Killian, and the two-hour meeting I had to attend once we returned to go over the game tapes, a hot shower is exactly what I need.

I grab my shampoo and wash my hair, then squirt some

body wash into my hands. As I scrub the dirty feeling from the nasty bus off my skin, I try to think of everything I need to get done. With it being the beginning of my junior year at North Carolina University, it feels like my to-do list is never ending. I need to pick up the textbook I ordered for the British Literature class I'm taking, go by the library to see if I can check out *The Hobbit* and *The Neverending Story* for my Fantasy Lit class... Shit! I also need to go by the writing lab to schedule the required tutoring session. Some days it feels like there aren't enough hours in the day, and today is definitely one of those days.

After rinsing off, I get dressed and head to the writing lab. "Excuse me, my name is Nicholas Shaw. I'm taking Professor Hughes's creative writing course, and he said we have to schedule a tutoring session."

"Yep! Let me pull up your name. What's your student ID number?" I give her my ten-digit number, and she types it into the computer. "Hmm...it seems you're no longer enrolled in that course." She types some more on her keyboard. "It actually shows you've dropped the course and switched your major." She prints something out and hands it to me. I read over it, and sure enough, my degree seeking states business and not English Literature. My classes are all basic accounting and business management shit. What the hell? I just picked my damn major not even two weeks ago when I met with my advisor.

"Okay, thank you. I'll get this figured out." I fold up the paper and put it into my back pocket and start heading toward Samantha's dorm, furious as hell. There's only one person who would do this. I hit his name on my cell phone, and not even one ring later, my dad answers.

"Dad, we need to talk."

"Nick, I'm glad you called. I saw your game, and I'm not the only one. There's chatter from several teams. If you continue to play the way you did yesterday, you'll be entering the draft this year instead of next, and most likely go in as a first round—"

"Did you change my major?" I ask, cutting him off.

"What?" my dad responds incredulously. "Did you hear what I said? There's a damn good chance you will be drafted this year."

"Yeah, I heard you. But I thought I was going to stay in college all four years so I can graduate with my degree."

"We talked about this, Nick," my dad says, frustration evident in his tone. "Football comes first. Your coach called and told me that you asked for permission to leave your practices early this semester because you need to attend some writing bullshit."

"Writing lab." I sigh. Since I was little, I've always felt a pull toward literature. When I'm not reading, I'm writing. Horror, Mystery, Fantasy, Nonfiction, I don't care what it is. When I was a kid and didn't really believe I stood a chance at playing pro ball, my dream was to one day delve into the world of books. My second grade teacher gave me a writing journal, and that year I filled the entire thing with story after story. Growing up, I read everything from *The Boxcar Children* and *Harry Potter* to *1984*. As an adult, I'll give anything a try. From James Patterson to Stephen King. Hell, I've even given Nicholas Sparks a go-round. I'm not sure, if given the opportunity, what I would do in the field—maybe write or edit. All I know is I love books.

Not that it matters at this point. I'm not being given the opportunity, and I won't be in the future. How many football players do you know of that have written a novel? And I'm not talking about the millions of autobiographies. Exactly...

"I don't give a shit what it is!" my dad yells. "We talked about this. You're majoring in business." I stop walking and sit down on the bench outside of Samantha's dorm. With my face in my hands, I close my eyes and take a deep breath.

"Does it even matter what I'm majoring in if I'm not going to graduate anyway?"

"It does when you're having to cut out of practice early." I want to argue with my dad, but I don't. It's pointless. It was stupid of me to sign up for those courses in the first place. When I met with my advisor, I thought maybe my choice of major would go under my dad's radar, and truth be told, had the creative writing class not required a tutoring session at the same time as practice, I might have gotten away with it. But it does, and I didn't.

"What if I can save that class for another semester?" I ask as a last ditch effort to convince my dad to let me keep my major as English Lit. When he sighs, I think for a moment that maybe he's going to relent. *How stupid am I?*

"Nick, you go to North Carolina for football. Your scholarship covers your classes and dorm. I pay for everything else. Your books, your food, your car, insurance, cell phone, clothes. Are you prepared to pay for all of that?" He already knows I can't. Not if I want to graduate debt free. What if football doesn't work out? Then I'll be stuck with loans, and who's to say I'd even be approved for a loan big enough to cover everything. And getting a job is out of the question. I can't even attend a damn tutoring session twice a week.

Without waiting for an answer, my dad continues, "Besides, an English degree is a waste of time and money. I went to law school, and so did your grandfather. The men in our family don't major in English," he scoffs. "Your coach has notified your professors that you'll be starting your new classes on Monday, and they know to give you time to get caught up. I need to go, I have a client calling. Don't forget we're having a dinner at the house for your mother's birthday next Sunday." And with that, he hangs up.

Just as I'm about to stand, my phone rings. Surprise, surprise, it's my mother. I consider not answering, but figure I might as well get it over with so she won't continue to call me while I'm hanging out with Samantha.

"Mother."

"Nicholas, please tell me your majoring in English was a joke." C'mon, who the hell picks a major as a joke? Clearly her question is rhetorical, but fuck...

"Yeah, Mom," I say dryly. "It was a joke." *And so were all of the books I had my nose stuck in throughout my entire childhood...*

"And what exactly would you do with that degree? What if, God forbid, you got injured? What would you do with a degree in English?"

Oh, I don't know...maybe write a book...work in publishing...maybe I could teach English...Of course, I don't say any of that to her. Speaking to her is the same as speaking to my father. A waste of time and energy.

"According to Dad, I won't even be getting my degree."

"I heard!" she exclaims. "Can you believe it? Not many football players get drafted their junior year. I told all the women at the country club today. Helen Grotowski, of course, tried to trump my news with news of her son's early admittance to law school. But I heard from Bertha Stein her husband had to make a rather large donation to the school." I sit back on the bench and close my eyes, knowing my mom won't be done gossiping any time soon. Once she starts, she can go on for hours.

I grew up in Piermont, a small town in North Carolina. It's split down the middle by a set of railroad tracks. On one side is where my dad grew up, in a wealthy gated community. On the other side is where my mom grew up—in a rundown trailer park. My parents met when my mom was eighteen and my dad was twenty-five and fresh out of law school. He had just moved back to Piermont and had begun working at Shaw Management—a sports management agency my grandfather started. He met my mom when she was waitressing at a restaurant he stopped into one night after a meeting ran late. They hit it off immediately. While my grandparents weren't thrilled about my dad and her dating, she apparently adapted into my father's life quickly, and soon she was the perfect Stepford wife—although, I'm pretty sure her getting knocked up by mistake has something to do with why he married her. I also think he loved that he was able to mold her into what he wanted her to be. I imagine when you come from nothing, if given the opportunity, you'd do whatever it takes to become something.

"...so then I told Bertha that if Sherry plans to come to

my birthday dinner with her mother, she needs to leave that good for nothing boyfriend of hers at home. All those tattoos. It's a disgrace. I can't believe she's dating him."

"Hey mom," I say, cutting in before she can continue. "I need to get going. I'm sorry. I'll see you Sunday, though, for dinner."

"And will you be bringing Samantha?" If my mother had it her way, Samantha would be out of the picture. While she approves of her coming from wealth, she hates that Samantha wants to work. According to my mother, women belong in the home. Which is ironic since my mom was home my entire childhood, yet I spent more time with my nanny than with both of my parents combined.

"She'll be there, Mom. Please be nice." She lets out an annoyed huff but agrees. We say goodbye then hang up. Standing, I take one more calming breath before I head into Samantha's dorm. We've been dating for the last year, and she's a junior like I am. She's majoring in business and planning to work for her father's company after she gets her MBA. Hence, the reason my mom isn't thrilled about us dating.

When I get to Samantha's door, I wiggle the doorknob, and when it doesn't open, I knock. I hear shuffling and then she opens the door slightly. Her hair is messy, and her lips are puffy. She looks like she always does when we finish having sex.

"Nick! Wh-what are you doing here? I thought you had a game."

"I did have a game…yesterday. We got back a couple hours ago, so I came to see you." Samantha's features contort into a pained expression, and I'm slowly putting the pieces together. Pushing the door open, I walk into her room to find Jesse, a friend of mine, shirtless and sitting on Samantha's bed.

"Are you guys serious?" I ask even though it's a dumb question. There's a fucking condom wrapper on the nightstand. It doesn't take a genius to figure out what the two of them were doing.

"I'm sorry, Nick, it's just that you're always playing football, and even when you're not, you never have any time to hang out." I thought she understood how important football is to me. It's not like I suddenly started playing. I've been playing since the day we met. *Hell, I've been playing pretty much since the day I could walk.* I'm attending NCU on a football scholarship, which means on top of taking a full load of classes, I have practice every day and games every weekend during season.

"How long has this been going on?"

"Since the beginning of summer. You're just always so busy and—"

"And instead of talking to me about it, you decided to fuck my friend?" I yell before I look over to Jesse. "Way to have my back, *bro.*" I cut across the room and deck him straight in his face. He falls backward onto the floor, then stands but doesn't attempt to retaliate.

"I swear, we didn't mean for it to happen," Samantha cries, but I'm already halfway out the door.

"Spare me. As far as I'm concerned, you're both fucking dead to me," I shout before I walk out of her room, slamming the door behind me.

I get back to my dorm and see my friend Celeste is waiting for me. Growing up, Celeste was always around. When my mom left the trailer park, she left everyone from her old life behind, except for her best friend, Beatrice. Beatrice and my mom grew up next door to each other— two peas in a pod. The only difference between them is while my mom got knocked up by my dad and crossed over the train tracks into a life of luxury, Beatrice fell in love with a biker in a motorcycle club. The story I've heard is that he told her he had something to take care of and promised he would return. Over the years, Beatrice had the opportunity to be with several wealthy men, thanks to my mother, but she's chosen to pine after Celeste's dad, hoping one day he will come back. Seventeen years later, and he still hasn't returned.

For whatever reason, she doesn't seem to care that she's living in a trailer park, and Celeste resents the hell out of her for that. She doesn't understand why her mom would choose love over money, especially choosing to love a man who left and never returned. Her mom might be content living in a trailer park and pining after the love of her life, but Celeste isn't. While she's sixteen and still in high school, because she looks a lot older, she only gives her attention to wealthy guys. Her goal is to marry a man who is the opposite of what her mother fell in love with—wealthy and emotionless. Her plan is to show her mom that money, and the comfort it brings, is more important than love.

Celeste is beautiful, and she knows it. She's five-ten with jet black hair and big black eyes. She has a model's body— thin and leggy with minimal curves, but a decent rack—and she wants a modeling career. I don't doubt one day she'll have it. She's determined. She's already been in several commercials and ads for local stores and such.

"I saw you play on TV. Good first game." She's sitting on my bed in a pair of tiny shorts and a low-cut shirt, despite it being chilly outside. "Did you go see Samantha?" Her voice is smug, which means she already knows.

"Yeah, I caught her cheating with Jesse."

"Don't worry...I won't say I told you so." She lays back against the headboard. "I saw them last night at the club all over each other. Smart girl, Jesse's loaded."

"Whatever, Celeste." I sit on my bed next to her. Between Samantha cheating and my dad fucking up my major, I'm annoyed as hell and not in the mood for Celeste's shit. Some days, despite our four year age difference, she's my best friend; other days, she's more like the annoying little sister I never had. "And why the hell were you even at a club? You're sixteen years old."

"It's called a fake ID. And even if I didn't have one, every bouncer in North Carolina thinks I'm of age." She rolls her eyes. "Don't change the subject. Everyone knows Jesse got his trust fund at eighteen, and he has no problem spending his money on whoever he's fucking. Maybe you should come with a warning label: I'm rich but broke." She cackles at her dumb joke. She's right, though. My dad is rich, but I'm not, which means that while my parents have always provided for me, I don't have a stuffed bank account I can access anytime I want. Hell, even after being married to my dad for over twenty years, my mom still doesn't have her own bank account. She might spend her days socializing at the country club, dining at expensive restaurants, going to the spa, or shopping for shit she will never use or wear, but it's all done with my dad's credit cards. Henry Shaw lives for control. Giving my mother or me money would mean losing a slice of that control, and that's definitely not happening.

In all honesty, I've never really cared. I have everything money can buy. I drive a nice-ass Audi A4, courtesy of my father. I have unlimited funds for food and clothes. My schooling is paid for. What I don't have is money to spend on women, and apparently, that's all women seem to care about. All through high school and college, it's been the same shit with every female. They hear I'm rich, so they expect me to be their meal ticket. They hear I'm the quarterback, so they want to latch on to my status. I'm so fucking sick of all the fakeness.

"I refuse to believe money is all people in this world care about. I'm going to find someone who couldn't care less about money, and when I do, I'm going to love the hell out of her." Celeste cackles again and shakes her head. Since we were old enough to understand the difference between our living situations, we've had an ongoing debate. She believes money trumps love, and I believe money destroys it. My parents have a ton of money and they're miserable as fuck.

"You've always been so naïve, Nick. This isn't some fairytale. This is real life. Love is nothing more than a wasted emotion. One that only gets in the way of the important things like nice houses and cars and clothes…and eating at expensive restaurants! Oh! And vacations! And don't get me started on social status…"

"There should be more to life than all that." I grab the

remote and switch the television on to Sunday football. "Money doesn't buy happiness. It just buys shit."

"You wouldn't understand," Celeste says, her voice serious. "Because you've never been without money. You've never had to worry about the electric or water being shut off. If you want to go to Colorado to ski, you go."

I don't even know why I bother to argue with her. It's always the same shit. I'm rich and my life is perfect…She's poor and her life sucks…

Celeste continues, "You'll see. All those broken hearts you've had because you keep thinking with your heart. Once you're in the NFL and making bank, you won't have to worry about all that. I guarantee once you're making your own money, girls like Samantha will be begging to be with you, but it won't be your heart they're after."

"They can come after me, but that doesn't mean I'll be with them."

"Let's be real here, Nick. Those that are poor, want to be rich, and those that are rich, only want to be richer. Plus, you've had how many failed relationships in high school and college? You should just quit while you're ahead."

I turn my head to Celeste and glare at her. "When I throw a shitty pass, I don't quit playing. I keep throwing until I get the pass right."

Celeste laughs. "You know what they say the definition of insanity is? Doing the same thing over and over again and expecting different results."

"You're such a bitch." I laugh, and Celeste hits me in the face with my pillow. "I'm going to find *her*…One day I'll find a girl who'll love me and won't want shit from me other than me."

"Okay…how about we make a pact?" She smirks. "If you haven't found love by the time you turn thirty, you'll admit I'm right. Money makes the world go round."

"Okay…" There's got to be more to this.

"And we get married."

At this, I crack up laughing. "Wasn't that in a movie once?"

"So?" She hits me with another one of my pillows.

"I'm pretty sure it didn't work out for them…"

Celeste rolls her eyes. "It was a movie. What do you have to lose? You have ten years to prove me wrong."

"Are you serious? You and me get married?" I rake my eyes down her body. Sure, Celeste is hot, in a Victoria Secret model sort of way, but she's not exactly my type. I prefer my women with a little more T and A if you catch my drift.

"Don't give me that look. I'm not attracted to you, either. If I haven't found a rich guy yet, we get married and do it my way. Not for love, but for money. I mean, c'mon…just about every NFL player you know has a model attached to his arm."

Before I can respond, my best friend, roommate, and teammate, Killian Blake, walks into our dorm, slamming the door behind him.

"What's up?" he asks, throwing his gym bag onto his bed.

"I caught Samantha fucking Jesse. Apparently she's been cheating on me with him all damn summer."

"I told you that bitch was money-hungry." Killian shakes his head as he plops down on his bed across from us.

I groan internally because apparently everyone saw it but me.

"And Celeste wants to make a pact." I laugh. "If I don't find love before I'm thirty, I marry her."

"You can't seriously be considering this?" Killian sits up, his eyes trained on me, not even acknowledging Celeste is in the room. Killian and I met our freshman year of college, when we were assigned to the same dorm room, and clicked immediately. He's a wide receiver, and I'm the quarterback. This will also be our third year sharing a room, and if my dad has it his way, it might be our last. "You realize you're making a deal with the she-devil, right?" he adds, and Celeste glares at him.

The two of them have never gotten along. Celeste has never hidden the fact that she wants a man who has money, and for that reason, Killian thinks she's a gold-digging bitch. The funny thing is, she's never denied it, never once tried to be someone she's not, and oddly enough I respect her for that. At least she isn't constantly getting her heart smashed on like I do.

I let out a low chuckle as I consider her proposition. For years, my mom and Beatrice have said Celeste and I will one day get married. I think deep down my mom is rooting for Celeste to get out of her situation like she did, but only because she's her best friend's daughter. Any other girl in Celeste's situation, my mom would be looking down on. But Celeste, she's always had a soft spot for. Like the daughter she never had.

"And what if I do find love?" I challenge Celeste.

"Well, then you'll restore my faith in love, and I'll stop looking for a rich guy and find myself a man to love." She snorts in disbelief at her own words.

"Yeah, right," Killian scoffs. "You wouldn't know what love looks like if it smacked you in the head with your high heel." I laugh, and Celeste shoots daggers his way.

"You're too young to be this jaded," I say to her.

"I'm only four years younger than you, and if we go by life experience, I'm actually ten years older."

Killian groans and falls back onto his bed, covering his face with a pillow.

"So, do we have a deal?" Celeste grins, extending her hand out to me.

"Fine," I say, and we shake hands. If by thirty, I still haven't found the one, maybe it will be time to admit Celeste is right…but I'm not ready to give up on love yet. Plus, the thought of finding love and Celeste having to give up on her 'marry-a-rich-man plan' to find her own true love will make it well worth it. "Better be ready." I smirk.

"For what?" she questions.

"To find your happily-ever-after. Once I find true love, it will be your turn." I shoot her a wink, and she rolls her eyes.

"You guys have lost your minds." Killian laughs. "Party tonight at Jase's new place. You down?"

"Hell yeah," I tell him. Jase Crawford has been a friend of mine since high school. We played football for two years together at Piermont Academy and then another two years at NCU before he graduated last year.

"I'm down," Celeste agrees, and Killian gives me a hard stare, telling me to shut it down.

"Not tonight," I say apologetically to Celeste.

"Really?" She scoffs. "It's like that?"

"Yeah, little girl, it is," Killian says. "You might have a fake ID that says you're older, but you're still only sixteen, and we're not going to be responsible for you. This is an adult party."

"Whatever." She stands. "I'll catch you later. Have fun at your *adult* party." She saunters out of the dorm room with an extra sway to her hips.

"That girl is nothing but trouble," Killian says as we watch her close the door behind her.

"Don't I know it."

One

NICK

Nine Years Later

"It's all going to come down to this final play. If Nick Shaw can pull off this touchdown, North Carolina will be the Super Bowl champions for the fourth time since Shaw was picked up eight years ago."

"If anybody can do it, it's Shaw."

"And he has a lot on the line. This has been a rough season for Shaw, and with his contract up this year, I imagine this will make a difference when the owners reevaluate whether to sign him again."

"It's almost as if he's a completely different guy out there. Now, I'm not saying he isn't good. We all know he is. But his numbers have steadily declined this season, and with three interceptions during this game alone, Shaw is in the spotlight."

"All right, here we go. With ten seconds on the clock, they're on Pittsburgh's ten-yard line—there's no room for error. North Carolina either scores a touchdown or Pittsburgh will be the new Super Bowl champions."

"They snap the ball...there's nobody open! The pocket's collapsing. Shaw better make a decision quick."

"He's scrambling toward the end zone!"

"He's reaching toward the goal line...he's been hit!"

"Did he get in?"

"I don't know. It's going to be close."

"It appears Shaw is still down. He's grabbing his arm, John. This can't be good."

"The ref is saying the touchdown is no good."

"They have the trainers coming out. He's still holding onto his arm."

I cringe as I watch the replay over and over again. Even with a broken arm and a dislocated shoulder, another few feet before getting tackled and we would've been the Super Bowl champions. Instead, I not only let my team down but my parents as well.

Not able to watch the video for a fifth time, I put my phone away and turn on the television. Of course, every sports station is analyzing the game. They all have opinions, assumptions, and predictions. I stop on a station that has the headline: **Will Nick Shaw be re-signed?**

"It's a tough loss, but Nick Shaw has earned them three championships. That's more than most players ever get in a career. He deserves a chance to come back."

"You're ignoring the fact he just broke his throwing arm and dislocated his shoulder. That's a lot to come back from. Plus, there's the fact he was showing a decline this year with a career high of fifteen interceptions."

Not able to take another second of listening to this shit, I turn the television off and toss the controller across the room. It hits the door and crashes down, the batteries spilling out and rolling across the floor.

The door opens and in walks my mother. Her heels clack across the tile as she flits across the hospital room like she owns it—and in her completely selfish, self-absorbed mind, she probably believes she does. Dressed impeccably in only designer labels—from her Chanel glasses to her Saint Laurent heels—you would think Victoria Shaw actually worked for a living. Well, I guess she does…if you count running my life and spending my dad's money as a job.

"Throwing another hissy fit, Nicholas?" She comes to the side of my bed and pats my arm like I'm a fucking dog. "Stop watching those shows. They thrive on negativity." One might think she's trying to give me some motherly advice, a pep talk of sorts to help me stay positive during the most fucked up time of my life, but I know better. She's trying to convince herself that her now imperfect son isn't about to disgrace the family name by becoming unemployed at twenty-nine years old.

"Would it be so bad if I did get released?" The words come out before I can stop them, and my mother looks like I just told her I'm having a limb cut off. And I guess in her eyes, it would be the equivalent, since all I am to her is the golden-boy child who plays professional football. Without my career, what would she have to brag about? What would she say to her stuck up country club friends? And my dad, if I'm released, he'll lose his twenty percent agent fee he makes off me. What would we even have to talk about? I mean, without football, what else is there?

"Nicholas! Don't say that!" my mom shrieks. "This is

because of your girlfriend, isn't it? I know she hates you playing. We didn't come this far for you to just give up now…" I tune her out as I think about how everything I've worked my entire life for is about to go down the drain, but for some reason, I'm not worried about what I'm about to lose, what my parents are about to lose, but rather what I might gain.

My girlfriend, Fiona, has made a few comments about wanting to get married and settle down. She doesn't like how often players are away from their families and said she would feel like she's a single parent. Maybe now would be the right time to settle down and start a family.

As my mom continues to nag me over my comment about getting released, I pray the nurse will come in soon to give me more pain meds. I was transported back home to North Carolina—from Baltimore—where the Super Bowl was held—immediately after I was taken off the field. Once the team doctors assessed and prepped me, they performed surgery on my arm. Then we had to wait for the swelling to go down enough for the doctors to see how it went. So here I am, stuck in this fucking hospital, living on pain meds and waiting for the doctor to make an appearance to read me my future.

The nurse, who was here earlier flirting with me, said she'll be back with the doctor in a little while when he makes his rounds. It doesn't matter what he says, though. Mandatory surgery due to a broken arm plus a dislocated shoulder can only mean two things: time off and physical therapy. And at almost thirty years old, even with three Super Bowl wins, there's no way North Carolina is going to renew my contract.

I replay my mother's words in my head. *We didn't come this far for you to just give up now.* What a fucking joke. My parents have ridden my ass for as long as I can remember. From playing pee-wee football to high school ball. From playing College ball to me dropping out of college a year early to enter the draft. I've done everything their way, worked my ass off, made choices I didn't want to make, and I'm fucking exhausted. *We* haven't come anywhere. I've come this far. Not my mom. Not my dad. Me! I'm the one who practiced every damn day. I chose football over having a life. And what the hell for? My mom wants me to play for the status and fame. My dad wants me to play for the money. What I can't seem to remember at the moment is why the hell I want to play.

"Are you listening to me?" I open my eyes and see my mother glaring at me, her resting bitch face even more prominent than usual. I can't even recall the last time she smiled. She's so concerned over the possibility of me choosing my girlfriend over football. She's my mom. Shouldn't she want her son to put his girlfriend first? Isn't that what you do when you love someone? Ha! Love…I don't think she's capable of such an emotion. At least not by the definition most would go by. Does she love her home? Yes. Her car? Definitely. Does she love shopping? Without a doubt. Does she love my dad? Or me? I think once upon a time she did…but now the only thing she loves is what we can do for her.

Before I can answer, my father strolls through the door. "Victoria." He gives her a chaste kiss on her cheek before approaching my bed. That's the extent of their affection. "How're you feeling?" he asks me.

"Shitty," I answer honestly. The door opens again and in walks my girlfriend. She smiles sadly as she approaches my bed.

"Hey." She leans in and gives me a kiss. Her lips are soft and sweet, and for a brief moment I feel like everything is right in the world. "How are you feeling?"

"Okay. Waiting for the doctor to come in and tell me my fate."

"If you can't play again…" Fiona swallows thickly. "It won't be the end of the world."

"You can't be serious!" my mom hisses.

"Mom, stop," I say, hoping to prevent an argument between my girlfriend and my mom. It won't be the first one.

"No, Nicholas! She doesn't want you to play, yet she has no problem spending the money you make from playing."

"I don't spend his money, Victoria," Fiona shoots back.

"Your school? Apartment? All the bills?" my mom volleys.

"Enough, Victoria," my dad snaps. "The doctor will be here soon. Please get control of yourself. Fiona, it's probably best if you leave. Nick can call you with an update."

Fiona's eyes widen.

"Dad," I hiss.

"Nick, we have a lot of shit to figure out. I don't have time for your mom and girlfriend to be going at it like children. I have a business to run. So, it's either your mother or your girlfriend."

My dad doesn't say another word—already back on his phone, furiously typing away.

"Fiona," I say with a sigh, and she shakes her head. "I want you here." I take her hand in my good one. "I just don't want to argue with them."

"You never do, Nick." She walks out of the door, and I wish I could chase after her, but I can't.

"Knock, knock," the doctor says before the door is even finished closing. His lips are upturned in a sympathetic smile as he walks into the room, the nurse from earlier following behind him. "How are you feeling, Mr. Shaw?"

"I'm in a bit of pain," I answer truthfully, hoping they can give me something to knock me out so everyone will leave me the hell alone.

"Nurse Karson can take care of that for you." He nods toward the nurse who then scurries over to my bedside and switches something on to release more meds into my IV.

My father gets straight to the point. "What's the prognosis, doc?" It's always about business with him, and since right now, I'm the highest paid quarterback in the NFL, if I can't play, my dad will be losing a shit ton of money. Because at the end of the day, twenty percent of zero is zero. With my contract being up this year, I don't see them keeping me on. There's a lot the team can do with the millions of dollars they pay me.

I glance toward my dad, who has a worried look marring his features, and feel a twinge of sadness. In my father's eyes, all I am is a football player. If it weren't for me playing, we wouldn't even have a relationship.

And if I can't play, where will that leave us? I won't be bringing anything to the table, and as a result, he'll no longer have any use for me.

"The surgery went smoothly. My recommendation is time off for ten months to a year, minimum. He's going to need extensive physical therapy..." He continues on with his doctor talk, but I'm no longer listening. I'm looking at the disappointment on my father's face. The sadness in my mother's eyes. Other than football, I can't remember a single thing I've ever done to make them proud. It didn't matter that I was a straight A student, or that I volunteered after school for the literacy program to help kids who couldn't read. They never went to any of my Math Elite matches or attended any of my engineering competitions.

But every Friday night, they would be in the stands to watch me play. My mom would cheer for me throughout the entire game, and my dad would spend the entire next day strategizing for the next game. And it was during those moments, I felt like they actually saw me—that they actually cared. I thought her cheering me on and him strategizing with me was us being a family. But now I'm starting to wonder if it was love or greed. My guess is toward the latter.

As I stare at the both of them, I consider telling them to go fuck themselves. That they can take my money and status and shove it up their asses. But I can't do that. Because at the end of the day, they're my parents, and like any child, I want them to love me and be proud of me. I let out a heavy sigh, my heart cracking as I come to the realization it might not even matter. Without my job or income, neither of them will need or want me.

"Nick." I snap back to the present to see the team owner, Edwin Smith, and my coach, Reggie Frazier, standing in front of me. The doctor has apparently left, and everyone is staring at me. "You okay?" Coach asks, and I lift my chin up and down robotically.

"We need to talk," Mr. Smith says, and I nod again. "The doctor filled us in…" Of course he did, because he's the team doctor. They probably knew my prognosis before I did. "It's not personal…" Like fuck it's not. I give them eight fucking years and three super bowl rings, and the minute I'm no good to them, they drop me like a bad habit. "We just feel at this time it's best to part ways. After careful consideration, we've made the decision to take the team in a different direction."

Fuck, have I always worn rose-colored glasses? How did I not notice all of the greed and selfishness around me? Probably because up until this moment, it's been smooth sailing. My numbers have only increased. My income and bank account only growing. I allowed everyone around me to use me while I basked in the artificial feeling of being wanted and needed while believing I was making everyone happy.

My mom starts to frantically argue and beg. She doesn't give a shit about my job, or about the fact that my entire life has been about ball since I was a kid and my father realized I could throw like a pro. She doesn't give two fucks that I'm not even thirty years old and my football career might be over. She cares about one thing: how this will look to her stuck up country club friends.

"Mom." She ignores me. "Mom!" I yell louder, but she just keeps going on and on. "Mom!" I shout, and everyone looks at me. "Stop!" I glare at her and see she has actual tears in her eyes. I don't think I've ever seen her cry before. "Coach, Mr. Smith...thank you for coming by to let me know."

"If anything changes..." Mr. Smith starts to say but doesn't finish. We both know my career with North Carolina is over. There's no point in making false promises he can't—and won't—keep.

"Thank you," I respond politely.

They leave, closing the door behind them, and then my father starts. "This is just a temporary setback. This isn't the end, Nick. Rest up, do your physical therapy, and next year we'll get you back on a team and making money again." He says all this while he's typing away on his phone. "I need to take this. It's Roger Cedarbeck, the rookie offensive tackle. We're in negotiations." Bringing the phone up to his ear—not even bothering to look at me—he walks out, leaving only my mother and me in the room. *Guess some things never change.*

"Well, since you'll be available, we can schedule luncheons and charity events. We can find ways to make you look good in the public eye. As soon as you get out, we'll go over the social calendar." She gives me a kiss on my forehead, and then she's gone, leaving me alone.

The doctor comes back in and lets me know I'll be discharged from the hospital by the end of the day tomorrow. Not wanting to text Fiona and ask her for a ride since she left here upset, I put a call in to the car service I use often and arrange for someone to pick me up tomorrow.

"I don't love you anymore, Nick, and I can't be in this relationship another damn day." I'm sitting on the couch in my apartment, listening to my girlfriend explain why she's leaving me. When I arrived home, I found all of her stuff already loaded into a U-Haul truck. The only reason why we're even having this conversation is because she thought I wouldn't be home for another couple days. She was planning to leave with nothing more than a note and her apartment keys on the counter.

"Okay, so let me get this straight. You loved me a week ago…hell, supposedly you loved me two days ago…but now you no longer love me?" I ask, confused as fuck. "So, all the talk about wanting to get married and have a baby…it was what, just talk?"

"It was me being stupid. I have no family or support, and your parents, they would make horrible grandparents." She cringes. "Plus, you always put them and your job first. I need a man who actually puts me first."

"I'm right here. I'm putting you first." *Was my paying for all of our bills and her schooling not putting her first?*

"Until next season…then you'll be back to playing football, and I'll be stuck here by myself. I have dreams, and I need to follow them, and starting a family with you is no longer one of my dreams. To be honest…"

Fiona pauses. Her eyes close, and a second later they reopen with a look of such contempt, I feel it down to my bones. "I would consider it a nightmare." She lifts her purse over her shoulder and says, "Honestly, Nick, I don't think I ever really loved you" and walks out the door, slamming it behind her.

Well, damn...okay, then.

My head hits the back of the couch as I think about how much my life has already changed because of my injury. My dad hasn't once called me since the doctor gave us the verdict—not even to see if I made it home okay. My mom's one and only text was regarding the charity functions she thinks I should attend to keep myself in the public eye. And Fiona, as you can see, just walked out the door and out of my life.

Maybe it's time for me to make a change. Time to put myself first. There's no way I'm staying here for the next year and attending charity functions with my mom. Grabbing my phone from the coffee table, I shoot a text to Killian. The year after I was drafted, he was drafted to New York. We might not be roommates anymore, but we're still best friends.

> Me: I'm out. Minimum 10 months. They let me go.
>
> Kill: Fuck. What are you going to do?
>
> Me: If it were up to my mom... charity functions.
> Kill: Fuck that.

Me: You up for some company?

Kill: Fuck yeah! But what about Fiona?

Me: Apparently she's looking for her next meal ticket.

Kill: Bitch. Where are you now?

Me: Home

Kill: Get your ass up here!

Me: I'll get everything settled here and be on my way in the next few days.

Kill: I'll get a room ready.

Me: And the women.

One thing that I've learned from Fiona is that it doesn't matter how much you give or try, it's never enough, and I'm done doing both. Fuck my parents, and fuck Fiona, and fuck love. It's time to get fucked.

Kill: That's a given.

He says women are a given, but the truth is, I haven't seen Killian with a woman in years, not since our sophomore year. The guy went from practically sleeping his way through the student body to barely looking at a woman. I'm not sure what happened, but he refuses to talk about it. Anytime I see him at a football function or charity event, he always has a woman on his arm, but in all the years I've stayed with him or vice versa, I've never seen him bring a woman home or spend the night out with one.

Two

NICK

Fourteen Months Later

We're sitting in a booth in Club Envy, partying like we do most nights. Only tonight, we're partying with a purpose.

"Bro! You fucking nailed those tryouts. You and me," Killian shouts over the music. "You and me! We're going all the way!" We clink glasses, and Killian announces "My boy is back!" before we both throw back our shots. It takes everything in me to tamper down the nagging feeling that once again somebody is after me for what I can do for him. But I remind myself that Killian isn't like that. He's not like my parents, who both went radio silent—after my mom threw a fit—when I up and moved to New York, or the women who only want me for what I can give them: materialistic possessions, trips, nights out at expensive restaurants. The tabloids say I'm a manwhore, a playboy of sorts, but you know what? Those women who spread their legs with dollar signs in their eyes aren't any better. I tried the hearts and flowers route and look where it got me…so don't judge me when I finally come to my senses and give everyone what they want.

For the last year, Killian is the only person who has had my back. After putting my condo on the market and having my shit shipped to New York, I chartered a plane and refused to look back. I've been living with Killian at his place, and it's been like one long party. On the days he's home, he helps me with rehab, and he's done it without knowing if I'll ever be able to play again. So, no, Killian isn't like that. I know that, but sometimes I have to remind myself. When it's all you know, it's hard to accept otherwise. I heard through the grapevine Fiona is still attending dance school and living it up in North Carolina in a nice as hell apartment. Seeing as she was broke as fuck when we met tells me one thing: she did, indeed, find her next meal ticket.

"I think I spot Melissa. I'll be back." Killian fist bumps me before walking away to find his friend. They hang out more often than not, but nothing seems to ever come of it. I look to my left and then my right. I've got a woman on each side of me, both fake blondes, and both vying for my attention. One is rubbing up on my dick while the other is licking down my neck. I bring another shot to my lips as I ignore the buzzing in my pocket indicating I have a phone call coming in—most likely one of my parents who are back to acknowledging I exist since there's a good possibility I'll be getting my career back tomorrow. I wouldn't be surprised if they're both on a plane heading to New York right now.

I press my finger against my pocket to stop the

vibration, and when it starts up again, I pull it out and shut off my phone. Tomorrow, I'll deal with them. Tonight, I'll pretend they don't exist. After all, they spent the last year pretending I don't exist.

When I look up from my phone, I spot the most gorgeous fucking woman I've ever seen, standing at the bar. She's wearing a black lacy top and matching shorts. Her brown hair is down in waves, and she's sporting the most adorable pout as she tries to get the bartender's attention.

Not giving the two women on either side of me another glance, I shoo them off me and make my way to the bar. "Can I buy you a drink?" I whisper into the woman's ear as I approach her from behind. She angles her head to look at me then graces me with the most beautiful, shy smile before she shakes her head no.

"No, thank you. I can buy my own…if the damn bartender would ever look my way." Her face scrunches up in anger, and I have to hold back a laugh. She waves her hand out with a bill between her fingers, and I can't take my eyes off her. Dark brown hair, chocolate-brown eyes, and creamy, porcelain skin. Her natural beauty stands out like a shiny diamond in a room filled with dirty stones. Amongst all the fakeness in New York, this woman screams, 'real.' Of course, that's what I thought about Fiona and look where that got me.

I raise my finger in the air, and the bartender immediately makes her way over. "What can I get for you, baby?"

I turn toward Brown-Eyes. "What would you like to drink?"

At first, she looks stunned, but then her face contorts into a look of annoyance mixed with anger. "Seriously?" She rolls her eyes, and I shrug. I don't know why she's shocked. Everyone knows who I am here in this city. "I'll take two vodka cranberries," she says to the bartender then places a twenty on the bar top. The bartender nods, then she turns her attention to me. "What're you having?"

"Her...I'm having her." I point to the woman next to me. This time, the bartender rolls her eyes, unamused, while Brown-Eyes snorts in amusement. "But for now, I'll take a couple shots of Patron."

"Sure thing." The bartender goes to grab the woman's twenty, but I pull out a fifty before she can. She takes my bill—leaving hers—slips it into her bra, and walks away to make the drinks.

"So, two vodka cranberries?" Please don't let her be here with another guy.

"One is for my friend. She's somewhere around here. She ran into a guy she knows when we were walking in." Thank God!

She looks around in search of her friend before her brown eyes come back to me, giving me a once over. This is where I expect her to recognize me, figure out who I am and milk it for all its worth, and believe me, I most definitely will.

But instead, she gives me a small smile, takes her twenty off the bar top, and says, "Thank you," shrugging nonchalantly.

"No problem. But now you owe me." I shoot her a playful wink.

"Oh really…even after I tried to buy our drinks?"

"Yep." I hold back a grin.

"And what is it I owe you?" She cocks her head to the side, a small ghost of a smile playing on her lips.

The bartender comes back over and sets our drinks down in front of us. I grab one of the shots and hand it to her. "A shot."

She throws her head back in laughter, and I know I've got her. And fuck, if her sexy laugh doesn't have me.

C⌒

"Shot! Shot! Shot! Shot!" Lifting the shot with my mouth from the middle of Brown-Eyes' perky tits, I tilt my head back and swallow it in one gulp. The Patron burns going down, the warmth settling in my stomach. I hold the shot glass up for everyone to see, and the crowd erupts in cheers and applause. We've been drinking for the last hour, and I still don't even know the woman's name. But what I do know is, I'm deeply and madly…in lust with everything about her.

She grabs her shot and downs it, her slim sexy-as-fuck neck on display, begging for my lips to kiss it. Closing the gap between us, I pull her tiny waist into my body. My arms wrap around her backside, and my hands land on her tight little round ass. "Dance with me," I murmur into her ear. My tongue darts out to lick the bottom of her earlobe. Chills rush down her arms as I feel her physically shiver.

She nods in agreement, and I pull her in closer. Our bodies are flush against each other. Our skin sweaty. I'm not quite drunk, but I'm definitely tipsy, enough that I'm nuzzling my face into her hair and sniffing her sexy perfume. It's sweet and has my dick twitching, wanting to know what else on this woman is sweet. My lips move to her neck, and I trail kisses downward toward her collarbone. Her head rests on my shoulder as our bodies grind against one another to the pulsating dance music that's infiltrating the club's speakers. It's loud, and we don't speak, allowing our bodies to do all the talking for us.

"Yo, bro!" I hear Killian yell to me over the loud music and chatter in the club. "I'm out." I look up long enough to lock eyes with him. I was curious as to why I haven't seen him much tonight, but the doe-eyed woman by his side answers my question. He found Melissa. I tilt my chin up in acknowledgement then bring my attention back to the woman in my arms.

Gliding my hand over her ass and up her back, I grip the back of her head, entwining my fingers in her thick mane, and pull back enough so she can make eye contact with me.

"Are you drunk?"

She looks up at me and shakes her head. "No."

"Want to get out of here?"

Her lids are hooded over with lust, and she bites down on her bottom lip as she considers my question. What I thought was an act—her not knowing who I am—I'm starting to think isn't one after all. Because let's be real, if she knew who I was, she wouldn't even be contemplating whether or not to leave with me. I'm Nick fucking Shaw. Any woman who knows who I am would be begging me to leave with them. I have a reputation of being stellar in the sack, which I take seriously. And even if I sucked in bed, they would still come because money talks. Now, with all the buzz about the possibility of me signing a multi-million-dollar contract tomorrow, women are all over me trying to get on this money train. So, as I watch this woman consider whether it's a good idea or not to leave with me, I'm thinking she has no clue who the hell I am.

"Okay," she finally says, a small smile playing on her deliciously bee-stung lips that look like they were made to be wrapped around my cock. "Let me text my friend and let her know I'm leaving." Her friend and the guy she ran into joined us earlier for a quick drink, but then they excused themselves to dance.

Grabbing her by her hand, I guide her toward the side exit of the club. I'm going to have to hail a cab since we've both been drinking. The last thing I need is to get a DUI when I'm about to be back on a team playing ball again.

Just as we're about to leave, I spot Celeste, and her eyes meet mine. I give her a chin-jerk toward the door to let her know I'm leaving, and she rolls her eyes at me. She's used to me leaving with a different woman from the club.

"I'm staying at the Ritz," Brown-Eyes says once we're outside. "It's only one block over."

"Sounds good to me."

We head to her hotel in silence. We walk through the lobby, and she presses the button for the elevator. Once we're inside, she says, "I know it's probably going to sound cliché, but I've never done this before." Her honesty paralyzes me. She's a complete contradiction to everything I've ever known. I'm used to women who make a career out of bedding guys like me.

Pushing her gently against the elevator wall, I brush my lips against hers. They're soft and plump and taste fruity, and they have me craving more. "I'll take care of you." I give her another kiss, this time my tongue pushes into her mouth. Our tongues swirl against one another as our kiss deepens. She pulls back slightly, her chest rising and falling quickly as she catches her breath.

"I don't even know your name." Her words come out breathless, and I find myself wanting to know what she'll sound like when she's calling out my name. Then it hits me. She just said she doesn't know my name, confirming she has no idea who I am. I look into her eyes, trying to find some type of untruth in her words, but all I see is a beautiful, brown-eyed woman staring at me with want in her eyes. Not want for my money or status or fame, but just plain and simple want. This woman is either going to win an academy award for her acting skills or she's telling the truth.

"I'm Cole."

"I'm Liv." Her lips upturn into a small, shy smile as I take her in. She's fucking beautiful. From her silky brown hair to the slight pink tint on her cheeks that tells me she really is this innocent. The elevator dings, and I follow her lead, not knowing where we're going. Once we get to her room, she pulls a key out of the back pocket of her short shorts, which show off her toned legs, and walks in first. I follow behind, my eyes raking down her body, landing on her muscular calves and her sexy fuck-me heels.

She stops in the center of the room and catches me checking her out.

Averting my eyes, I notice this is a multi-room suite. "Is your friend staying here with you?"

"Yes, the one you met briefly at the club. She's still there catching up with her friend, but she'll be back later." Smart woman...letting me know someone will be here soon.

"Got it."

Placing her hand in mine, she guides me to her room, closing the door behind us. The room is dark, the only light shining in through the curtains from the New York City skyline. The light hits her face, and she looks worried.

"You okay?" I ask, framing the sides of her face with my hands. Her cheeks are warm, and if it wasn't so dark, I would bet they are flushed pink with need.

"Yeah."

"You sure?" I ask again, wanting to make sure we're on the same page.

"I'm sure. I want you. I want this." Her hands grip my shirt, lifting it over my head. Her fingers trail down my torso, landing on my belt. When I don't move, she stops. "Do you...want this?" Her question is filled with self-doubt. She thinks I've changed my mind. Has this woman lost her damn mind?

"Fuck yes, I do. I've wanted you since the moment you walked into the club."

Instead of continuing with my belt, Liv steps forward and places a soft kiss on my pectoral muscle right above my heart. I stand there, frozen in my spot, watching her place kiss after kiss along my chest and down my torso. She kneels down so she's parallel to my crotch and looks up at me, her brown eyes connecting with my green. She has a look of mischief on her face as she places an open-mouthed kiss right where my dick is bulging through my boxers and jeans.

"Fucking tease." I laugh, and she giggles. Her eyes break the connection as she becomes a woman on a mission. She unbuckles my belt, unbuttons my pants, then pulls the zipper down. When she yanks my jeans down, she takes my boxers with them, and my hard cock springs to attention. Toeing off my shoes, I kick them, along with my pants, to the side.

My eyes stay trained on her as she takes my shaft in her hand. She lifts it up until it's almost hitting my stomach and then she languorously licks the entire underside like she's savoring every fucking inch of me. I let out a groan at the feeling of her wet tongue running along my flesh. When she gets to the head, a bit of pre-cum is beaded over. Her tongue darts out and licks the cream, and I about lose my shit. I grab her by her hair, my hand fisting her mane. Pulling her up, I lack all the patience she possesses. She pulls her top off and unclasps her bra. I toss her onto the bed, then yank her shorts and panties off.

I push her legs back, and my head is between her thighs in mere seconds, lapping at her wet fucking cunt. The heady moan she lets out in response only spurs me on. I lick and suck on her clit, but it's not enough. I need more. I need to feel her. I push my fingers inside her. She's warm and wet, and fuck, she's so goddamn tight. I want to be inside her, but I need to make her come first. I lap and lave up her slit, my tongue pushing on her clit, and finally, she fucking comes all over my tongue and fingers, her juices spilling onto the bed sheets.

Not able to wait another second, I'm up on my knees, condom ripped open and rolled on, and pushing into her. Her head rolls back, her chin lifting, as her back arches. And then she's meeting me thrust for thrust as we chase our orgasms.

"I. Need. It. Harder," she groans out. Grabbing her ass, I flip her over onto her knees, her round ass in the air. I give it a hard smack, and then I'm pushing back into her from behind. My fingers dig into her hips as I piston in and out of her, bottoming out. I can feel her trembling around my cock in pleasure, and then her cunt starts to choke my dick like a goddamned vice grip as she comes for a second time. Not able to last a second longer, I pull out and rip the condom off my dick, preparing to come all over her ass. But before I do, she turns around, and taking my dick in her hand, strokes me up and down until I'm releasing my seed all over her luscious fucking tits. And holy hell, if the sight of my jizz dripping down her breasts doesn't have me hard all over again. I swipe my finger across her taut nipple, and her body shivers.

"Open your mouth," I demand, and she obeys. I run my cum-covered finger over her lips, painting them a creamy white, then I push my finger inside her mouth. Her tongue darts out and her lips close. She sucks my finger clean, her eyes closing as she lets out a breathy moan. When her eyes open back up, she grants me a mischievous grin.

"How about a shower?" I suggest, and she nods in

agreement.

Once we're both cleaned up, we lay down in her bed. Usually this is the moment when I make up some bullshit excuse as to why I need to leave, but for some reason, I don't want to go anywhere.

"Tell me about yourself," I find myself saying.

"What do you want to know?" she asks.

"Tell me something you love."

"I love art." Her smile is bright and wide. "What about you? What do you love?"

"Playing football." The words are out before I can stop them. I expect her to ask me about it, but she doesn't.

"Tell me something you hate," she asks instead.

"Playing football."

She gives me an incredulous look. "Explain."

And for the first time, I tell Liv something I've never told anyone. "I love playing football because I'm good at it. I love the rush I feel when I'm out on the field. The thrill of the plays. What I don't love about football is everything else."

"Like?"

"Like the fact that if football didn't exist, my parents probably wouldn't know I'm alive." And now I sound like a whiny little bitch…"Tell me something you hate," I say, changing the subject.

"Switzerland."

We both laugh. "Switzerland? What the hell did Switzerland ever do to you?"

"A guy I was dating left me to move there." She shrugs. "I gave him three years, and he didn't even give me a second thought as he packed up and left."

I pull Liv closer and into my arms. "It's his loss, trust me." I bring my lips to hers and thank my lucky stars for that dumbass leaving her. His loss is definitely my gain.

My eyes open slowly, but quickly close when the sunlight shining through the window adds to my fast-growing headache. I groan as my head throbs. It takes me a second to remember where I am and what I did last night—or I should say who I did last night. The sucking, the fucking, the talking for hours, the falling asleep with Liv in my arms. Waking up and needing more of her. Pulling her on top of me, and her riding my cock until we both came. Falling asleep sticky and satiated.

Some would think I'm crazy, but I think I could fall in love with this woman. What started out as lust turned into something more as the night went on. Between the fucking and talking, I found myself craving Liv in a way I haven't wanted a woman since Fiona left me. And if I'm honest, I don't even think I ever wanted Fiona like this.

I roll back over, feeling for Liv's warm body, wanting to hold and touch her. I want to ask her for her phone number. One night wasn't enough. I need more time. More nights and days. Only there's no warmth. It's cold. My eyes dart open, and I glance around until I spot a note on the pillow.

Have a flight to catch. Check-out is 10:00.
Thanks for last night.
—Liv

My heart constricts as I crumple up the note and throw it onto the floor, suddenly feeling pissed off and used. Why doesn't it surprise me the one woman I've met in the last year I thought might be different, isn't? Just like everyone else, once I was no longer of use to her, she walked out without even a backward glance, showing me once again people are only in it for what they can take from you.

After I'm dressed and make sure I have everything I came with, I head out. As I'm snagging a cab, Celeste texts me, asking to meet up for breakfast. She moved here after she graduated from high school in hopes of having a career as a model. Using my connections, I was able to get her into a summer internship program with a modeling company, which got her foot in the door. She now makes a more-than decent living and her name is definitely out there. You can find her picture on several billboards throughout the city. She also has her own successful makeup and accessories line and has been on shows like America's Elite Model as one of the judges. But she's still not satisfied. She's always striving for more. She's one of the most hard-working and determined women I've ever known.

When we were younger I thought for sure she would latch on to some rich guy and ride his coat tail, but I was wrong. Celeste is independent and career-focused. Don't get me wrong, the men she dates are always wealthy, and if it's possible she's even more cold and emotionless than she was when she was younger, but since she moved here she's different. She no longer comes across like she needs a man. Maybe it's because she has her own money. I don't know. As close as we are, she doesn't open up to me about that kind of stuff. She travels a lot for work, but when she's in town we hang out often.

We meet at Buvette in West Village and are seated immediately. After she orders a mimosa, and I order a coffee, she says, "So today's the big day, huh?"

"Yep, I find out in a couple hours if New York is going to take a chance on me."

"You nervous?"

"I guess." I shrug. The truth is my mind is still on the beautiful brown-eyed woman who rocked my world and then skipped out.

"You guess? What's up with you?"

The waiter sets down our drinks, and Celeste takes a sip of her mimosa while I pour a bit of milk into my coffee.

"That woman last night…"

"The one you left with?"

"Yeah. She skipped out on me this morning."

Celeste cackles. "Aww…you poor baby. You got left before you could do the leaving."

"It's not that." I take a sip of my coffee. "I thought maybe…" I shake my head. "I thought maybe there was something there. Something more." I cringe at my confession as I wait for Celeste to give me shit.

And of course she does. "Oh God, Nick. You didn't

really think a woman you met at a club was going to fall in love with you. You're an NFL player."

"She didn't know that, though," I point out.

"Oh, c'mon! Of course she did." Celeste laughs. The waiter comes back over, and we order breakfast. Once he leaves, Celeste says, "Sometimes I wonder if you're really related to Henry and Victoria. You're so damn gullible."

"Because I wanted to fall in love instead of being in a money and status driven marriage like my parents?" I volley back.

"No, because even though you've had your heart stomped on and used repeatedly by everyone around you, you refuse to see life for what it really is." I notice when she says this, her lips turn down into a frown, and I wonder if maybe Celeste has had her heart broken. I don't bother asking, though. If she has, she would never admit it. She hates appearing weak or vulnerable.

"Well, then you'll be happy to know I've given up. Money makes the world go round. Women are heartless, and my parents don't know the meaning of love. You win, I lose."

"Are you saying what I think you're saying?" Celeste leans in toward me, and I'm confused by her question.

"That I'm done with love? Yeah." I shrug. "I mean, I pretty much gave up on it after Fiona left me. And after Liv left me a note this morning..." I release a humorless chuckle. "I think it's time I throw in the towel and admit defeat."

"No, not all that." Celeste shakes her head. "Although, that information definitely helps. But what I meant was..." She bites her bottom lip nervously. "You're thirty."

"Yeah, so?" I shrug. "And you're twenty-six," I point out, not understanding her need to remind me of my age. The waiter sets our food down in front of us, and I grab my fork to dig in.

"Our pact when you were in college," Celeste says. "If you didn't find true love by thirty, you would marry me."

My fork falls out of my hand and clatters against the plate.

Three

NICK

"Your tryout and evaluation were top notch, and the doctor signed off on your physical..." I'm trying to focus on what's being said in probably the most important meeting of my career, but my mind is completely fucked up at the moment. First off, I can't seem to get Liv off my mind, which is really fucking stupid because other than knowing her first name, nothing else I know about her will help me find her. She said in her note she had a flight to catch, which most likely means she doesn't even live here...or maybe she does and she's leaving on a trip. But then why would she be staying in a hotel? I tried to get the front desk to give me some information on her, but they wouldn't budge. I shouldn't have even tried. If she wanted to see me again, she would've woken me up or left her number. She did neither.

And then there's the fact that I'm actually considering making good on the pact I made with Celeste all those years ago. When I agreed to her terms, I imagined by thirty I would be married with kids. But after having dealt with Fiona, my string of one-night stands this past year, and then Liv leaving this morning, I'm beginning to think maybe Celeste has the right idea. Fiona said it herself, I would make a horrible father, and the one woman in the past year I actually wanted to get to know better left without a trace the morning after. Clearly, I'm doing something wrong here, so maybe it's time I do things Celeste's way... Jesus, to even be considering this must mean I've lost my damn mind.

"We would like to offer you a one year contract, ten million—"

"Absolutely not!" my father booms, cutting off Declan Thomas, the owner of the New York Brewers. "You know damn well Mr. Shaw is worth double those numbers."

"If he's successful," Stephen Harper, the new coach, points out. "It's a risk, but one I'm willing to take."

"He's hardly a risk," my dad says. "You saw him out there with your receiver. This team's about to get its first Super Bowl win in over a decade."

"Henry, let's not get ahead of ourselves here," Declan says.

"I'll take it." Everybody's gaze swings to me.

"What are you doing?" my father hisses. It's been over a year since I've even seen the man who walked out the door at the hospital and has barely spoken five words to me since then. When Killian mentioned our college playing days to the new coach, he asked to meet with me. Of course, that meant contacting my agent on file. My dad was on the next flight out, dollar signs flashing in his eyes—my mother right beside him. For a while there, I forgot why I was playing football. I was so caught up in trying to make my parents proud of me, I lost my love of the sport along the way. This last year has been eye-opening.

Now, playing football is about me—what I want. If I'm going to bust my ass, it's going to be because of my love for the game and not because of the money, status, or fame. And it's definitely not going to be to make my parents give a fuck about me. Being with Liv last night, I thought maybe was a sign—reminding me love could still exist—but her walking away only reconfirmed why I'm done. Football is the only damn love I have left, and I'm going to give it my all.

"We're coming up to the end of free agency. I'm happy here, and I want to play." This past year has been fun, like an extended vacation. I've worked hard in physical therapy, and I've partied even harder. But now I'm ready to get back out there and play again. I didn't bust my ass this last year rehabilitating my throwing arm to be out for another year because I refuse to take a deal from a team who's willing to give me a shot.

Sure, with a month left of free agency, there's still a chance another team will offer me a deal, but what if they don't? And even if they did, that would mean moving. Plus, signing with New York means playing on the same team as Killian.

"Does your ass hurt?" my dad asks. I know he's pissed because, for once, I'm actually going against him. Up until I was injured, I've done everything he's advised. Where to go to college, what to study, when to leave college, who to play for…but I'm done going along with everything he says.

"I'll make sure to ask for some lube." I shoot him a condescending smirk, and he throws his hands up in the air. He's only peeved about this deal because the less I accept means the less he pockets. He doesn't give a shit that I'm actually going to be on a team and able to play. He doesn't give a fuck that I busted my ass day after day in physical therapy. Most guys at my age would've said fuck it and retired. I've made enough in the last eight years to last me a lifetime. I'm no longer playing for the money—I'm playing for the love of the game.

"There is one condition," Mr. Thomas says slowly.

"Okay."

"We need you to settle down."

"What?" I ask, confused.

"This past year you've managed to party in probably every club on the East Coast, as well as screw most of the female population. You've lost most of your endorsements, and nobody is going to take you seriously if you don't start acting like the thirty-year-old man you are."

"I lost those endorsements because of my injury," I point out.

"True, but you won't get them back if you keep acting like the playboy of NYC."

"What are you saying?"

"I'm saying, it's time to settle down."

"What the hell does that mean?"

"It means no more partying. No more drinking. No more one-night stands." Mr. Thomas places a piece of paper on the table. "You were seen leaving a hotel this morning in the same clothes you were seen in last night."

I pull the paper closer to examine it. It's a printout from something a trashy tabloid posted online. In the image my tall frame is hovering over Liv's petite body, hiding her face.

"I didn't know we were being watched."

"You've spent the last year being filmed and photographed while partying. We can't have that if you're playing for this team."

Coach Harper adds, "You're going to be the face of this team, the man who's hopefully going to lead us to a championship, and you're going to need to act like it. Nobody wants to root for a guy who's spending his time sleeping with half of New York. Got it?"

"Got it," I agree.

"Excellent!" Mr. Thomas clasps his hands together. "Now that we have that figured out, let's get this contract signed."

Four

NICK

Nine months later

"All right, guys. This is it. We've worked too hard not to make it to the playoffs now. Let's finish this." We're huddled up on San Francisco's twenty-yard line. There's only twelve seconds left in our season, and we're down by four points. As I look around at all the cheering fans in the stadium, I have a bout of déjà vu. Only this time, I'm not playing for North Carolina but instead for New York. We get this touchdown, and we make the playoffs. We don't, and there's a chance this is the last game I'll ever play. I feel a twinge of pain radiate down my arm, reminding me this game has to end differently.

The guys are all pumped up and ready to win this game. I call out the play, "FB West right slot 372 Y stick on three, break!" And then we take our positions on the field. On my three-count, the center hikes the ball. Taking a three-step drop, I find Killian and see he has a step on the defender. I throw the ball to him, a bit too high—my nerves getting the best of me—to avoid the interception—and like always, he comes through in the clutch, catching the ball in the end zone for the touchdown. The rest of the team joins him as we celebrate our win and our spot in the playoffs.

Every game we win leaves me feeling exhilarated. I've learned over the last several months my one and only true love is football. It's all I need. Sometimes when I wish for more, I remind myself of what *more* means in my life. And then I accept my life for what it is. I'm damn blessed, and it would be selfish of me to want more.

We head back to the locker room to shower—adrenaline still coursing through our veins from our win. The guys are shouting and joking. It's the week before Christmas, and this is without a doubt the best gift I've ever been given.

"Reservations at El Tao," Brian McCaldon calls out to the team.

"We fucking did it!" Killian jumps on my back. Then as he comes down, he pulls me in for a side hug.

"We still have a long way to go…but yeah, we fucking did!"

"You going to El Tao?" he asks.

"Yeah, might as well. I'm alone for the night." I shrug. "Want to play some Madden at your place afterward?"

"Hell yeah."

A few months ago, I moved out of Killian's condo and into my own place. I didn't want to, but I had to. After accepting the contract with New York, my life changed drastically, and while I know it's what needed to be done, sometimes I wonder if I made the right decision.

"When does she—" His words are cut off when I hear a version of my name being called. The version I have only told one woman. I put my hand up to stop him from speaking and look around, wondering if I'm hearing shit. Wondering if it's possible, after all this time, I'm imagining *her* calling my name.

"Cole," I hear again, and my eyes swing over to the woman who's calling me. And sure as shit, standing there in the locker room is *her*.

"Brown-Eyes." I say the nickname I gave her. So many times I've tried to remember what she looks like, but my memory of her didn't do her justice at all. Her hair is a bit longer, a little lighter. Her eyes are still a beautiful shade of brown that remind me of melted chocolate—sweet like the taste of her pussy on my tongue.

My eyes move downward, lingering on her voluptuous breasts, before I continue farther down, stopping on her...stomach. What the fuck! She's...pregnant? "You're pregnant?"

She follows my gaze down to her protruding belly and then gives me a *duh!* expression.

"What're you doing here?" I ask a bit too coolly as I suddenly remember the note she left the morning after the night we spent together.

"Well...I saw you playing..."

Coach Harper cuts in, making his presence known. "How do you two know each other?"

Liv darts her gaze from Coach to me and then back to him. "He's the father," she says softly. Her eyes close slightly, and the guys gasp and curse around us.

Coach makes eye contact with me, his glare like nothing I've ever seen before. It's a look that says he's about to kill me, and it has me repeating what she said over and over again in my head, hearing the words but not comprehending them. Why the hell is she saying I'm the father? And why is she telling my coach?

"You're...the father?" Coach asks, but I don't answer him. I've lost my voice. I'm in shock. A minute ago, I was remembering how this woman was the best damn lay of my life, how I woke up wanting more, wanting to get to know her, how she walked away without looking back, and now she's trying to fuck me over. She didn't want anything to do with me the morning after when she thought I was a nobody, but now that she knows who I am, she wants to cry baby?

"Bullshit!" I say, finally finding my voice. "We had a one-night stand." I turn to Liv. "If you think you're getting a dime from me, you've lost your mind."

"Son, what did you just say?" Coach's face is turning beet red. I've never seen him this pissed. I'm not sure why he cares, but he needs to have my back or mind his own business. "I would watch what you're saying."

"What the hell, Coach? You expect me to just stand here while this gold-digger tries to fuck me over?" I nod toward Liv who looks like she's not sure whether to be mad or upset. "You're supposed to have my back."

Without saying a word, Coach cuts across the room, and before I can duck, he punches me in the face. My back hits the wall as the guys all jump into action, pulling him off me.

"That *gold-digger* is my daughter!" Oh, hell...shit just got real.

And this is when I should close my mouth, but I'm too worked up—too pissed because I thought she was different, too disappointed that she's like everyone else in my fucking life. "That may be so, but can't you see this for what it is? She's a fucking groupie." I turn to Liv. "What do you want? Huh? Money? A house? A car?"

Coach pushes through the guys, but Killian grabs him before his fist can connect with my face for a second time.

"Nick, stop!" Killian shouts, but I don't listen.

"C'mon, you come at me, what—" I quickly do the math in my head—"nine months later. What do you want? And don't tell me nothing. *Everybody* wants something."

She stares at me for a minute, her face bright red with anger and her hand resting on the top of her swollen belly. "I didn't know…I lived in Paris…I didn't know who you were that night, *Cole*." She emphasizes my name to prove her point. Anybody who knows me calls me Nick. My mother calls me Nicholas. I told her my name was Cole.

Coach goes to his daughter's side. "Olivia, honey, what the hell happened?"

Five

OLIVIA

Nine months ago

"Olivia, I hate that you wouldn't let me fly over for your graduation." I'm sitting on my terrace, talking to my dad, but my mind and heart are a million miles away as I stare at the Eiffel Tower. It's nighttime, and the beautiful tower monopolizes the area. The twinkling lights glitter, making it look like a white Parisian Christmas tree.

"You came for my graduation when I got my bachelor's degree. You didn't need to come for my master's as well. Plus, I was thinking of coming to visit you." I wasn't really, but in light of recent events, I'm thinking a vacation across the Atlantic is just what I need.

"Yeah?" My dad's voice raises several octaves in excitement. "I haven't seen you since the wedding. I would love for you to come and visit." My thoughts go back to the day my dad married my stepmom, Corrine. The way he smiled with unshed tears in his eyes. After losing my mom—his soulmate—to breast cancer seven years ago, he didn't think he would ever fall in love again. Then he met Corrine. I remember when he called me. His voice wavered, scared I wouldn't be happy for him. How could I not be? He loved my mother until she took her final breath. Nobody deserves to live the rest of their life alone because they lost the love of their life too soon.

"I would only be able to come for a week, though. The museum has asked me to come on fulltime as their Arts Education Coordinator now that I've graduated."

"That's amazing! I'm so proud of you. You took your passion for education and your love of art and seem to have found a job you really enjoy."

"Well, I have to make a living somehow."

My dad chuckles. The truth is, my mother was an extremely wealthy woman, and when she died, she left everything to me. I have enough money to never have to work a day in my life. When I asked my dad why she didn't leave it all to him—he was her husband after all—he told me his job was to take care of her. She never had to touch the money while she was alive, and it was her last wish to know I would be taken care of.

"I miss you, Olivia," my dad says. "I would really love to see you, even if it's only for a week." Six months after my mom died, I turned eighteen and received my inheritance. I made the decision to leave New York and attend college in Paris. My mom was from there, and I wanted to spend some time seeing for myself all the stories she used to share of her childhood in France. And if I'm honest, I needed some distance from the home I grew up in. My mom was my best friend, and losing her hurt my heart beyond belief. Everywhere I went, it reminded me of my mom and the fact that I would never see her again.

So, I moved to Paris to attend college, which is where I met my best friend, Giselle Winters, my freshman year. She had a horrible flat mate and was looking to move. I had an extra room, and we hit it off immediately. A bachelor's and master's degree later, and we've created a home here. I never thought that six years later I would still be living here, but I love it, and so does Giselle. The funny thing is, we're both from New York, but because we're from different areas, we never met until we were going to school in Paris.

"Are you excited to be starting your new job?" I ask my dad.

"Yeah, I am. I loved coaching college ball. I've been doing it for the last fifteen years. But I'm excited to take this team on. You know I love a good challenge."

"Yes, I do."

"How is Victor?" And this is the part of the conversation that I've been dreading. I don't lie to my dad. I don't keep secrets from him.

"We broke up."

My dad is silent for a moment before he asks, "What happened?"

"He was offered a job in Geneva."

"Switzerland?"

I laugh softly. "Yes, Switzerland. He didn't ask me to go. Not that I would have…but he didn't even ask. Didn't even consider me when making his decision."

"He's a dumbass."

I love that my dad always has my back. "It hurts. I gave him three years, and he gave me a thirty-hour notice he was moving out."

"I bet Giselle is thrilled," he points out.

"She is." Giselle and Victor never got along. Last year, after dating Victor for two years, he suggested we move in together. My flat was the obvious choice. Giselle swears he only asked so he could crash somewhere in luxury. She might've been right, especially since he made more excuses than not to keep from contributing on a monthly basis.

"All right, well, you talk to Giselle, because I know you won't be coming here without her, and let me know the dates. I'll make sure I'm available to you. We can stay at the house in the Hamptons. It will be great."

"Sounds good, Dad. I love you."

"Love you, too."

It's our last day in New York. We've been here for nine days. Five of them spent at our beach house in the Hamptons, two of them exploring all the museums I love to visit while here—during which time my dad mentioned a million times I could do the same job I'm planning to do in Paris, here in New York. Yesterday was spent at the spa with Giselle, Corrine, and her daughter, Shelby, who is in town visiting from Connecticut, where she lives with her father and his family.

Earlier today, I met my dad for breakfast, and then I spent the rest of the day doing some shopping since he had to attend a meeting for work and Giselle was visiting with her family. Tonight, Giselle and I are meeting my dad, Corrine, and Shelby at a new club my dad heard about.

After we've perfected our hair, makeup, and outfits, we walk the few blocks over to Club Envy. I'm about to call my dad to see where we should meet them when my phone pings with an incoming text. It's from Shelby, letting me know her dad needed her to babysit for him and her stepmom, so she had to drive back early. She says she's going to try to come back tomorrow for breakfast. I text her back that it's okay and if she can't make it I understand. Her dad relies on her a lot to help with her half-siblings.

Just as I'm swiping out of the message, my phone rings.

"Hey, Dad! We just got here. Where are you guys?"

"Hey honey! I'm at home. Corrine thinks she might've gotten food poisoning from the sushi she ate earlier. She's been hugging the toilet for the last hour."

"Oh, no! Do you want me to go over there?"

"No, no. You should still go to the club and have a good time. I heard it's all the rage." I laugh at my dad trying to sound cool.

"Shelby had to cancel too. Her dad needed her to babysit. Are you sure you don't need me to come over?"

"No, there's nothing you could do here, and I'm almost positive Corrine would kill me if I allowed anyone to see her in her current state. Besides, there's no reason for you girls to be stuck in on your last night in New York. Go. Have a good time…but not too good of a time," he adds, and I roll my eyes.

"Fine, but we'll see you before we leave tomorrow, right?"

"Damn right you will. We're still meeting for breakfast after you check out. I moved my meeting back to the afternoon, so I can take you to the airport myself. You know I'm still annoyed you insisted on staying at a hotel instead of with me."

"Dad…" I groan. "You downsized. Your two-bedroom condo is beautiful, but it's not big enough for us women and our luggage." I giggle, and he grunts. My dad finally made the decision to sell our family home and buy a condo closer to the stadium in Lower Manhattan since he will be spending a lot of his time there.

"I know, I know. I'll see you in the morning," he says.

"Okay, Dad. Tell Corrine I hope she feels better soon."

"Will do."

"What happened?" Giselle asks once I end the phone call.

"Corrine has food poisoning, and Shelby is stuck babysitting. I guess it's just us."

"Well, that sucks! But we're going to have a fabulous time."

We approach the bouncer and, after paying the cover charge, enter the club. We aren't even down the hall when Giselle's name is called.

She turns around, yells, "Oh my God," and then runs into a man's arms.

"Christian, this is my best friend, Livi; Livi, this is

Christian. We dated for a while in high school." Her cheeks flush pink, and I remember her telling me about the guy she left in New York to move to Paris. He's now the lead singer of some huge band here in the U.S.

"Nice to meet you." Christian shakes my hand. "Are you back for good?" he asks Giselle.

"Actually, this is our last night here."

"Then you have to give me tonight," he says forward as ever, causing Giselle's pink-colored cheeks to deepen to a dark crimson.

She glances my way, and I nod my encouragement. "Go and catch up. I'll order us a couple of drinks and bring them over."

"Are you sure?" Giselle asks.

"Yes! Go! Christian, would you like something to drink?"

"I'm good, but thanks," he says, "I have my beer over at my table. It's in the back corner just behind the bar. I spotted Giselle and didn't want to take a chance of losing her in the crowd." Christian gives her a soft smile. "I can't believe after all this time we ran into each other here."

Giselle smiles back. "I know…it's been a long time."

"Okay, I'll get us drinks and then find you guys," I say, wanting to give them some privacy. They obviously have a lot of catching up to do.

Giselle throws her arms around me in a tight hug and whispers, "Go find a guy to get under." I just shake my head. Earlier, she told me the best way to get over a break up is to get under someone else. I love Giselle to death, but she's freaking crazy.

She and Christian head to a booth nearby, and I go to the bar to order us a drink. The club is packed, and the bartenders seem to be picking and choosing who they're serving. I attempt to get their attention, waving my bill in the air, but it's not happening.

Just as I'm about to give up and go beg Giselle to dance on the bar to get their attention, I feel a whisper of a breath in my ear. "Can I buy you a drink?" I turn slightly to see who the owner of the voice is and find myself staring at one of the most sexiest men I've ever laid eyes on. Messy light brown hair that looks like he just climbed out of bed, dark green eyes that scream trouble, and day-old scruff that has me clenching my legs together as I imagine his face buried between my thighs. I back up slightly to get a better look at him. He's built but not bulky—lean and fit. He's dressed in an expensive light green button-down shirt that makes his eyes pop even more.

My eyes drag back up to his face and land on his cocky grin, telling me he knows how hot he is. He knows he can get any woman he wants, and that look has me wanting to show him that not every woman bows down to guys like him. When I politely tell him I can buy my own drink, he laughs, and the melodic yet masculine sound has my insides melting. He shoots one glance over to the bartender near us, and she comes running our way. Of course he has no problem getting the female bartender's attention.

We order.

We drink.

We dance.

And several hours later, I do the craziest thing I've ever

done in my twenty-four years. I invite him back to my hotel room, where we have the hottest, most passionate night of sex I've ever experienced. Our chemistry is undeniable and off the charts, and for a moment I think about what it would be like to be with this man again. But I quickly check that thought, remembering what this was about. *My attempt at getting under someone to get over someone else.*

The next morning, I wake up and leave him sleeping in my bed.

I check-out.

I have breakfast with my dad.

I board my flight.

I arrive home.

My luggage gets lost.

A week later it's found.

Three weeks after that I find out I'm pregnant.

Giselle and I search the football roster for a Cole, hoping we might find him on there. He did mention he loves—and hates—to play football. Giselle calls Christian to see if maybe he's heard of him. They only briefly met, but it's worth a try. Unfortunately, he doesn't know who he is.

I ask my dad—as nonchalantly as possible—if he knows a Cole. He says he doesn't.

I search the headshots on the ESPN sites. What I don't take into account is that because he's a free agent, he hasn't been put on the roster since the season hasn't officially begun.

So, I do the only thing I can do. I move on with my life with my growing baby inside me. I don't tell anyone how much it hurts every time I think about my baby never knowing his father. I keep it to myself how much my heart breaks whenever I think about being a single mom. Not because I can't do it, but because that's not what I want. I wanted the fairytale like my parents had. I wanted the happily-ever-after. There's no Disney book where the mom gets knocked up from a one-night stand and raises the baby alone.

When my dad asks who the father is, I tell him the truth. It was a one-night stand. I can hear his disappointment. I was raised to believe in the power of love. He's been with two women his entire life: my mom and my stepmom.

He asks me to come home.

I agree to come back temporarily.

Giselle graduates in December, and we pack up the flat and head to New York.

I've been here for three weeks, focusing on buying a place and then getting it ready for my baby.

My dad asks me to attend a game since I haven't been to one all season.

I look out from the owner's suite and see *him*.

The father of my baby.

Six

NICK

"Olivia, honey. What the hell happened?" Coach Harper asks his daughter.

"He..." She points directly at me, her perfectly manicured fingernail pressing into my chest. "He said his name was Cole! Not Nick!"

"My name is Nicholas," I point out, "and what does it matter what I'm called?"

"It matters"—her voice raises several levels—"because I looked for you! I searched the roster for Cole! I asked my dad if he knew of a Cole!" This woman is so mad right now, I'm thankful she doesn't have a weapon in her possession, because if she did, I would be a dead man. I can't imagine her getting this worked up is good for her, and really...what is she so mad about? I'm the one finding out a one-night stand I had nine months ago—who I might add, left me—might've left me a father. Something I've decided this past year I'm not at all interested in becoming.

"First of all, you're the one who walked out the door the morning after, leaving me with nothing but a 'thanks for the fuck' note. Second of all, I'm not sure you should be yelling and screaming and getting all worked up in your condition."

And I don't think that was the right thing to say because that finger that was in my chest a moment ago becomes several fingers as she pushes my chest in frustration.

"It was a one-night stand! What did you want from me? To ask you to marry me? I was leaving back to Paris! And this…" She points to her belly. "It's not a goddamn condition! It's called pregnancy, you moron!"

I hold my hands up in a placating manner. "Okay…but I don't get why you're yelling at me. You left me that morning. I woke up, and you were gone. I didn't do anything wrong."

She looks around the silent locker room as if just now realizing our conversation is taking place in front of the entire New York Brewers football team. Using a lower, more controlled tone, she says, "Umm…maybe because you said your name was Cole when everybody else calls you NICK! And…you're the one who put me in this *condition*, as you call it."

Oh. Hell. No. "Like fucking hell I did…we used protection. You better go figure out who else you slept with that you didn't use protection with." I shrug. *Glad we cleared that shit up.*

I turn to walk away not wanting to continue this pointless conversation. The locker room is still radio silent, and then I hear a loud screech. I turn back around to see what the hell that noise is when I'm decked in the head with a hard object. I grab the side of my face as it radiates with pain. "What the fuck!"

I look down, and there's a water bottle rolling across the ground. "Did you just throw that at me?"

"You're lucky that's all I did!" she shrieks again, this time grabbing a Gatorade bottle off the table and chucking it at me. I duck out of the way this time as the bottle hits the wall with a bang.

"Coach, get your crazy fucking daughter away from me."

"I'm going to kill him," she says to her dad, and then she's coming after me. Thankfully, her father pulls her back before she reaches me.

"Olivia, calm down, please." She relaxes slightly at his words, but then her eyes go wide, and she looks down. There's liquid dripping down her leg. Is she so upset she peed herself? My conscience gets the best of me, and I almost feel bad. I didn't want to upset a pregnant woman. She's clearly distraught over not knowing who the father of her baby is.

"Dad," she whispers, her voice coming out soft, reminding me of the woman I met at the club and spent the night getting to know in the most intimate way. "It's too early." She shakes her head then glances toward me, tears welling up and glossing over her brown eyes.

Her dad looks down at the puddle, and he must know

something I don't, because he says, "Let's get you to the hospital." Our argument completely forgotten, she nods in agreement. Holding onto her arm, he walks her through the locker room while pulling out his cell phone and calling someone. "Corrine, can you pull the car around? Olivia is in labor." Well shit, apparently peeing yourself means you're about to have a baby.

Killian's eyes meet mine with shock and worry. "Are you going to go to the hospital?"

"For what?" I step around the mess on the floor as the janitor comes over to mop it up.

"She's about to have your baby." He says the words slowly like I'm an idiot.

"She's about to have *a* baby." I shake my head. "Not mine."

"Nick, is there any chance that kid could be yours?"

I think back to that night. I was tipsy, but I wasn't drunk. I'm positive we used protection: in the bed, against the dresser, me on top, her on top…Fuck! Did we use one when I woke up in the middle of the night and pulled her on top of me?

"Nick." Killian pulls me out of my memory. "Are you one hundred percent sure?"

"I-I'm pretty sure." But as I say the words, I know they might be a lie.

"If there's any chance you could be the dad, you need to go to that hospital. You don't want to live with that regret, man." His words sound ominous, almost like he can empathize with what I'm going through.

Killian drives me to the hospital in his car, since we drove together this morning. I was hoping to get in the doors without being seen, but it's just my luck the fucking paparazzi followed us here. It shouldn't surprise me, though. With Killian driving his fucking Bugatti, we stick out like a damn sore thumb. He drives me around to the side, but there's no way to get in other than through the main doors or the emergency room entrance.

"Fuck it. I'm just going to have to make a run for it."

"Good luck, man. I'd wait in the waiting room for you, but I don't want to draw any more attention to you. Text me once you know anything." Killian pats me on my back before I jump out of his car.

Photos are taken and questions are slung my way, but I ignore them all. When I get inside, I'm met by none other than my dad and Amber, my publicist. They pull me into a private room where nobody can overhear our conversation.

"Dad? What are you doing here?" My publicist, I understand, as it's her job to keep my name squeaky clean. Plus, I called her on my way over here. But I'm not sure why my dad would fly all the way from North Carolina when he could just call me or Amber. And how the hell did he get here so fast?

"Your mother and I flew in last night for the game!" he barks. "In case you forgot you're in the middle of the goddamned playoffs!"

"Yeah, I'm well aware," I snap.

"So, is it true?" he asks. "Did you knock up this woman?"

"I-I don't know. She says the baby is mine, and we did spend the night together..." I can't believe this is happening. The last thing I wanted was to be a dad. I had it in my head being a father wasn't in the cards for me.

"Damn it, Nick! Have you not listened to a single word I've said to you over the years!" My dad shakes his head in disappointment. He's engrained it into my head a million times over the years to be careful. Too many guys end up paying half of everything they've earned by being cavalier when it comes to wrapping their dicks up. I also think, while he's never said it, him knocking up my mom meant he was forced to marry her. I've never asked them, but I'm almost positive my dad has cheated on my mom several times over the years—and vice versa.

"You have everything going for you," he continues. "You have your career back, your personal life is on track. I can't believe you would be this careless." He curses under his breath as he storms out of the room.

Jesus, he's acting like I'm the first guy in professional sports to get a woman pregnant by accident. He's a damn sport's agent. Half his clients probably have kids from one-night stands.

"Did you call my dad on your way here?" I ask Amber once my dad is gone.

"No, but I'm pretty sure it got leaked by a fan or someone. There's footage of the pregnant woman and Coach Harper leaving the stadium, and then you and Killian following almost directly after."

"Her name is Liv…Olivia. She's Coach Harper's daughter."

Amber's eyes go wide. "I'll make a statement right away. I'll keep it simple. We don't know anything at this time, and you're requesting privacy while you get it sorted." She gives me a sympathetic smile.

"All right, thank you."

Seven

OLIVIA

My feet are in the stirrups, and the doctor is sitting between my legs. When we arrived several hours ago, I was checked in and then brought back to labor and delivery. The nurse hooked me up to several monitors and took my blood. When I requested an epidural for the pain, she frowned apologetically and said I was already too far along for it, but she could give me some pain reliever. Once I was situated, I called Giselle to fill her in, and she immediately left her mom's house to meet me here. The doctor has come by numerous times to check on my progress, and my family has been in and out of my room to make sure I'm okay throughout my labor. A few minutes ago, after checking on the baby's status once again, the doctor informed me it's time to push.

Since I made the decision to only have Giselle in the room with me when I give birth, my dad is outside with

Corrine and Shelby, while Giselle is next to me currently holding my hand.

"Okay, Olivia. Here comes a contraction," the doctor says. "Push for me." I push through the contraction, and the pain is like nothing I've ever felt before. I almost feel bad I might break Giselle's hand from squeezing it too hard. "That's good…and relax." This process goes on and on and on for God knows how long. Each push hurts worse than the last. My body is tiring out.

And then finally in the middle of another push, the doctor says, "I see hair. You're close." I stop pushing, taking a small break, and wait for the next one to hit. My throat is dry from screaming and exerting myself, and I'm seriously questioning this so-called pain reliever the nurse insisted she gave me.

"Sir, you can't go in there!" the nurse shouts, and I look over to see Cole's large frame filling the doorway.

"I might be the father," he says, ignoring her and walking inside. I'm about to kick him out when another contraction hits, and I find myself pushing.

"Oh my God!" I scream in pain.

"Keep going. Keep going," the doctor commands. "There he is!" My body finds relief as the doctor holds the baby up. "Congratulations."

The nurse comes over and cleans up my baby boy, then she sucks all the stuff out of his nose. He's screaming and crying, and it's the most beautiful sound I've ever heard.

"Would you like to cut the umbilical cord?" the doctor asks Nick, and I shoot him a warning glare, which he ignores—Nick, not the doctor.

"Oh, I'm not a doctor." Nick shakes his head, and the doctor chuckles while I roll my eyes.

"I know, I am. Sometimes the dads like to cut the umbilical cord that connects the mother to the baby."

Nick nods and slowly steps forward. The nurse holds my baby while the doctor hands Nick the scissors to cut the umbilical cord. I want to yell at him and tell him not to touch anything involving *my* baby. Not even a few hours ago he was accusing me of lying and saying the baby isn't even his. But I don't say a word because I can't. My heart is pained, and there's a huge lump in my throat. This was supposed to be my husband cutting the umbilical cord. I read about this in a baby book. It's a tradition for men to feel like they're part of the delivery—to help establish an emotional connection between the father and the baby. Tears blur my vision as I watch Nick carefully cut the cord. I feel Giselle's hand on my shoulder, and when I look up, she's snapping pictures with her phone camera. I, both, hate and love her for that.

"Good job!" the doctor says, taking the scissors back from Nick, who nods once and backs up out of the way. The nurse finishes cleaning off my still-crying baby, then she wraps him up in a blanket and places him on my chest. "Shh...it's okay," I coo. "Mommy has you." I bring my hands up to hold him as his warm body rests against mine. "I love you, baby boy." I place a kiss on his forehead.

"I'm going to get him checked out," the nurse says, taking him from me far too soon. "As soon as you're stitched up and moved to recovery, I'll bring the baby to you."

I watch as she takes my entire world away from me. "Is

he okay?" I ask another nurse. "I wasn't due for a few more weeks."

"We'll know more once the tests are run, but he seems perfect." I close my eyes in relief as everybody bustles around me getting the room cleaned up. The doctor lets me know the placenta has passed, then he stitches up a cut he had to make so I didn't tear. I'm lifted and transferred to a clean bed, given a fresh gown, and moved to a new room.

The entire time I feel Cole still lingering in the background, but I ignore him. I have nothing to say to that asshole. He might've been the best sex of my life, and I'll never regret that night because it gave me the most precious miracle in the world, but still…fuck him.

Once I'm situated in my new room, my dad, Corrine, and Shelby come in and join Giselle and me. That's when I notice Cole isn't here anymore. Well good fucking riddance. "We saw the baby being brought to the nursery for tests. He's beautiful," Corrine gushes, and I smile.

"I took like a million pictures." Giselle holds her phone out for me to take.

"Thank you!" I pull her in for a hug before I begin swiping through each photo.

"Is that Nick?" my dad asks when I stop on the one of him cutting the umbilical cord.

"Yeah, he snuck in and declared himself *possibly* the dad, and the doctor asked if he wanted to cut the umbilical cord." I swipe to another photo.

"I can still remember when I got to do that with you." My dad smiles at me. "One of the greatest moments of my life."

"Yeah, well, I doubt Nick felt the same way." Fresh tears surface, and I will them away. *Damn hormones.*

"Okay, here he is." The nurse comes in, pushing my baby in a rolling bassinet. "His Apgar scores were perfect." She hands me a piece of paper that shows the tests which were given, along with the scores. "His lungs are fully developed. It says in your birthing plan that you're planning to bottle-feed. Here are a couple different kinds." She pulls the bottles out. "This one is good, but if he has reflux or a sensitive belly, try this one." She points to the different formulas.

"Thank you." She picks him up and brings him to me. I shake the bottle gently like I read in the baby books and bring the nipple to his mouth. He starts sucking and drinking immediately. Giselle comes over and snaps another picture. A few minutes later, there's a knock on the door and the nurse opens it. Nick walks in and glances around the room.

"Now's not the time," my dad says.

"Dad, it's fine." I lean over and give my baby boy a soft kiss on his forehead before I pick him up to burp him. "Can you guys give us a few minutes, please?" It's best to get this over with. Reluctantly, everyone leaves.

"Sorry for barging in earlier. I was waiting outside your door, but when I heard you scream, I thought something was wrong."

"It's called giving birth," I say dryly. "Why are you even here?"

"I'm not really sure."

"Look, if you don't want to be a dad, you don't have to be."

"And what is it you want?" He stands at the end of my bed, his arms crossed over his chest. His question comes out cold and distant. He's nothing like the man I spent the night with all those months ago. Or maybe I just convinced myself it was more than what it really was.

"It doesn't matter to me…" I start to say, but he shakes his head.

"No, I mean what do you want in order for me to sign over my rights? How much? You're right, I don't want to be a dad." My heart breaks when he says this. My mind going back to my fantasy—the one where I have a baby with a man who loves me. We would get married, buy a house with a backyard like the one I grew up in, and we would start a family together. I didn't realize it until right now, but when I watched him step forward and cut that umbilical cord, something in me felt a sense of hope that maybe he wanted this too.

My little man burps. When I lower him from my shoulder to take a good look at him, his eyes are already fluttering shut. I swaddle him in his blanket, but instead of laying him in the bassinet, I hold him, hoping that having him in my arms will help heal my broken heart.

Just as I'm about to respond, a woman comes barreling through the door. "Ugh! Do you know how hard it was to get through the hospital without being photographed?"

Having no clue who this woman is or why she's in my room, I say, "Excuse me?"

"Celeste, what are you doing here?" Cole walks over to her. *Okay… I guess he knows her.*

"It's all over social media! Do you not understand how

bad this looks? And I'm your fiancée! A phone call to let me know would've been nice." Taking a closer look at the woman, I spot a gigantic engagement ring on her left hand, the hand that's waving around in frustration as she drones on about being blindsided. She's skinny and tall and lacks any major curves, yet she's stunningly beautiful. Her hair is long and black and smooth. She's wearing what I recognize as a Valentino dress from his couture winter line, and her makeup appears to be professionally done. I can't put my finger on it, but I recognize her from somewhere…

"I was forced to leave the shoot, and now it will need to be rescheduled for another night." Oh, yeah! She's a model. I've seen her on billboards. And…wait a second…holy shit! She's Celeste Leblanc. I only purchase my makeup from her line. It's the best. Jesus, Olivia…now is not the time to fangirl over her and her amazing makeup line. She's your baby-daddy's fiancée for God's sake.

"I didn't ask you to come here," Cole points out. "And I was going to call you, but everything happened so fast."

"Ahem." I clear my throat, and both of them whip around to acknowledge I'm in the room. "If you guys wouldn't mind, maybe you could discuss this…oh, I don't know"—I lift my shoulders in a shrug—"out of my room." I hold my sleeping baby up slightly. "I just gave birth, and I'm a bit tired." I'm aware my words come out bitchy, but we'll blame it on the new mom hormones. Okay, no, screw that. I'll take responsibility. I just don't want to hear them.

"Look, Celeste. I didn't know she was pregnant. I just found out. And I didn't know the press and paparazzi figured it out until I got here." He looks at me. "I'm going to call my attorney and find out about having a paternity test done."

I would rather not do this with an audience, but I guess I have no choice.

"You said you didn't want to be his dad," I point out.

Celeste's eyes swing from him to me, and she gives me an incredulous look. "Wait a second, you're not pushing for Nick to be the father? Then what's your angle?"

Refusing to discuss this with a woman I don't know—and also mentally making a note to throw away all of my makeup—I say to Cole—or shit, I guess it's *Nick*, "I told you, you're the father. If you don't want to be the dad, you don't have to be." I try my best to keep my crazy emotions from leaking out. "I don't know what happened that night, but I didn't get pregnant on purpose. I'm not going to force you to want our son." I hear my voice crack on the last word, but I will myself not to cry. It's not like I'm in love with the man—I don't even know him. I just always thought I would raise my children in a two-parent loving home like my parents gave me. I never thought at twenty-five I would be a single mother.

With his eyes trained on my baby in my arms, he says, "I still want to know."

Celeste steps closer to him and says, "If you take that test and it proves you're the dad, there's no going back. You're the one who said you don't want to be a dad. The last thing that baby needs is a father who doesn't want him."

He nods once and then says, "If I'm the father, I'll pay you whatever it is you want."

"Will you stop saying that?" My voice comes out harsh, and my baby jumps in his sleep. "I don't want or need your money, and if you don't want to be this baby's father then I don't want you to be. If you want a paternity test, fine. I know he's yours. Now both of you...*get out*."

Nick opens his mouth to argue but closes it. Both of them walk out and close the door behind them.

A few minutes later, my dad, Corrine, Shelby, and Giselle all come back into the room. Nobody asks what happened. Instead, we focus our energy on the beautiful, healthy baby.

"Do we have a name?" Giselle asks.

"Yes, we do. Reed Cameron Harper." I look to my dad, and he gives me a warm smile.

"Oh, sweetie!" Corrine coos. "That's perfect. Both of your parents' middle names." Tears well in her eyes as my dad cuts across the room to my bedside.

"If your mom were here, she would be loving on her grandson. She'd be so proud of the woman you've become."

"What is there to be proud of? Getting knocked up from a one-night stand?" I joke, but even I can hear the embarrassing truth in my words.

"No, for taking responsibility. You're going to be an amazing mom just like yours was."

NICK

It's been a week since I walked out of the hospital with Celeste and argued with her for hours over the Olivia and baby situation.

"I can't believe this is happening," she says. "Everything was going perfectly fine. And now it's all about to be destroyed because of your one-night stand. I shouldn't be surprised." She throws her arms up in exasperation. *"You're a man, which means keeping your dick in your pants is impossible."*

"This happened before we got together!" I shout in frustration. She's acting like I asked for this to happen. *"You knew I was sleeping around. It's part of the reason I agreed to make good on our pact."*

After I was told I needed to settle down, figuring I had nothing to lose, I called up Celeste and agreed to go through with our pact. At least with her, I knew what I was getting myself into. A business arrangement. We dated for a couple months and then announced our engagement. Celeste let the lease on her apartment go and moved in with me once I purchased a place in Lower Manhattan near the stadium—and directly above Killian.

"I know." She nods. "I just…I thought being with you would be safe," she whispers.

"I'm sorry," I say, "But it's not as if I cheated on you." Despite the fact that Celeste and I have never once had sex, I've been one hundred percent faithful to her. It's not that we didn't try. We did. But the foreplay was robotic, and neither of us could get into it. After getting her off, I ended up finishing in the shower using my hand. We've never spoken about it or tried to have sex again.

"I know that," she says, her voice rough with emotion. "That's not what I meant." She swallows thickly.

"Celeste, what's going on?" I've never seen her like this. Celeste doesn't do emotion. She doesn't get her feelings hurt. "Talk to me."

She opens her mouth to speak then closes it. She stands taller, straightening her back and squaring her shoulders. "Nothing is going on," she says. "I just meant that I thought you would be safe for my reputation. I guess I was wrong."

"I can't change what happened," I tell her, "but this doesn't have to change anything between us."

"Don't you get it?" She shakes her head. "This changes everything." She sighs in defeat and sits down on the couch. I walk over and sit next to her. "I didn't sign up for this, Nick."

I know from the outside it may seem like Celeste is being a bitch, but she's right. She didn't sign up for this. In the beginning of our relationship, we hammered out all the details. Celeste wanted to make sure we were both on the same page. She told me she didn't want to have kids and I agreed. I feel bad that my past is complicating what we have. Celeste doesn't deserve any of this.

The truth is, from the beginning, being with Celeste has been easy.

Because of our high-demanding careers, we're rarely ever home, both busy living our lives. There's no expectations. No emotions involved. She's more like a roommate than my fiancée.

We both sit in silence for a few minutes, and then she asks, "What are you going to do?"

"I don't know," I admit. "I don't know what the right answer is."

"You said you didn't want to be a dad," she says, "You told me you felt like you were never good enough in your parents' eyes. And you said that Fiona not getting pregnant was for the best."

"I know." She's right. I did say all that. But at the time I said all that I didn't think there was a chance of me actually becoming a dad. Now, there's a baby who I might share DNA with.

"And what about Olivia?" she asks.

"What about her?"

"You said it yourself the morning after you two hooked up that you thought there could be something more between you guys. Are you telling me you honestly haven't thought about how she plays into this picture?"

I let out a low groan, regretting my decision to confide in Celeste the morning after. "She walked away that morning, leaving me with nothing more than a note. Her only role in my life would be as my son's mother." As I say those words, my heart strings feel like they're being tugged. Watching her deliver the baby was probably the single most amazing thing I've ever witnessed. She was so strong through it all. And then when she held him in her arms...the love that shown through in her eyes... In all my years growing up, I don't think I ever saw my own mother look at me the way Olivia looked at her son. Had she not left without giving me her number, who knows how things would be different right now. But it doesn't matter because she did leave, and now I'm engaged to Celeste. It's pointless to focus on the what-ifs.

"She probably wants to trap you."

"Did you not see her in the hospital? She can barely stand to be in the same room as me."

"Then she's doing it for the money," Celeste states.

"I don't think so," I say honestly. "She said she doesn't want my money."

"There you go being all naïve once again."

"I'm not being naïve," I argue.

Celeste turns her body slightly in my direction and our eyes lock, neither of us saying a word as she tries to determine if there are any hidden emotions behind my features. She's trying to figure out what I'm thinking but not saying. Finally, she sighs and says, "It's like we're teenagers all over again. How many times are you going to let a woman manipulate your emotions?" She gives me a pointed look. "You said it yourself. She's the same woman who left you the morning after with nothing more than a note. Who knows what her angle is now that she knows you're a professional athlete."

I hear everything she's saying, and had she mentioned all this before I watched Olivia give birth I probably would've agreed, but the problem is I saw the little boy who might be my son. Hell, I even cut his damn umbilical cord. I saw the way Olivia's love for her son shone through. And while I won't admit this to Celeste, it made my heart feel something I haven't felt in a long time. Does that scare the shit out of me? Hell yes, it does. But it also feels damn good to feel something, anything, again.

"I really don't think she has an angle."

Without her eyes leaving mine, she says, "You want her." Her tone as she says those three words contain zero emotion, as if she's simply stating a fact. A fact I'm not ready to deal with yet. Because those three *words, if they are true, will change everything, just like Celeste said.*

"This isn't about her," I say, deflecting. "This is about a baby who might be my son."

"Yeah, okay, Nick. We both know you think with your heart. It won't be long until you've ditched me to play house with your baby mamma."

"Celeste…" I begin to say, but she cuts me off.

"Don't 'Celeste' me. Just think about this before you make any rash decisions. You agreed to give this relationship a chance, not only because of your reputation but because you were tired of getting your heart stomped on. Since we've been together, how many times has your heart been broken? Zero." I don't point out that my heart can't be broken if it isn't on the line.

"You want to go play Daddy to this baby, fine." She lets out a frustrated sigh. "I'm not going to stop you. I would never try to stop a father from taking responsibility. But don't be so naïve to think this woman is your one true love. You aren't going to find out you're the dad and live happily-ever-after, Nick."

I can hear the fear in her voice. She won't ever admit it, but one of Celeste's biggest fears is not being put first. Her dad never came back for her mom or her, and in her eyes, he chose someone else over them. And then for years, her mom put her love for her dad above her own daughter. Beatrice chose to stay in that trailer park and work at that diner over creating a good life for Celeste. Now she's afraid I'm going to choose my son and his mother over her, leaving her once again on her own. She comes across so tough on a day-to-day basis that sometimes I forget how insecure Celeste really is.

"All I want to do is find out if that little boy is my son."

"And what if he is, Nick? What then? What will that mean for us?"

"I'm not breaking off our engagement," I tell her.

"Yet." She huffs and snatches her purse off the table. I know I should stop her and convince her she's wrong, make her feel secure about us, but for some reason I can't bring myself to do it, to say the words she needs to hear.

"I need to get going," she says. I watch her walk to the door, but then she stops and turns around. "You might not see where this is all going, but I do. And as your best friend I'm going to warn you just like I did when we were younger. She's going to break your heart." I open my mouth to argue, but she doesn't give me a chance. "And when she does, this time I will *say I told you so." And without waiting for me to respond, she swings the door open and then slams it shut behind her.*

I hate to admit it, but on some level Celeste is right. Olivia walked away that day. She didn't want a future with me. If she did, she would've stuck around or left me her number. She did neither. I was nothing more than a one-night stand to her that left her knocked up.

The next morning I called my attorney, and he put a petition in to the courts to establish paternity. I went to the hospital, got swabbed, and left. Now, I'm just waiting to find out the results.

Yesterday, my mom called to find out when she would see me for Christmas—which really meant she wanted to find out my side of what's going on. Luckily, we had an away game, so I was able to put off her inquisition temporarily. But at some point I'm going to have to deal with her. There's no way she's going back to North Carolina until she gets some answers. My dad has already mentioned them finding a short-term lease here in New York. I'd like to think it's so they can be near me for moral support, but I know better. I've been spending every day at practice or in the gym to keep busy. I need to stay focused. We're too damn close to becoming champions for my drama to fuck it all up now.

The negative tension between Coach and me has been awkward to say the least, and I was worried it would rub off on the rest of the team, but we made it through our game— winning 24-21. We already clinched a spot in the playoffs, but this game determined if we would have home-field advantage. It was a close game, and it had the commentators talking, questioning if I'm regressing with the new weight and stress on my shoulders. Celeste was right in that regard. The tabloids and gossip rags are all talking, and none of it is projecting me in a positive light.

I was hoping when we returned today, I would come home to a quiet house, but instead, I walk in to the opposite. Groaning when I spot everyone, I consider sneaking back out and heading to Killian's place, but before I can, Celeste spots me and calls out my name.

"Thanks for letting me know everyone is here, *babe*." I glare at my fiancée, and she shoots daggers back at me. Nobody besides Killian has any clue about our pact-slash-fake relationship.

"Of course we're here!" My mom huffs. "Yesterday was Christmas and you were away. I was thinking we can open gifts. Celeste said your results are back. They came in this morning. Has this *woman* told you what she wants yet?"

I grab the envelope off the counter and notice it's been opened. "Really? You guys opened the results for me?"

"We need to know what we're working with, Nick," my dad says. "I saw your game yesterday. You can't let this baby news affect your game, and if you don't nip this shit in the bud, she'll be suing you for child support."

"So, I'm the father?" I ask, pulling the papers out to read them myself.

"Yes," Celeste answers, zero emotion showing through her rough exterior. "But this doesn't have to change anything." She comes over to me and puts her hands on my arms.

"I need to think about all this," I tell her honestly. Now that I officially know I'm the father, there are a million different thoughts swarming around in my head. It was one thing to consider the possibility, but now it's fact. I'm someone's dad.

Not liking my answer, Celeste squeezes my arms. "What is there to think about?"

"A lot, actually," I say, moving my arms out of her grip.

"Like what?" she presses.

"How about the fact that I have a child with my coach's daughter, for starters?" That's not really high on my list of worries, but it's the safest thought to say out loud.

"That's hardly a concern," my dad says. "Your season is almost over, which means so is your contract, and with the way you've been playing, every team is going to want you."

"Like who?" Celeste asks.

"LA for one," my dad says. This gets Celeste's attention. I can already hear the ideas forming in her head of moving across the country and away from Olivia. LA isn't really where Celeste wants to live, but since she sometimes travels there for work, it wouldn't be the end of the world.

"I don't know what the future holds. For all we know, I could end up in Michigan or somewhere." I name the last place in the world Celeste would want to end up just to fuck with her, and it works. She shudders then glares.

"Don't be ridiculous, Nick," she seethes.

"I need to go speak to Liv about the paternity. Now, as my fiancée, do you want to go with me?" I know she won't want to go, but at least I can say I tried.

"I need to catch my flight soon."

"Mom, do you want to go with me to meet your grandchild?"

My mom scrunches up her nose. "How about you send me a picture? At that age, all they do is eat and sleep anyway."

"Dad?" I ask stupidly, but before he can answer, my mom cuts in.

"Can we please open presents?"

"And that's my cue to leave," my dad says. "Money doesn't get made by itself. I have a meeting with a potential client." He glances down at his watch to check the time. My mom doesn't even ask him to stay, like it's perfectly normal for her husband to choose work over spending Christmas with his family. And I guess it is. It's how it's always been.

Once he's gone, the three of us make our way to the living room, and my mom grabs the gifts under the small tree Celeste paid to have brought in.

Both women open their gifts, squealing with delight. Celeste throws herself into my arms, giving me a kiss on my cheek. "Thank you so much." She puts the stainless-steel Tiffany watch on her wrist then shows it to my mom. "Isn't it gorgeous?" *I'm not sure why she's acting so shocked, she picked the damn thing out herself.*

My mom agrees. "It is. Thank you, Nick." She holds up

the certificate for the week-long cruise I purchased for her and my dad. That gift I did pick out myself. Regardless of how frozen my heart has become, I don't think I'll ever stop trying to help my parents rekindle the love they once had for each other, even if I've accepted it's most likely not going to happen. I figured a cruise would be a good place for them to get away and enjoy each other's company.

"You're welcome, Mom."

She leans over and gives me a kiss on my cheek. "I love you, sweetie."

I nod absently as the women open up the other gifts I got for them, the smiles on their faces never faltering, and I wonder what it would take to put a smile on Olivia's face. Most women are simple. Expensive jewelry, clothes, vacations, and they're good to go. Olivia, on the other hand, that day in the locker room and then in the hospital room, didn't want anything I had to offer. Then I question why I'm even thinking about what it would take to make her happy. It's not my job to make her happy. I shouldn't *want* to make her happy.

Celeste may think I'm going to end up with Olivia, but she's wrong. Olivia chose to walk away that morning after. She's one of the reasons I agreed to the pact with Celeste in the first place. No emotions. But even as I try to convince myself what I'm thinking is how I really feel, I can't overlook the fact that Olivia has crossed my mind a dozen times since Celeste and I talked. I may not want her to be in my thoughts, but that isn't stopping her from being in them.

"All right, I need to head over to Olivia's."

"Wait, I have a gift for the two of you." My mom runs

to her purse and pulls out an envelope.

Celeste opens it then jumps up off the couch. "Oh, Victoria! Thank you!"

"What is it?"

"It's an appointment with Dedra Fray, one of the most elusive wedding planners in the world! How did you do this? I heard she has a wait list a mile long."

"I've become close with Kelly Parks."

"The mother of Zack Parks, my teammate?" I question.

"Yes, she's so sweet. Anyway, his wife used Dedra, and when I mentioned Celeste would be looking for a planner soon, she called in a favor. Turns out Dedra is a huge fan of yours, Celeste."

"Oh, wow! Thank you. I can't wait to start planning our wedding. You'll come with me, right?" she asks my mom.

"Of course. Maybe we can finally get your mom to fly up with me so she can join us."

"I doubt it," Celeste says with a frown. "It's been ten years since I moved to New York, and she hasn't once agreed to leave Piermont. Not even for a weekend."

"I know, but maybe I can convince her," my mom says.

"Yeah, maybe." Celeste shrugs.

"You know, when I spoke to Dedra, she mentioned a few locations that have availability. She thinks the Seversky Mansion might even have an opening for a summer wedding."

"This summer?" I choke out. My throat feels like it's tightening and blocking my airflow.

"Yes, Nicholas. This summer." My mom shoots me a hard glare.

"I thought we were going to do a longer engagement," I mention to Celeste, who is now shooting daggers my way. *I guess the excitement over the gifts has worn off.*

"Are you having second thoughts?" Celeste asks. She raises one brow, challenging me to lie to her...or maybe to admit the truth. The problem is I don't know what answer would be a lie or the truth.

"Can we please talk about this when you get back?" I ask. "I really need to head over to Olivia's to discuss this paternity situation."

Celeste nods once. "Of course." The hurt that comes through in her voice is evident, and I hate that I'm the reason she's hurting, but I don't know how to fix any of this.

"Don't be like that." I attempt to grab her hand as she turns to walk away, but she yanks her hand out of my reach. "I'll see you when you get back," I say to her as she walks down the hall toward our room.

She ignores me, and knowing how stubborn she is, I don't attempt to apologize. Instead, I say goodbye to my mom and then head out.

Nine

OLIVIA

"Do you think the couch would look better against this wall?" Giselle points to the wall across from the fireplace. "Or maybe this wall?" She points to the wall adjacent to the one she just pointed to. We've been settled into our brownstone in Brooklyn Heights for close to a month, but I'm beginning to think Giselle will never be settled with our décor. We put up a small Christmas tree in the corner, and now that it's gone, Giselle's back to rearranging our furniture. The woman didn't even wait until New Year's Day to take the tree down.

When I found this brownstone online, she insisted we keep all the furnishings in our flat in Paris there. She claimed it was because she didn't want us to spend the money shipping it all to New York, but we both knew she just needed an excuse to decorate while she's job hunting. With a bachelor's and master's degree in Interior Design, my best friend better know everything there is to know about decorating a place. Who even knew you could go to school for six years to learn how to decorate a room?

"I think it should stay right where it is." And yes, my answer has everything to do with the fact that I'm currently sitting on the couch in question. Giselle pops her hip out and glares, knowing me way too well. I laugh, setting Reed down in his bassinet.

Her phone beeps indicating an incoming text. When she looks at it, her face lights up.

"Christian?" I ask.

"Yeah." She grins, typing something back. "I just can't believe we're back together again."

"Why? Because he's a famous musician now?"

"No...well, yeah, I guess that's a little bit of it." She giggles, throwing herself onto the couch next to me. "I'm just so happy. You would think after not seeing each other for six years, it would be awkward. But it's not. It's like we picked right back up where we left off all those years ago. It just feels so surreal, like any moment I'll wake up and it will all have been a dream. When I left to Paris, I honestly never thought we would be together again, and I had accepted that, you know? Christian needed to follow his dreams, and I needed to chase mine."

"But you guys found your way back to each other. You deserve to be happy." Giselle doesn't talk often of her home life, but from the little bit she's mentioned over the years, she didn't have it easy growing up.

"I know, but sometimes I feel guilty."

"You can't feel guilty for living your life. Your mom has

your dad, and it's his job as her husband to help her. You visit all the time, and you're there for your sister. You can't do it all."

"I know. I know you're right, but it doesn't stop me from still feeling that way."

"Well stop feeling that way!" I pull Giselle into a hug. "You know if you ever need anything I'm here, right?"

"You do enough, but yes, I know. Thank you."

"I'm going to take a quick shower before we head out to brunch. Can you keep an eye on little man?"

"Of course."

Yesterday was Christmas, but because my dad was away for a game, we're all getting together today to celebrate. As I stand, the buzzer goes off indicating someone is downstairs, so I press the button. "Hello?"

"I have a certified letter for Olivia Harper to sign."

"Okay." I buzz him in.

"Paternity results?" Giselle questions.

"I'm sure." I roll my eyes as I walk to the door to wait for him so he doesn't knock and wake up Reed. We're on the third floor, so the courier will have to take the elevator up. When I see him walking down the hall, I notice he's not alone. Cole—shit, I mean Nick—is with him, and holy hell does he look hot. He's standing to the side of the courier in a baby blue collared Lacoste shirt that fits his arms and chest way too well, distressed jeans, and a pair of Nikes. The guy definitely knows how to do casual—No! No! I will not go there. He's a dumbass who doesn't even want his own baby and that makes him ugly as fuck, NOT hot.

"Hand delivering your own paternity results?" I say to

give him attitude, and he actually has the nerve to sneer at me.

"He was coming up at the same time I was, so I tagged along." His lips contort into a *fuck you* kind of smile that has me wanting to slap the smirk right off his too good-looking face.

"Next time, buzz." He gives me a confused look. "That way I can deny you access," I explain. He hits me with a hard glare, and I shoot one right back.

"Real mature," he mutters. I ignore his jab and take the envelope from the poor kid who looks unsure of what to do. I show him my identification and sign, then give him a tip. He thanks me and scurries off. *Smart kid...*

Before I can invite Nick in, he takes it upon himself to walk through my door. "Sure...come on in." I slam the door behind me in frustration and immediately regret it when Reed starts whimpering. "Damn it."

"What's he doing here?" Giselle hisses, her nose scrunched up in disgust. Have I mentioned how much I love my best friend who totally has my back?

"I'm the dad," Nick states matter-of-factly.

"No, you're the sperm donor," Giselle lobbies back. "A dad is a man who claims his baby and cares for him. You simply shot your load into her vagina. X plus Y equals baby. You're the sperm donor, not Reed's father."

Nick lets out an annoyed huff, and I stifle a laugh. Reed's cries quiet back down, telling me he's fallen back asleep. "Would you like something to drink?" I ask Nick, my manners winning out over my desire to tell him to go jump off the GE building. He shakes his head, and I head to the kitchen to grab myself a bottle of water. Untwisting the cap, I chug half the bottle down, dying of thirst. Giselle and I just finished doing some yoga. I've been doing it since I was a little girl with my mom. It's a great stress reliever, and a good way to slowly begin to get my body back in shape. I'm still in my workout clothes, and I'm hot and sweaty.

When I walk back out to the living room, Giselle is standing near the bassinet looking like a human watch dog, and Nick is on the other side. "Everything okay?" I come up next to Nick, and he's looking down at Reed sleeping.

He clears his throat and steps back. "You named him Reed?"

"Yes, Reed Cameron *Harper*." I make it a point to place emphasis on the fact our son has *my* last name. "Reed is my dad's middle name, and Cameron was my mom's." He nods, and we both stand here staring at each other. I don't know what to say, and he's not saying anything either.

"Why are you here?" Giselle asks, breaking the silence. Nick ignores her question, glancing back down at Reed. Giselle and I lock eyes, and I shrug.

"I'm going to shower," she says, but it comes out more like a question, asking me if I want to be alone with Nick.

"Okay." I give her a tight smile. Once she's down the hall, I turn to Nick. "Why are you here?" I repeat Giselle's question, only this time he doesn't ignore it.

"I never thought I would become a dad."

"I never thought I would get pregnant from my one and only one-night stand." I lean against the arm of my sofa, not leaving Reed's side.

"I really thought we used protection."

"Look"—I tilt my head toward our sleeping baby and give Nick a sarcastic grin—"it really doesn't matter now. I'm assuming the results state you're the father."

"Yeah."

"Great, glad we got that sorted out without having to go on Maury."

Nick sighs in frustration, his eyes briefly closing. When he opens them, he hits me with a hard stare. The bright green in his eyes remind me of the fresh green grass in Central Park, the first sign of spring and warmth after a long, cold, white winter. Reed has his eyes. They're still dark since he's a newborn, but the emerald is already shining through.

I should say something, but I don't. I refuse to make this easy for him. I didn't ask to get knocked up, but here I am with a baby. I don't regret having my son. I love him with every fiber of my being. But I didn't plan or ask for this. My life has completely changed while Nick's has remained the same. Every day I live in fear I'm going to mess up my son's life. Make the wrong decision. What if he one day blames me because he doesn't have a dad? Being a new mother is a lot of work. I'm exhausted. I'm emotionally and mentally drained. I'm doing the best I can, but I'm scared my best won't be good enough.

"I don't know what to say, Liv," he finally says, using the name I gave him, and I have to force myself not to go back to that night all those months ago. When everything between us clicked. When his kisses alone had the ability to drive me insane.

"You don't have to say anything, Nick." This is so freaking awkward. You would never know less than a year ago, the man standing in front of me fucked me just about every way possible and then held me in his arms while we talked for hours.

"I wouldn't make a good dad." His lips turndown into a frown, and the sadness in his voice has my heart tightening. My natural instinct is to reach over and comfort him, tell him he can do it, just like I would with one of my art students when I give classes and they feel like they're failing. When they're afraid they can't draw or paint good enough. But I don't because he's not a student or a child, and it's not my job to comfort him. My job is to care for Reed, and if Nick doesn't want to be his dad, that's his choice. There's a reason why adoption is an option. Not everybody is cut out to be a parent.

"Now that paternity has been established, you can have your attorney draw up papers to relinquish your parental rights." Nick flinches slightly, almost like the words I just said pained him, but I ignore it. "Once you do, have them sent to my attorney. I gave Reed's and my information to your attorney the other day at the office when I brought Reed in to be swabbed. There's no reason for you to come back over here ever again."

"I can give you money…" he begins to say, but I put my hand up to stop him.

"We already had this conversation. I don't want or need your money. Does it look like I'm living on the streets?" I glance around my home to make my point. We're standing in a multi-million dollar brownstone for God's sake, in one of the wealthiest areas in New York. "I can afford *my* son just fine."

"I didn't say you couldn't." His jaw clenches. "I just—I'm just trying to do the right thing here."

"Well, you don't have to worry about doing the *right thing*. I walked away that morning without telling you anything about me or getting your information. You didn't have a say in any of this, and I'm not going to force anything on you."

He sighs in frustration and then says, "If it's not money you want, then what is it?" He runs his fingers through his already messy hair, messing it up some more. "Damn it, Liv. I don't know what you want from me." His eyes are pleading with me to give him the right answer, but I can't do that because what I want isn't possible.

What I want to tell him is that I want to give Reed a family. One with a mom and a dad who love him and love each other. I want to be able to tell my son he was conceived out of love and not from a half-drunken one-night stand. I want to beg him to change his mind about wanting his son. But I don't tell him any of that. Instead, I say, "I don't want anything from you. Now if there's nothing else, I'm stinky and sweaty"—I glance down—"and I could really use a shower before Reed wakes up. I think it's best you go." I shrug my shoulders in total nonchalance when really I feel the complete opposite. He has me riled up and wanting to punch him while also wanting to crawl into my bed and ugly cry.

"Okay." He nods slowly, his eyes darting from Reed to me. He turns and walks to the door. He opens it then twists back around like he wants to say something. And a small part of me—the part that stupidly still believes in fairytales—

holds on to the hope that maybe he has changed his mind. While another part of me considers, even for a brief moment, blurting out everything I just thought and seeing where the chips fall. But the biggest part of me wants to push him out and lock the door behind him so he can't hurt me any more than he already has.

Okay…and maybe, just maybe, there's a small part that wants to pull him back in because holy shit! The man is swoon-worthy…Nope! Not going there…he's engaged and doesn't want his kid. He's off limits!

However, I neither push or pull him anywhere. Instead, I stand frozen in place, waiting to see what he does. His mouth opens and closes like he's at war with himself, and for a second I think he's actually going to say something, but he doesn't. He lifts his hand, and with a sad smile, gives me a small five-finger wave before walking out the door.

I don't realize until the door is shut that I wasn't breathing, and I let out a much-needed breath, the tears releasing I didn't know I was holding in. They race down my cheeks one after the next until Giselle comes out and finds me. She holds me to her chest as I let out every emotion I have had locked up inside of me.

As I come to accept every dream I ever had as a child, and even as an adult, of finding the kind of love my parents had—the kind of love I long for—won't be coming true.

Ten

NICK

Well, that sure as shit didn't go as planned...Then again, what the hell did I think would happen when I showed up at Olivia's home unannounced? It's not as if I exactly had a plan. I went there with the intention of discussing me being Reed's dad, but then I took one look at him and choked. And Instead of doing what I set out to do, I once again, like an idiot, offered Olivia money. I knew in the back of my mind she wouldn't accept it, but I had to try. Because for the first time in my life I'm at a complete and total loss as to what somebody wants from me. I have no clue how to make any of this right. She's just so...mad. It's obvious in the way she looks at our son and talks about him, she loves and wants him. But then why is she being so hostile toward me? God forbid she just tell me what the fuck she wants from me. And despite her denial, I know damn well she wants *something* from me...

Just like she wanted something from me nine months ago…That night I knew exactly what she wanted and gave it to her…but then again that want was mutual…fuck, was it mutual—until she walked away. I guess what has me going crazy is that when she showed up in the locker room, I thought for sure she wanted something from me. Everybody wants something. My dad wants money and respect. My mom wants to be accepted through status. Celeste wants to be financially stable, to feel taken care of while still feeling independent. But Liv's a whole different story because according to her, she wants nothing. But if that's true, then why the hell did she seek me out?

As I walk down the sidewalk away from her home, I think about how angry I made Olivia when I offered her money. I tried to explain I was just trying to do the right thing, but she wasn't exactly understanding.

Liv reminds me of a mystery novel. One that keeps you guessing the entire time. The more I read, the more clues she lays down for me to find. But with every clue, I'm left even more confused. At least with a novel, you know when you get to the end, the author will tie all those clues together in a neat package. Everything that was confusing will finally make sense. And, with a novel, if you lack patience you can always flip to the end to see how it all turns out. But with Liv, there's no end to turn to. I'm trying like hell not to run out of patience, but I'm afraid I may never figure out the mystery that is this woman.

I stop at the corner and pull the paper out of my pocket, needing to read the paternity results again. Like somewhere on this paper is the answer to all of my problems. I still can't believe I'm actually a dad. A week ago, I was a football player, a son, a fiancé…Now, I'm a fucking dad. I shake my head in disbelief. What the hell do I even know about being a dad? Giselle wasn't too far off base with what she said. The results may label me the father, but I haven't the slightest clue as to what to do with a baby. And then what happens once he's older? I grew up wishing for a dad who would love and pay attention to me. Wishing for a mom who would put me above herself just once. I grew up spending more time with Ms. Kelley, my nanny, than I did with my own parents. The day Fiona left, she looked at me and said having a baby with me would be a nightmare. A woman who had the shittiest life out of anyone I've ever known—raised by a drunken and drugged up mother in the worst part of North Carolina— actually left me because the thought of marrying and having a family with me was so terrible in her eyes.

I glance up and spot the old movie theater across the street. It reminds me of when I was younger and would ask my dad to take me to see the latest Star Wars film, but he would tell me he was too busy. The only time he would ever say yes to spending any time with me was when I would ask to play catch. I remember throwing the ball and his face lighting up. It was the only time I ever saw him truly get excited. The only time he would praise me. My heart constricts as I think about how good it would make me feel. I would've thrown that ball a million times if it meant having his attention. If it meant him telling me I was doing a good job. I didn't want shit from him. I just wanted my dad.

My mind goes back to what Fiona said: "*You always put your parents first.*" She walked away because she needed someone who would put her first. It's the same thing Celeste is afraid of—not being put first. Is that what Olivia needs? For me to put Reed first?

I lean against the brick wall, watching a family walk down the street. A flashback surfaces of my mom and me walking hand-in-hand through the park. I couldn't have been more than eight years old. We stopped at the ice cream truck, and she bought us the biggest ice cream cones. We sat on the edge of the sidewalk, talking and laughing, as we ate our cones. I smile, remembering that day like it was yesterday. She may not have ever looked at me the way Olivia looks at Reed, but I would like to believe in her own way my mom does love me. I just think somewhere along the way she got sucked up in the life of the rich and famous. And she was so scared of going back to where she came from, she ran as far as she could in the opposite direction—losing herself along the way.

A father and son pass by, and the dad grabs him in a chokehold, making the boy laugh. I try to recall even a single memory of my dad and me acting like that, but I can't. Celeste's recollection of what I once told her comes to the forefront of my mind: *You never felt you were good enough in your parents' eyes.* I don't want a child to ever experience the heartache I've felt over and over again, every time my parents have let me down, or when, in their eyes, I've let them down. All I wanted was for my parents to put their wallets and expectations away and love me.

And yet, here I am with a son of my own, who's not asking anything from me, and I'm walking away. And why? Because I'm scared of the idea of failing my son? While I'm over here judging my parents, they're exactly who I've become—only worse. I threw money at Fiona, paying for her school and the bills, and justified it as loving her. I've seen Olivia three times, and every time I've offered her money to make things right. I've agreed to a relationship of convenience with Celeste just so neither of us has to deal with any real emotions. Holy shit! I've literally become my father. But I can still change this. I can give my son the love and attention without the expectations and strings attached. I can show my parents what it looks like to simply and unconditionally love someone else.

My feet start moving of their own accord, and before I know it, I'm buzzing the intercom. Giselle—with contempt dripping from every word she speaks—lets me up. And once I've taken the elevator up to their floor, I'm knocking on their door.

Giselle swings the door open, eyeing me up and down with disgust. "Livi is in the shower. Didn't you do enough damage?"

"Damage?"

She holds the door open, and I walk inside.

"You're so fucking blind. Livi might be selfless, letting you off the hook, but I'm not her. You come up in here, waving your dollar bills around like it's going to make up for the fact that you knocked her up and want nothing to do with being a dad. Your money means jack shit to Livi." I listen to her as she confirms everything going through my head, but also adding to what I was thinking. Olivia does want something from me. She wants the same damn thing I've wanted from my parents my entire life.

"She wants me to be a dad," I confirm, and Giselle gives me a *duh!* expression, reminding me of Olivia. Well shit, I can do that. That's why I came back here. She looks at me like I'm crazy, and I realize I'm grinning. But I can't help it. It feels like a huge weight has been lifted off me. Olivia doesn't want anything from me except for me to be a dad to our son, and not one like my father is to me, but one that's hands-on. Reed whines, so we walk over to his bassinet. "Can I hold him?"

Giselle gives me a hesitant look, but after a few beats, relents. "Fine. Have you ever held a baby before?"

"No." The little guy's cries pick up.

"Reach down and pick him up, but when you do, make sure you hold his head and neck steady. Newborns don't have control of their neck muscles yet."

Reaching down into the bassinet, I pick him up the way Giselle said to. He's tiny in my hands, yet solid. Definitely my kid. When I lift him up, I hold the back of his head in one hand—the rest of his tiny body resting on my forearm—and he stops crying for a second, confused.

Giselle's phone rings in her pocket, and she pulls it out. "I need to take this. It's the interview I've been waiting for. I'll be right out there." She points to the patio. "Be careful with him." She gives me a pointed look. I hear her answer the phone as she closes the door leading to their outside patio.

I watch Reed as his eyes work to focus, and once they're open, I can see the dark green irises that match mine. His lids flutter a few times, his eyes moving all over—not quite sure what he's looking at—and then he lets out an ear-piercing wail.

"Oh shit!" I'm not sure what the hell to do. I look over at Giselle, and she's still talking on the phone. Not wanting to interrupt her interview, I make my way down the hall with the crying baby. "Liv!" I whisper-yell, having no clue which room she's in. My eyes stay trained on the screaming baby, making sure he doesn't fall out of my hands.

Olivia opens the door, and holy shit, she's a fucking wet dream, standing there in only a small plush towel with her wet hair pulled up in a messy bun, the ends dripping wet. I watch as the droplets run down her neck—that same neck I spent hours sucking and kissing on—over her collarbone, and disappear down into her luscious tits.

"What the hell are you doing?" She cuts across the hallway and plucks Reed out of my hands. "Who let you in here?" She glares my way while she rocks him gently, his cries lessoning by the second.

"Giselle let me in. She had to take a call…an interview, I guess, and he started crying."

She huffs loudly in frustration, then walks down the hallway toward the kitchen, her ass swaying in the towel as I follow behind her. She stops at the counter and grabs a can of something with one hand. When she reaches for what looks like a bottle, it falls to the ground. She sighs, the baby still crying in her arms. She bends down to pick it up and the bottom of the towel rises, giving me a peek of her ass. *Jesus, I'm going to hell…*

"Here! Let me help." I reach down, needing to focus my attention on something other than her sexy-as-sin body, but she snatches the bottle off the ground before I can grab it.

Once she's standing upright again, I reach for the baby in an attempt to help her.

"What are you doing?" she snaps.

"I'm trying to help."

"I don't need your help." *Alrighty then…* Olivia finishes making the bottle one-handed then sticks the nipple-looking thing into Reed's mouth. He immediately stops crying and starts sucking. She carefully wipes the tears from his eyes, gives him a kiss on his forehead, and then looks at me. We stand in the kitchen, staring at each other for a moment, neither of us knowing what to say. These awkward moments just might be the death of me. I've only known Olivia for a second, but she has got to be the most challenging person I've ever met.

"He has my green eyes," I say, trying to break the silence. She glares, and I close my mouth. Just as I'm about to say what I really came here for, there's a knock on the door.

"Jeez!" she huffs out. "It's like Grand Central Station over here." Still holding the baby and the bottle, and still in her towel, she opens the front door.

And it's her dad. His gaze moves back and forth between Olivia and me. "Why are you standing in a towel with Nick here?" Olivia's eyes dart down to her lower half then back up to me, embarrassment coloring her cheeks.

"Oh my God!" She carefully thrusts the baby with his bottle into her dad's arms before scurrying out of the living room and back into the bathroom, slamming the door shut behind her.

I chuckle, and her dad hits me with a hard glare. "Why

are you here with my daughter while she's in a towel?"

"The baby was crying, and she just got out of the shower."

He lifts the baby up, burping him like he's done this a million times. "Doesn't explain why you're here." Reed burps, and Coach lays him back down across his arms, giving him some more of the bottle.

"I came here to see Reed." I study Coach for a few moments, comparing him to my father. I would bet my dad never fed or changed me. He probably never even held me. Ms. Kelley was a part of my life from as far back as I can remember. I doubt either of my parents actually took care of me more than they were required to. Meanwhile, Liv is doing it all on her own here—with the help of her friends and family. Not with the help of her baby's father.

"You okay?" Coach asks, concern evident in his eyes. I glance from my son to him, and I know what I need to do. My words aren't going to make a difference with Liv or her dad. I need to show them through my actions.

"Yeah."

"We're going out for brunch to celebrate a belated Christmas. Would you like to join us?"

I consider it for a moment, but then Olivia walks back out, dressed and shooting daggers at me, and I figure it would be best not to upset her further.

"That's okay. There's something I need to take care of. I'll see you tomorrow at practice." I'm about to walk out the door, but before I do, I stop and lean down and give my son a kiss on his forehead.

When I get home, I put a call in to my attorney with my

request. He says he'll file the paperwork today, and Olivia should receive the papers in the next two to three days. Next, I call Celeste, not wanting her to hear it from anyone else. When it goes straight to her voicemail, I remember she's on a plane to Los Angeles.

I text Killian and ask him to meet me at the baby store, and he agrees. I'm scared as shit at the idea of being someone's dad, but I'm confident that with time I'll get the hang of it. Practice makes perfect, right?

I'm pretty sure we purchased every item imaginable at the baby store. Luckily, they deliver, and I won't have to deal with any of it until tomorrow when it all arrives. I have practice in the morning, so I scheduled it all to arrive in the afternoon. Seeing that it's almost nine o'clock here, I call Celeste since she more than likely arrived in LA a couple hours ago.

"Nick," she answers.

"How's it going in LA?"

"Good. It's a quick visit for a last minute shoot for my spring line. I'll be back tomorrow."

"I need to talk to you."

"Look, if it's about me not going with you to see Olivia…"

"I've decided to file for joint custody. My attorney is filing the paperwork today."

When she doesn't say anything, I continue. "I want to be Reed's dad."

"Reed?" Her voice is soft, very unlike Celeste.

"That's his name. I saw him today, and he has the most beautiful green eyes and a thick mop of brown curls. He deserves to have a dad. I know you of all people can understand that." Celeste stays quiet, so I keep talking. If we're going to work in any way she's going to have to be on board with my son staying here in our home. "I got a bunch of baby stuff today. It's all being delivered tomorrow."

"Where's it all going to go? We only have three bedrooms."

"Killian is helping me move my desk and files into your office. I figured we can just share one office. And that will open up a room, so that I can turn it into a nursery for when Reed comes over." When Celeste doesn't say anything, I pull the phone away from my ear. It shows she's still on the line. "Celeste?"

"Yeah," she says quietly. "I need to run."

"Okay…have a good night."

"You, too."

Eleven

OLIVIA

"That motherfucker!" I throw the papers onto the table, and Giselle swipes them up. I'm so pissed I could murder him!

"He filed for joint custody?" she questions after reading the top document.

"Yep! The last thing he said to me was that he didn't want kids! He said he wouldn't be a good dad! Now...he wants shared fucking custody! Fifty-fifty!"

I sit down at the table, my head resting in my hands. I don't know what happened, what changed his mind, but he could've let me know. "We could've discussed this. I don't understand what happened that made him not only change his mind but file for joint-fucking-custody."

"It says he agrees to pay child support as well." Giselle sets the document on the table. "Maybe he's just trying to do the right thing."

Do the right thing...those are the same words Nick threw at me the other day.

"I should've known he was up to something when he came back the other day." I pull out my phone and call my attorney. His assistant puts me through.

"Olivia, I just received the petition."

"He said he didn't want kids." My voice cracks at the thought of my baby having to go with him and his evil fiancée—which reminds me that I still need to throw away all of the makeup with her stupid name on them! "He didn't want Reed. Why is he doing this?"

"I'm not sure. But as a father who has established paternity, he's within his rights. You have thirty days to respond, but he's requested he be given visitation in the meantime."

"How long do I have before I need to respond to his request for visitation?"

"Fourteen days for the temporary visitation and thirty days for the shared custody."

"Okay, can you please hold off until the last day? Maybe he'll change his mind."

We say goodbye, and I call my dad. When he doesn't answer, I remember it's Friday. Tomorrow is game day. I look online and see it's a home game. Good! That means I won't have to wait for Nick to get home to kill him. Then an idea forms. He wants to fuck with me, well two can play this game.

I've rallied up my girls—Corrine, Shelby, and Giselle—and we're in the owner's box getting situated. I didn't tell them my plan, in fear they would try to stop me, but I still wanted them with me in case anything goes down. I know they'll have my back regardless if they think I've done something stupid. Reed is sleeping, and I'm looking around for my target. If she's not here, my plan won't work. I spot her, and when she notices me, I set my plan into action. Immature, sure. Dirty, definitely. But so was Nick filing for custody without telling me!

Gently, I shake Reed awake—don't judge me. He begins to cry, and everyone's eyes start darting over to us. Giselle shoots me a confused look, but I ignore her, standing up and pretending to soothe him. The truth is, he hates it when you rock him too much. He prefers to be swayed. His cries continue to get louder. Out of the corner of my eye, I see Nick's fiancée staring at Reed in horror, her mouth pinched in annoyance and her eyes squinting in pain at the loud cries coming from my baby. I hold back my grin, pretending to look concerned, meanwhile Reed is now pissed off and wailing at the top of his lungs. I want nothing more than to soothe him, and I will soon.

Celeste continues to glare daggers my way, her eyes squinting from Reed's ear-piercing screams. And then when she can't take it any longer, she swipes up her purse and stomps out of the room. As soon as the door closes behind her, I immediately slow down my rocking, and my baby boy instantly lowers his cries. "Shh…Mommy's sorry, baby," I coo softly, wiping his tears away. His eyes begin to flutter closed.

"You're bad." Corrine smirks knowingly.

"I don't know what you're talking about." I play stupid, trying to hide my triumphant grin.

"I've seen her here several times. She shows up once in a while to support her fiancé. She's always dressed impeccably and always makes sure to speak to the media."

"If I've learned anything from watching my dad with my mom and then with you, it's that men follow their woman's lead. If he's filed for custody because she wants to play house, hopefully this will have her thinking twice."

"And if he filed because he wants to be a dad?" I still at her question. I hadn't thought about that. I've been so mad over the fact that he filed behind my back, I never considered his motives, or that they might be pure.

"I'll cross that bridge when I get to it. Based on her reaction to Reed crying, if she did want to play house, she'll more than likely be begging him to drop his petition for joint custody. I guess we'll find out soon enough what his motives are."

Corrine gives me a soft smile, the one moms give their kids right before they're about to give them advice. "I know you're hurt and nothing is happening how you imagined it. But the one thing I learned from my divorce with Shelby's dad is that it's better to get along and play nice than to piss everyone off. If he's serious about being a dad, you both will be raising Reed together for the next eighteen years."

We stay for the entire game. Eventually Celeste returns, but I don't play any more games—not wanting to upset Reed again. New York wins, and after the teams make their way off the field and into the locker rooms, Giselle and I take off. I had wanted to confront Nick, but Corrine's words have me wanting to avoid him while I come to terms with the harsh reality of this situation. If he's filed because he wants to be a dad, I'm going to have to share my son...*our* son with him— as well as with his soon-to-be wife.

We get home and I lay Reed down to sleep in his crib. Grabbing a glass of wine and my laptop, I pull up a couple museum sites in the area. While I love being home with Reed, one day I'm going to want to find a job doing what I'm passionate about—sharing my love for art with others. I had planned to go back to France one day, but now I'm not sure that will be possible.

Giselle has taken off to go have dinner with Christian, so when there's a knock on the door, my thoughts are that it's probably my dad. Corrine asked if she could tell him about the petition Nick filed, and I told her she could.

I look through the peephole, and when I see it's Nick, I swing the door open. "Don't you know how to use the intercom system downstairs like everyone else?"

He shrugs. "I figured Reed might be asleep, so I followed someone in." He steps into my home without invitation. "Have you received my petition yet?"

Guess we're getting right to it. "Yep, thanks for the heads up." I go to slam the door but catch it. My anger isn't worth waking up my newborn baby.

"I was going to tell you, but you weren't in a good mood. I figured it would be best to show you through my actions."

"Oh, you sure showed me." My hands go to my hips.

"Okay…" He gives me a confused look, and I glare at him, silently wishing for a space shuttle to come down and kidnap him. "Well, I haven't heard back yet, so I wanted to ask if I could see Reed."

An oversized lump forms in my throat, and I have to swallow several times before I speak. "I just got the papers. I have fourteen days to respond."

"Yeah, I know, but I was thinking I could spend some time with him while we wait for it all to go through the courts and become official."

"No." The word is out before I can stop it, and Nick's confused look morphs into anger.

"No? You're going to keep my kid from me?" His eyes glance over my shoulder and around the room for Reed.

"He's sleeping. I think it's best if you go. As I said, I have fourteen days to respond, and until then there's no agreement." My palms are sweaty, so I rub them down my jeans to calm my nerves.

Nick gives me an incredulous look. "I don't get it." He scrubs up and down his face with his hands and then locks eyes with me. "You gotta give me something here, Liv. You can't really be considering fighting against me for wanting to spend time with our son. You came to me. That day in the locker room. You came in there and flipped my world upside down. You said you didn't want anything from me. You just wanted me to know I'm the father. What did you think the outcome would be when you told me? If you didn't want me to be a dad, you shouldn't have said anything when you recognized me. You fought for this, and now you're fighting against this. What you're doing doesn't make any sense."

He's frustrated and confused, and I don't blame him. He hit the nail directly on the head. I didn't think any of this through. I saw him playing, and all I thought was that I would be able to give my baby his father. I never imagined that he would be engaged and we wouldn't be a family. I never considered I would have to give up my son fifty percent of the time. I was blinded by wanting that stupid effing happily-ever-after. But none of this is Nick's problem. He's doing the right thing, and he's right, I can't keep our son from him.

After I take a calming breath, so I don't cry in front of him, I force my tears back and say, "You're right." I nod once. "It's late, and like I said, he's sleeping. Would tomorrow be okay?" I only suggest this because tomorrow is New Year's Eve. There's no way he'll agree to take a baby on one of the biggest partying nights of the year. I'm sure he and his fiancée have plans.

Nick's shoulders sag in relief. "Yeah, I'm off tomorrow since we played today. I can come by in the afternoon."

"It's New Year's Eve," I point out, but he simply shrugs.

"I'm pretty sure our only plans were to go to the team

party, but I'll cancel them, or she can go alone."

"And when would you bring him back?" *Please say in a few hours. Please say in a few hours.*

"I bought a crib and stuff, so I can keep him for the night and bring him back in the morning. We don't have practice until the following day." Not able to speak, I nod again, then walk over to the door, opening it up to indicate I want him to leave. He gives me a quizzical look, but I avert my eyes, not wanting to look at him. "Okay. Well, I guess I'll see you tomorrow."

He shoots me a small smile, thanks me, then leaves. When he's just on the other side of my threshold, he turns around like he's going to say something but changes his mind. *He seems to do that a lot.* I shut the door, lock it, and close my eyes, wishing that this entire ordeal is one big nightmare that I'll soon wakeup from.

Twelve

NICK

It's close to noon, and I'm lying in bed, half-awake, when the bed dips down slightly. By this time of the day, I've usually gone for my daily jog and been to the gym to get a workout in, but with everything going on, I've taken the day off. I roll over and Celeste is facing me. She had to attend a photo shoot last night after my game. Because it ran so late, she ended up staying at a hotel near where they were shooting.

"What are you still doing in bed? It's almost noon."

I sit up and take a sip from my water bottle I left on the nightstand. "I took a day off. What's up?"

Her eyes go wide, and her grin is huge. "I heard back from Richard Ford."

"The designer?" Celeste has been looking into expanding her company. As of right now, she has a makeup and an accessory line, both of which are excelling far beyond what she'd ever imagined. Now her goal is to start her own clothing line. She's been pitching said line to several different investors, but who she really wanted to partner with is Richard Ford. According to Celeste, he's one of the top designers in the world.

I offered to lend her the money to make it happen, so she wouldn't have to partner with anyone, but she told me this is something she wants to do herself. I had invested in the initial startup of her company a few years back and was shocked when she'd paid off her loan in full—interest included—sooner than what we'd originally agreed upon. To say that I'm damn proud of her is an understatement. From the outside, Celeste may *look* like she's nothing more than a beautiful model, but don't let her cover fool you. Inside is a damn smart and savvy businesswoman.

"Yes! He's all in!" she squeals. "I can't believe it, Nick." She clasps her hands together in excitement. "Production will start early spring."

"That's amazing!" I pull her in for a hug.

"And there's more. Several of the department stores and boutiques I reached out to have verbally confirmed that they're interested in carrying my line. If all goes well, my clothes will be in stores next Christmas! And not just in the United States! I'm talking international…Milan and Paris…Italy!"

"Look at you, conquering the world." I give her hand a squeeze.

"My dreams are finally coming true." She looks at me with a watery smile, and before I even know what's happening, her mouth crashes into mine. I back up quickly, confused. "What are you doing?"

"Kissing my fiancé," she says, hurt evident in her tone.

"Since when?" I ask. We've been together for the last nine months, and aside from the one time we tried—and failed—to have sex, Celeste has never once kissed me in any way other than as a friend.

Celeste lets out a soft sigh and then follows it up with a loud huff. I watch as her eyes go from appearing hurt to being cold. "Do you not understand how bad this all looks, Nick? You're going to be raising another woman's baby."

"No...I'm going to be raising *my* baby."

"That you had while engaged to me!"

"No," I repeat. "He was created before us. He was *born* while engaged to you."

"Everything is about to be destroyed."

"Nothing is going to be destroyed."

"You don't know that." She shakes her head. "If a scandal arises, Richard might change his mind about wanting to partner with me, or the department stores might decide that carrying my name isn't in their best interest."

"It's hardly a scandal. I'm not the first guy to find out he has a son. The stores aren't going to think like that about your name. They want you because you're the best. And Richard Ford isn't going to change his mind. He would be stupid to." I take another sip from my water bottle and then add, "I thought I had your support, Celeste. You told me Reed deserved more than to have a dad who doesn't want him."

"I do support you," she insists.

"Okay, good. I really appreciate it." I throw the sheets off me and get out of bed. "I need to get ready. I'm having lunch with Killian and then going by Olivia's to pick up Reed."

"What? Why?"

"I'm assuming that you're referring to me picking up my son and not me having lunch with Killian." I smirk, and Celeste rolls her eyes. "I told you earlier in the week, I petitioned for joint custody. The room is ready."

"It's New Year's Eve," Celeste deadpans.

"And I'll be bringing in the New Year with my son. You're more than welcome to join us."

"I saw her at the game. That baby…it kept crying!" Her eyes go wide.

"She was at the game?"

"Yes! And the baby was screaming his head off. Maybe you should suggest she hire a nanny," she says, scrunching her nose up in disgust.

I internally groan. Every time I've seen Olivia, the baby is fast asleep or being cared for. "Babies cry. What's really going on?" I cross my arms over my chest and stare down at Celeste.

"I-I…" She throws her arms up in frustration. "I can't do this! I can't be the other woman." Tears prick her eyes, and I know there's more to all of this than what she's saying. But Celeste is a vault, and she'll never open up to me—or anyone.

"You're my fiancée."

"Exactly! So can we maybe…try for real?" She gets up from the bed and approaches me. "I know you went from getting laid on the regular to not at all. I don't want you to be unhappy." Her hand moves to my dick, and she grips it through my boxers. She's right. I did spend a lot of time inside women, and obviously sex is on my mind. For one, I'm a man, therefore, it's pretty much always on my mind, but also, ever since Olivia came back, I can't get our night together out of my head. She was the last person I was with before I agreed to this pseudo relationship with Celeste. She was the last woman I sank my dick into, and I can still remember the way her tight cunt felt... *Fuck!* I can't think about Olivia like that.

Removing Celeste's hand from my crotch, I back up slightly. "We already did once and there was nothing there. As a matter of fact, I'm pretty sure your exact words were, 'I can't do this. It feels like I'm about to fuck my brother, if I had one.'"

"Well, maybe we didn't try hard enough. What does she have that I don't, Nick?" *Oh, hell no...there's no way I'm going there, not even with a ten-foot pole...*

"Celeste, you're a beautiful woman. You know this. But you're my friend, and I can't see you as anything more than that. Just like you don't see me as anything more. If you're scared I'm going to cheat on you, I wouldn't do that. You know I've been cheated on, and I wouldn't do that to someone else." I walk over to the bathroom door.

"I'm not scared of you cheating," Celeste says, but the way her voice cracks as she says the words tells me otherwise. "It's just...you spent an entire year only having one-night stands, and not once did you want more...until her."

"That might be true, but she left," I point out, opening the bathroom door.

"And now she's back."

Celeste doesn't wait for me to respond. She walks out of our room, and I watch her walk away, having no clue what to say to her to ease her mind. Closing the bathroom door behind me, I strip out of my clothes and jump into the shower. Celeste was right. I slept with way too many women last year, but it wasn't until Olivia that I found myself wanting more. Fuck, how could I not? The chemistry between us was like nothing I'd ever experienced.

Reaching down, I fist my cock as I think about her, my mind going back to our one and only night together. How brazen she was. The way she sucked and fucked me like a woman on a mission. How responsive her body was to my touch—the way we connected on a deeper level. My fist tightens around my hard shaft, stroking it up and down as I recall Olivia's mouth around my cock. The way she took me with abandon.

My fist pumps harder, my grip tightening. I can feel the pull in my balls beginning. My forehead hits the shower wall as I recall the way she rode my dick in the middle of the night. The way her tits bounced up and down. Her hands splayed across my chest as she milked my cock until it was completely drained. My fist tightens, my strokes get more frantic, as I chase my release. I remember the way she kissed me with such passion. The way her body felt against mine. The way we fit so goddamned perfectly together. Letting out a low groan, I watch my cum shoot out and coat the wall before the water washes it away.

Letting go of my cock, I feel a sense of relief for about a minute, until it hits me that I just got off to the visual of Olivia, the mother of my son, the woman who *isn't* my fiancée. And with that thought comes the sobering realization that this engagement isn't going to last. So much has changed in the last couple of weeks. Everything I thought I wanted, I'm quickly realizing isn't actually what I want at all. I've been living in denial, not wanting to deal with the reality of this situation—that when I got together with Celeste, it was because she was the safe choice. Olivia had just walked away, the New York Brewers' owner and coach had said I needed to settle down, and Celeste was there, ready to make good on our pact. We were on the same page. But now, in light of recent events, I don't think we're even reading the same book.

Finding out about my son was eye-opening, a game changer of sorts. I've spent all these years wishing things would change between my parents and me, but when I was injured and then Fiona left, I gave up. I took the easy way out. From the one-night stands to agreeing to the arrangement with Celeste. But now that I have my son to think about, I'm ready to try again. I'm ready to open my heart and be the type of father he deserves. The change has to start somewhere and what better place to begin than with my son and me.

I flip the switch to turn the water off, grab a towel and dry off, then get dressed. Once I'm ready, I head out to the living room. Celeste is on the phone making plans, so I slip out quietly. Usually I'd call for a car service to keep it simple, but since I'm picking up my two-week-old son, I decide to grab one of my vehicles from the garage.

The valet brings around my BMW X6—and even helps me install the car seat—and then I'm heading out to meet

Killian. We meet at one of our favorite hole-in-the-wall cafés. New York may have many big-named restaurants, but it's the small ones that nobody's ever heard of that are actually the best.

"Olivia is letting me take Reed tonight," I say after the waitress sets our drinks down.

"By yourself?" Killian looks at me incredulously.

"Yes, by myself, *dick*."

Killian chuckles. "Calm down, I was just asking. So you're not going to the New Year's Eve party tonight?"

"Nah, I know Olivia did that shit on purpose. Told me I could take him on one of the biggest party nights of the year."

"Hoping you would say you couldn't," Killian adds with a smirk.

"Yep." I take a sip of my water. "But I'm not about to choose a party over my son. That's the shit my parents did, and my new goal in life is to be the opposite of them."

Killian nods in agreement. "Can't go wrong there. I bet Celeste is pissed."

"Yeah, but I can't really blame her. This isn't what she signed up for. We agreed to no kids, and now here I am with one."

"Can you imagine Celeste with a baby?" Killian laughs so loud that people look our way. "I would pay half my salary to see her change a shit diaper!"

I laugh along with him as I try to picture it—I can't. The waitress comes over and takes our order. We both go with a Club sandwich and a salad.

"Are you bringing Melissa to the New Year's party

tonight?" I ask Killian once the waiter walks away.

"No." Killian takes a sip of his drink. "She actually met someone, and I guess it's serious." He rolls his eyes. "She's talking about moving across the country with him or some shit." Killian's been friends with her for years, and while I'm almost positive she's always had a crush on him, he's never shown interest in being anything other than friends with her. Guess she finally moved on.

"So, who are you bringing then?" I ask.

"Nobody special." He shrugs nonchalantly then changes the subject, just like he always does when the topic of him dating gets brought up. "Are you heading over to get Reed after lunch?"

"Yeah, wanna join me?" I'm only joking, but the truth is that I could definitely use the moral support when dealing with Olivia. Between her and her friend, I don't stand a chance.

"Hell no!" Killian laughs. "That's all you. I have an appointment with Jase to get some ink added to my sleeve." Killian lifts his shirt sleeve to show me where he's planning to get the work done.

"Damn, I need to go by and see their shop soon. That's awesome that he and Jax opened a tattoo shop here in New York." Jase Crawford is an old friend of mine and Killian's from back home. Even though Jase was a couple years ahead of us, because we all played ball together, we ran in the same circles. While in school, Jase was also apprenticing to become a tattoo artist. Shortly after he graduated, he got a job at the same shop his brother Jax was working at. They always said their dream was to open their own place. But when Killian told me a few months ago that they opened their shop, Forbidden Ink, in East Village, I was surprised. Jase and Jax always seemed like the type of guys who'd prefer to live in a small town over a big city. New York definitely isn't for everyone. It's fast-paced and will eat you alive if you aren't quick enough.

"Planning to get some ink?" Killian jokes. While his body looks like an art canvas, I've never really considered getting a single tattoo. Guess there wasn't ever anything worth putting permanently on my body.

"Who knows?" I laugh. "If I were going to get one, he's the guy I would trust to do it."

After we're done having lunch and Killian tells me he's only a phone call away if I need any help with Reed, I head across the Brooklyn Bridge into Brooklyn Heights. I find fifteen-minute parking in front of Olivia's brownstone and then head up, buzzing for her to let me in. *See? I know how to work the intercom…*

When I get to her front door, her dad opens it up. He's dressed to the nines in a three-piece tux. He must've stopped here on his way to the team party. He enters the hallway and closes the door behind him instead of letting me inside. "Do you know what you're doing?"

I'm confused as to what he's talking about. "Coach—"

"Not here. Outside of the locker room, I'm not your coach. I'm Stephen Harper, the father of the woman you created a baby with…a baby you initially said you didn't want. I'm the grandfather to the baby you're now demanding to take."

We commence in a stare-down for a few moments

before he closes his eyes and sighs. When he opens them back up, he says, "Just tell me this, are you taking him to prove something? To punish my daughter?"

I take a second to think about my answer. Growing up I never had a man to look up to. When I was in college and then playing pro for North Carolina my coaches were assholes. It wasn't until I was picked up by New York I felt like I truly found my place in the world, a place I felt at home, and a lot of it has to do with the man standing in front of me. The day we found out I slept with his daughter, our relationship changed. We should've had this talk a couple weeks ago, but like the men we are, we both avoided it.

"I didn't know she was your daughter." I blow out a harsh breath. "I never would've slept with her had I known. I'm sorry for all of this. I never wanted to hurt her. You of all people know the shitty relationship I have with my dad. My initial response toward becoming a father was out of fear that I would end up like him. I shouldn't have reacted the way I did. I know my word doesn't hold a lot of weight right now, but I'm going to do everything in my power to make sure the relationship I have with Reed is nothing like the one I have with my parents. So, to answer your questions, I guess I'm trying to prove something to myself, but it isn't to hurt Liv. I want to be a good dad."

"Okay," he says, "as a father, I can respect that." Without waiting for me to respond, he opens the door wide, allowing me to walk through first. There are several people here: Olivia, Giselle, her stepmom, and stepsister. They're all sitting around her and appear to be comforting her.

"Is everything okay?" I ask, suddenly worried something

has happened to Reed. The women all turn to face me, four pairs of glaring eyes that have me taking a step back.

Olivia stands, wiping her eyes, her chin raising in defiance. "Yep." Giselle goes to say something, but Olivia stops her. "No." She shakes her head.

"Is Reed okay?" Something is going on, but nobody is saying anything.

"Yes." She hands me a diaper bag. "Reed's formula and bottles are in here, as well as a change of clothes and diapers and wipes in case you don't have any yet. He usually eats every three hours, and he was just fed." Her voice cracks, and I want to ask why she's crying, but I don't. "Do you have a car seat?"

"Yeah, my car is parked in the short-term parking in front of your building."

She nods and heads down the hallway.

"You're such an asshole," her stepsister hisses, but before I can ask what the hell I did, Olivia reappears holding Reed.

"Okay, sweet boy," she murmurs to him. "Mommy is going to miss you so much." She gives him a kiss on his forehead, her eyes closing and her lips lingering. When her eyes open, the tears she's trying to hide, escape. "I love you," she whispers to him.

She hands him over to me, and looking me dead in the eyes, she pleads, "Please take care of him."

"Of course." I take him from her, and when he squirms slightly, I tighten my hold on him. "I'll bring him back in the morning."

Since I'm almost positive every person in the room

hates me, I quickly say goodbye as I head straight for the door.

"Wait!" Olivia runs over and hands me a piece of paper. "This is my number. Can you please text me yours in case of an emergency? This paper also has Reed's doctor's information and anything else you need to know about him."

I take the paper from her. "I'll text you once I get him settled in the car."

"Thank you."

The car ride back to my condo is uneventful, and after pulling up to the valet, the attendant informs me I can keep Reed in the car seat to bring him up. I give him a large tip in appreciation, and he laughs, telling me he has four kids and if I need any help, to ask.

When I get inside, I see Celeste is dressed in a floor-length silver gown. Her hair and makeup are done, and she looks beautiful as always. I set the car seat down on the coffee table, and she comes over to check him out.

"He looks just like you, Nick." She smiles, but it's sad.

"Yeah, he does, doesn't he?" I grin. "You look beautiful."

"Thank you. I spoke with Mercedes, and she referred me to Quality Nanny. I wasn't sure with it being New Year's Eve, but they were able to find a nanny who's available." Mercedes is a model Celeste is friends with, who recently had a baby. She's also the wife to Brandon Evers, one of the linebackers on our team.

Carefully taking Reed out of his car seat, I place him into the swing and click it on just as the YouTube video I watched showed me how to do. "I told you I'm not going out. Olivia let me take him for the night. I'm not leaving him with a nanny."

"You act like nobody leaves their children with a nanny. You loved yours growing up," she insists, and she's right, I did love Ms. Kelley. She was beyond sweet and maternal in a way my mother had no desire to be. When Celeste would come over after school, Ms. Kelley would make us snacks and take us to the park and on picnics.

"I know they do, and you're right, I did love Ms. Kelley. But I saw more of her than my own parents. It's not happening. I can't let it happen. You want to go out, go."

"We were supposed to go together. As a *couple*. It's your team party. I can't believe you're really going to make me go alone." She snatches her handbag off the table, and with a huff, swings the door open and slams it shut behind her.

The loud sound reverberates through the walls and Reed starts to cry. "Hey there, little guy." I stop the swing and pluck him out, giving him his pacifier since it's not quite time for him to eat yet. Sitting down on the couch with Reed, I set him between my legs and create a vibrating motion with my thighs by shaking my feet back and forth. I read that a lot of parents do this to help calm their babies down. Within minutes, his cries cease and soon after he's asleep. Afraid that if I move in any way he'll wake up, I carefully reach for the remote control and turn the television on and then switch the channel to ESPN.

I'm not sure how long I watch the highlights of today's game for, but when Reed starts to stretch his tiny little body, I glance outside and see it's already dark out. His pacifier drops out of his mouth as he starts to cry. Taking him with me, I grab a bottle from the diaper bag to feed him, but it's empty. Then I remember Olivia had to put stuff in it. With one hand holding him, I use my other hand to sift through the bag. I find a can of formula and pop the lid open. It's powder and smells like shit. *Do I add water or milk?*

Reed's cries get louder as he grows more frustrated by the second. "Hold on, little guy." He was asleep for a while, so I imagine he must be starving. I read the back of the can and it says to mix with water, but it doesn't state how much he should take.

Remembering I have Olivia's number, I dial her. It barely rings once before she answers. "Everything okay?" She sounds distraught.

"Yeah," I answer her over Reed's crying. His face is now red, and hot tears are pouring down his face.

"Nick, why is he crying?"

"He's hungry, but I don't know how much he takes."

She's quiet for a second, and I think I hear her sniffle. Then she says, "I included it all on the paper I gave you." The paper! I should've read the paper. I only glanced at it long enough to get her number from it.

"Okay, thanks! I'm sorry for bothering you."

"You're not a bother. You have our son. Please call me if you need anything."

We hang up, and after reading the directions on the paper she gave me, I make Reed a bottle and feed it to him. His cries stop immediately, and a few minutes later, his entire bottle is gone and he's content once again. Laying him down on the ottoman in front of me, I snap a few pictures of him and send them to Olivia, figuring she might enjoy seeing them. She texts back a thank you.

"All right little man, it's just you and me bringing in the new year together. What do you want to do?"

Reed kicks his feet out.

"Sorry, buddy. No partying for you, you're too young." Reed's feet start kicking faster and faster. He looks like he's becoming agitated, and then a second later he starts to cry. I pick him up and walk him over to the swing. He seemed to like it earlier. I set him in it and try to give him his pacifier, but he immediately spits it out, his cries getting louder. Well, hell. He can't still be hungry. Maybe he needs to be changed?

Taking him out of his swing, I bring him into his room and place him on the changing table. I go about changing his diaper, and after several attempts of trying to get the tabs to stick, it works and he's in a fresh diaper, but the crying continues.

Not wanting to bug Olivia—and if I'm honest, I want to prove I can handle being a dad on my own—I pull up a baby site the sales associate told me about and search reasons for babies to cry. Holy fuck! There's like a hundred different reasons!

"Okay, let's go down this list," I say out loud to Reed, who isn't listening. I go through each reason, one by one: Hungry, wet diaper, fever, teething, constipation…the list keeps going. I haven't the slightest clue about half this shit. One reason for a baby to cry is being overtired. He just woke up from a nap, but then again, I have no idea how long babies stay awake for. Could he already be tired again? A mom mentions that she takes her baby for walks or for a drive when he's tired and needs help going to sleep. Spotting the car seat in the corner, I set Reed in it and buckle him in.

About two minutes into our drive, Reed's cries get louder, angrier. It sounds nothing like his cry of hunger. It's painful to listen to. I glance in the review mirror into the mirror facing his seat. His face is bright red, and my heart begins to pound as I consider something might be wrong with him.

Putting my pride, as well as the need to prove I can do this by myself, aside, I grab my cell phone and call Olivia while turning the car around to head toward her place. "I think something is wrong." I explain everything I did—from feeding him, to changing his diaper, to taking him for a drive. While we're talking, his crying never once lets up.

"I'll be right there."

"I'm already on my way."

We hang up, and roughly ten minutes later, I hand Reed over to her. She takes him out of his car seat, sits down on the couch, and starts checking him out. Then she places him on his belly across her lap and starts patting his back.

Within minutes, his crying has ceased. She glances up at me with a ghost of a smile playing on her lips. And it's then I notice her nose is red, her cheeks are blotchy, and around her eyes are puffy. She's been crying.

"He's gassy, but it's trapped. When you press on his belly, it helps release the gas. You have to make sure when he eats, you stop him several times to burp him. He's a little pig and will suck it all down too fast."

"Fuck!" I say aloud, "I forgot to burp him." I'm already sucking at this parenting thing.

"You'll learn," she says, "it just takes time."

I sit down next to her and glance at Reed, who is still on his belly across her lap. His eyes are open, but he's totally content. "Why didn't you go out tonight?" I ask her. She's sporting a pair of fleece sweatpants and a matching hoodie. Her hair is up in a messy bun, and her face is free of any makeup.

"Umm... maybe because I just had a baby a couple weeks ago." She nudges me playfully. "I was surprised you wanted to take him on New Year's. My dad and Corrine are at the team party."

"Yeah, Celeste is there too. I don't really care about that stuff."

"That's not what google says." My eyes meet hers, and she immediately tries to backpedal. "I mean..."

"You googled me?" I waggle my eyebrows playfully, and her cheeks turn an adorable shade of pink.

"I wanted to know about the father of my baby."

"And what did you find out?"

"Nothing I didn't already know." Reed makes a cooing sound, and she picks him up.

"Tell me why you were crying." She averts her eyes, but I'm not having it. "Liv, talk to me."

"He should be good now." She ignores my question and hands him back to me. I notice she has a movie going, but it's been paused.

"What're you watching?" When she doesn't answer right away, I look at her and see that she's blushing. "What is it? Porn?"

She slaps my arm. "No! Here." She hands me the

pacifier, and I put it in Reed's mouth. His eyes roll back, and I laugh.

"He loves that thing. So, what are you watching?"

"Titanic."

"Ahh…good old Leo." I glance around the room. "Where's your roomie?"

"I made her go out." That's when I notice on the coffee table is a box of Kleenex and a tub of ice cream.

"Liv, why were you crying?"

She huffs. "You can't be that oblivious, Nick." She hits me with a pointed look, but I have no clue what she's talking about. "I was crying because you took my baby. My very new, very fragile, newborn baby," she whispers, her eyes shooting up toward the ceiling as she tries to stop the tears from falling.

"I told you I'd bring him back tomorrow."

"I've never been away from him." Her voice cracks. "I wasn't prepared for this, prepared to let him go. I went from thinking my son would never have a father, to you saying you didn't want to be a dad, to being blindsided with a petition for joint custody. I just gave birth a couple weeks ago for God's sake. It's just…" She swipes at her eyes but the tears come anyway. "It's just a lot. I'm a new mom. I don't want my baby out of my sight."

"Fuck…" I was so caught up in trying to do the right thing, I didn't even think about how my taking our son would affect her. Most women in my life wouldn't care. Look at Celeste. She was trying to hire a nanny before she even officially met Reed. My mom had a nanny hired before I was even born. I spent more time with her growing up than I did with my own parents.

"I didn't think any of this through. I grew up with a nanny who was more of a parent to me than my own parents. Unless it was football related, my dad didn't know I existed. And the only time my mom showed me any attention was when she would drag me to family functions."

Olivia's eyes meet mine, and I can tell she's paying attention—actually listening to what I'm saying—so I continue. "You were so mad that I didn't want to be a dad. When I realized I could do this, and that I wanted to do it better than my parents did, I didn't stop and think about your feelings, or what all of this would mean for you. I'm sorry. We'll figure it all out. I promise."

"Thank you." She grants me a sincere smile.

We look down at our son and see that he's fast asleep. "I should get going. Let you get back to your movie."

Her lips turndown into a slight frown, but she nods. "Or we can watch the countdown," she suggests.

"I'm leaving Reed here with you, Liv. He's exhausted and finally asleep."

She bites down on her lower lip for a second and then softly says, "You could still stay and watch the ball drop. I mean, if you want to…or you could still make it to the party."

"I'll stay here," I tell her without giving my decision a second thought.

Our eyes lock for a brief moment and then she nods. "Okay." She switches the movie off and finds the New Year's Eve show on the television. "Have you ever been?"

"To Times Square for New Year's? Once. It's a damn

madhouse. You?"

"Growing up, my parents would always stay home. They said there were too many drunks on the road. My dad would pick up take out, and they would let me stay up to watch the ball drop on TV. Once I was old enough to go out, New Year's Eve was the only night they would make me stay home, but I didn't mind. It had become a tradition of sorts, plus they always let me pick the food."

"Where's your mom now?"

Olivia frowns. "She passed away from breast cancer when I was seventeen. She was born and raised in France until she came here at eighteen to meet with a photographer. She was a model. She met my dad on the subway on the way to her meeting." She laughs. "It was love at first sight."

"Is she why you were living in Paris?"

"Yeah...after she died, it was hard to be here without her. I moved over there after graduation in hopes of learning about my roots and ended up staying there."

"What made you move back?"

"Reed. My dad wanted me to be near family. Giselle graduated a few weeks ago, and since she's from here as well, she agreed to move back here with me. She's the best friend a woman could ask for."

"She hates me."

Olivia giggles. "With good reason."

"Hey, you're the one who left me."

"It was a one-night stand!"

"Says who? It was never specified. I woke up and you were gone. If you wouldn't have hightailed out of your room the next morning, I would've asked for your number."

"Oh God! You're so full of it, *Cole!*"

"Okay, *Liv.*" I chuckle, and she snorts.

"Just watch the show."

Thirteen

OLIVIA

The door slams closed and I jump slightly, my neck groaning in pain. My hand comes up to massage the kink as I attempt to sit up, only I can't. My body is overheated and I'm being weighed down by... Nick? I glance around. Why the hell is Nick's body wrapped around mine on the couch?

"Oh shit!" Giselle shrieks, and Nick rolls off the couch, landing on the wood floor with a loud thump.

"What the hell?" His voice is husky and has me tightening my thighs as I remember the last time I heard his voice like that—when he was pulling me on top of him at three in the morning, so I could ride his hard...Shit! I can't think about that night. He's freaking engaged!

"What's going on here?"

I sit up and notice Giselle has her hands on her hips, and she's still wearing her clothes from last night. Her makeup is also completely messed up like she's been crying.

"What's wrong?" I ask, rubbing the sleep out of my eyes. "And what time is it?"

"It's four in the morning. I spent the night at Christian's hotel…" Her words drift off, and her eyes brim with tears.

"Giselle, what happened?" I've never seen her look this upset.

"Christian and his friends threw a party. Before the clock even struck midnight they were completely wasted and I had enough, so I went to bed alone. I woke up around two to go pee and he was still partying hard. He had left his phone on the counter and it went off several times. I couldn't help being nosy, so I checked it. It was from another woman."

"Oh no! He's seeing someone else?" Giselle was just saying she felt like it was too good to be true. *Dammit, Christian!*

"Not someone…some-*ones*. Plural. I could tell that he's changed, but I didn't want to admit it to myself. He was drinking a lot, and I caught him with drugs. He kept making excuses, but I knew deep down that's just what they were…excuses. I ran out of his room upset, but after thinking about it, like the idiot I am, I went back up to his room to talk to him. I guess I was hoping he would convince me it wasn't what it looked like. I wasn't even gone an hour and he had already replaced me with some groupie-whore. I'm so stupid. I walked in and caught him fucking her in his bed. I should've known. He's a damn musician who travels around the country on tour. Of course he has a different woman waiting for him on speed-dial in every city."

"Hey now, that's not fair," Nick cuts in. "Not every guy who travels, cheats. I've never cheated while on the road."

Giselle glares down at Nick who is still on the floor. "That you'd admit to," Giselle hisses. "But there's more, and it's not about me." She frowns.

"Jesus, what else happened?" I ask.

"While I was waiting for my Uber to arrive, I was checking my social media and saw something…" She glances toward Nick, who has moved from the floor to the couch and is sitting next to me. "You know what. We can discuss what I saw later. What I'd like to know is what your baby daddy is doing here and not at home with his fiancée."

"We must've fallen asleep while watching the countdown. Nothing happened." I stand. "Now tell me what's going on. You have me freaking out and assuming the worst." Her eyes dart toward Nick. "Is it about Nick?"

"No." She shakes her head.

"Then just tell me!"

"Fine. Victor the asshole posted on social media."

"My ex?"

"Do we know any other asshole named Victor? Yes, *that* Victor. He announced his engagement to Heather."

"Heather? Our friend from college?"

"Yes! And according to their post, they've been together for two years."

"But that would mean…" I do the math in my head. "He cheated on me?"

"Apparently they were keeping it all under wraps the entire time. Nobody knew."

"Wow, I guess that explains why he didn't ask me to move with him to Switzerland."

"He was a self-absorbed dickhead anyway," Giselle

points out. "Plus, he was shitty in bed. Remember you said you didn't know how bad Victor was until…" Her eyes glance toward Nick, and I will her not to finish her sentence. The last thing I need is for Nick to know that the night I spent with him was without a doubt the best sex I've ever experienced. I had no idea how crappy my sex life with Victor was until Nick and I spent the night together.

Reed lets out a wail, and I get up way too quickly to grab him, needing to end this potentially awkward moment. I change his diaper and clothes, and when I come back out, Nick is still sitting on the couch.

"You okay?" he asks.

"Oh yeah." I wave him off. "Nothing I can't handle. We've been over for a while. Before you and I—well, anyway, I should've known, but I was too blinded by trying to find that stupid happily-ever-after. Speaking of which, shouldn't you get home to your fiancée?"

He looks like he wants to respond but thinks better of it. "Yeah…umm…is it okay if I come by Tuesday to see Reed? It's my day off from practice. Once you respond to the custody petition we can figure out a set schedule."

"Sure." I leave the living room and head to the kitchen to make Reed a bottle, and Nick follows. "Reed has a doctor's appointment tomorrow afternoon. It's just a routine check-up. I don't know what your plans are but—"

"I only have practice in the morning. I'll go." Nick takes Reed from me so I can make the bottle, and I let him.

"Right…okay." Nick is standing close to me, our son nestled in his arms. He smiles softly, and I allow myself a minute to check him out. Reed has a lot of his features. From his bright green eyes, to his messy hair, which curls at the ends. His jaw is chiseled with day-old scruff. He's a handsome man, and my son will most likely look similar to him. He leans over and gives Reed a kiss on his forehead, and the beauty in the moment sends shivers down my spine.

To an outsider, we look like a family. A mother and a father looking down adoringly at their baby. The false illusion has me frowning. All my life I watched my mom and dad live in a fairytale. I imagined one day I would have that. Instead, I'm a single mom with a baby by a man who's engaged to another woman. It sounds like the making of a Lifetime movie instead of Disney.

I finish making the bottle then take Reed from Nick, situating him into my arms and giving him the bottle. We're walking out of the kitchen and into the living room when Giselle comes running out from her room, freshly showered and looking like she's ready to take on the world.

"I got the job! I got it! Lydia emailed me last night! I'm officially employed by one of the most elite interior design firms in New York. I mean, it's only an internship, so I won't get paid much, but it's a start."

"Fresh Designs?"

"Yes! This is a dream come true. Do you know what this job will do for my resumé?"

"I'm so happy for you! When do you start?"

"Next Monday. They're off for the holidays. She said to come in early Monday morning to get all the paperwork filled out. We need to celebrate. Let's go out for lunch."

I glance down at Reed. "I'm not ready to bring him in public yet."

"You brought him to the game," Giselle points out.

"Yeah, but that was only..." My eyes dart to Nick, remembering he's still here.

"To scare the hell out of Celeste?" he says dryly, and I flinch.

Giselle giggles, and I do my best to hide my grin. If Nick knows, that means Celeste went home and told on me.

When I don't answer right away, Nick says, "I don't know all the details, other than the fact that Celeste thinks you should hire a nanny."

"What?" I screech. That wasn't my intention!

Nick smirks. "That poor baby was crying and being neglected."

"He was not! He is perfectly taken care of." My heart starts racing. Is that why he's here? Does he think I'm incapable of taking care of our son? "I just let him cry for a few minutes. I was hoping she would freak out and run back to you, and you would go away!"

Nick's grin widens. "Nice try. I'll give you credit, though. Your plan worked...partially. She wants nothing to do with a baby unless it comes with someone else to handle the crying, but you aren't getting rid of me that easily." He taps my nose with his pointer finger and chuckles. Then he says goodbye to Giselle and gives Reed another kiss. "See you tomorrow."

"Yep," I say, watching him walk to the door.

"Well, well, well," Giselle says slowly, once Nick is out the door. "I must admit, I didn't see these change of events coming, but now it makes sense."

"What are you talking about?"

"You and Nick." She nods slowly.

"I wasn't trying to break them up. I was hoping to scare her, so she would convince Nick not to seek custody. I was desperate. It was stupid." I sit on the couch and continue to feed Reed his bottle.

"But did you hear what he said? His fiancée won't be getting anywhere near the baby. I give that engagement two more weeks tops. He's committed to this daddy gig, and she's committed to the runway." Giselle plops down on the couch next to me.

"And if they split up, that will be their issue. It has nothing to do with me."

"So, you haven't thought about what it would be like to give Reed a mommy and a daddy?"

"I am giving him one of each." Setting the bottle down, I lift Reed up against my shoulder and pat his back until he lets out a loud belch.

"You know what I mean."

"In the beginning…when I first found out I was pregnant, all the time. Then when I spotted him playing football, the thought ran through my head…until he spoke." Giselle laughs. "We have nothing in common other than one night of hot sex."

"Explain."

"He's a freaking pro football player who's engaged to a gorgeous, successful supermodel. I bet they jet off on his days off to the Caribbean or some shit. Nick probably lives an extravagant, over-the-top life while I prefer mine to be more…low key. Sure, right now he says he wants to be a better parent to Reed than his were to him, but that's only because Reed is like a shiny new toy. Once Nick gets bored of playing dad, I'll be the one who is left to pick up the pieces of our son's heart when I have to explain to him why his father doesn't want him."

Giselle gives me a pointed look. "Your mom was a model, in case you forgot, and your dad played football before he became a coach." My heart tightens at the mention of my mom.

"Are you defending them? Because she's nothing like my mom, and he's definitely not like my dad."

"No, I'm simply pointing out that you're making a lot of assumptions and judgements without knowing all the facts. In case you forgot, you're rich. You could out-vacation both of them."

"Whatever…"

"Don't 'whatever' me. What if Celeste wasn't in the picture? Could you see yourself with Nick?"

"No way. My life might've taken a detour, but I'm not giving up on true love. I want what my parents had. I want a man who is in love with me."

"You had to have seen something in Nick to bring him back to your hotel room that night…"

"Victor had just broken my heart, and Nick was nothing more than a hot guy who helped me get over him." But even as I say the words, I know they aren't completely true. That night with Nick felt like more than just a one-night stand. It felt raw and real, like we connected on a whole other level—something I never felt with Victor. It scared me, and I ran.

"Judging by your expression, I think I've made my point." She puts her hands out wanting to hold Reed, so I hand him to her. "What your mom and dad had was beautiful and magical, but you're never going to find your happily-ever-after if you keep comparing every guy to your dad, and every relationship to the one your parents had. What they had was theirs…maybe it's time you find your own."

"Enough about me. I'm sorry Christian ended up being a cheater," I say, changing the subject.

"It's not your fault, but I can tell you one thing. I'm never dating another musician again. And while I'm at it, I'm banning all athletes too! Who else travels?"

"Pilot," I say, going along with her rant.

"No pilots! Who else?"

"Umm…Military guys travel, right?" I ask.

"Yeah, but don't they go to like Afghanistan? Do you think they cheat with Afghani women?"

"I'm not sure," I say. "We could look it up."

"Well, to be on the safe side, I'm banning all men in the service! Oh! And truck drivers too!" I bite my bottom lip to stop from smiling, but when Giselle cracks a smile, I can't help but giggle.

"You're banning everyone!" I say through my laughter, and she throws her head back in a fit of giggles. "There's going to be nobody left."

"Maybe I'll turn lesbian like my sister!" She laughs.

"What? Since when is Adrianna gay?"

"Since she called me last night and told me she wants me to meet her girlfriend!"

"My goodness. This New Year's is jam packed full of surprises!" I say. "Speaking of your sister. How is she doing? Aside from her switching teams?" I wink dramatically, and

Giselle laughs.

"She's good. Living and enjoying the college life. She was accepted into some sorority, so she's ecstatic."

"And how's your mom doing?"

Giselle sighs. "It's a good thing we came back. My mom has gotten worse, and my dad is almost never home. I've been visiting her, trying to help around the house, but she's just too much to be around sometimes. I asked my dad about getting her help, but he doesn't want to deal with it. Every psychiatrist she sees says the same thing. She's depressed."

"I'm sorry, sweetie." I pull my best friend into a hug. "If you need anything, all you have to do is ask...no, not ask, just tell me."

"I know, which is why you're my best friend and I love you."

"Love you more."

Fourteen

NICK

As I'm leaving Olivia's place, my mom calls me. I've barely said hello when she starts ripping into me.

"Nicholas, you weren't at the party last night." Immediately, I regret answering the phone call. Before I can respond, my mom continues, "That was a team party. There was a lot of press there. It looks bad when the face of the team doesn't show up." Stopping in front of my car, I close my eyes and lay my head against the side. Holy shit! I'm a thirty-year old man whose mom is still keeping tabs on him. It was so nice during the year I wasn't playing and they left me alone. The holidays need to seriously be over so she and my dad can go back to North Carolina.

"Mom—" I'm about to tell her I need to call her back when she puts my dad on the phone. *Great...*

"Nick, I have three contracts for endorsements, which need to be signed. I've already okayed them all. I'll bring them to you later today with all the details. I had Amber make sure the commercials and photoshoots will take place after your season is over."

Before I can ask any questions or even say okay, he's already put my mom back on the phone. This is what he always does, though. He handles my career. My mom rattles on about the next function and how important it is for me to be there, and just like my dad, when she's done saying what she needs to say, she hangs up. Unlocking my door, I get in my vehicle, feeling suddenly drained. Has dealing with my parents always been this exhausting? And yet, it doesn't even feel like I've participated in the conversations with them. What exactly did I say? Hello?

Needing to let off some frustration, I head over to the stadium. There's no practice today, but the gym is always open for us. When I walk inside, I spot several of my teammates working out. Not wanting to talk to anyone, I change into my workout gear and head out to the field. My workout of choice for today is sprinting up and down the steps. Plugging my ear buds into my ears, I start jogging upward. The music is playing, but I can't focus on the lyrics. My mind goes back to my non-conversation with my parents and then to last night with Olivia. The two of us watching the countdown—talking and laughing and getting to know each other. I've never felt that at ease around someone. When I talked, it felt like she was actually listening.

Since as far back as I can remember, everybody in my life has talked at me instead of with me. They've always wanted something from me. From my parents, to my coaches, to my girlfriends. Everybody has these expectations that are exhausting to live up to. But when I was sitting on the couch with Olivia, watching television and eating her microwaved snacks, something felt different. Real.

We fell asleep on the couch, and even without anything sexual happening, I felt closer to her than I have felt to anybody I've ever been with. It has me wanting to find out where things might lead to, but I know I can't do that as long as I'm engaged to Celeste.

Fuck...Celeste. I hate that I agreed to this pact and to this engagement, and now I want out. I never should've agreed to it in the first place, though. It doesn't matter how many times I get hurt, I don't think I can give up on love. Sure, I took a break from it. I had my fair share of meaningless hookups, but I never really gave up on the idea of love. I'd just accepted that it probably wouldn't happen for me. When Fiona told me the thought of having a family with me was the equivalent of a nightmare, I took her words to heart. And I don't blame her...I know I put my parents and my career before her. But now that I'm recognizing that, I'm hoping I can change things. It wasn't until I walked away from both of those things that I found some happiness. Now I have my football career back, but with it came my parents. I'm not about to let history repeat itself, which means I have some tough decisions to make. First one—being honest with Celeste.

"Oh good! You're home!" I'm not even through the door and Celeste is on me. "I leave for Milan in an hour. I've been thinking about our conversation yesterday, and I know I had said that I only viewed you as a brother before, but I really think—"

Grabbing Celeste's hand, I pull her to sit next to me. "We need to talk," I say, cutting her off. Her brows furrow with worry. "Last night I was—"

"Nick, whatever it is you're about to say, don't. I don't want to know."

"I spent the night at Olivia's place."

"I said I don't want to know!" Celeste stands.

"I'm not going to hide shit from you."

"I can't handle knowing if you cheated on me. Please, just don't tell me," she pleads. Tears fill her lids, but she quickly blinks them away. "Don't tell me," she whispers.

"Celeste, did someone cheat on you?" I ask. Her eyes go wide for a split second before she schools her features. "You know you can talk to me," I add.

"There's nothing to talk about," she says, her voice now completely devoid of all emotion. I assess her for a moment, but when it's clear she's not going to open up to me, I give up on trying to get anything out of her.

"Nothing happened," I say, needing her to know that I would never cheat on her.

"Okay, good." She nods her head up and down several

times. I stare at the beautiful woman I've known my entire life. When I was told I needed to settle down and Celeste had reminded me of our pact, I thought it was fate. I was done with love and relationships. We agreed on a marriage of convenience with a prenup and no kids. She knew exactly what she wanted, and I thought it was what I wanted as well. But now as I look at her, I know all I was doing nine months ago was taking the easy way out. I didn't want to go up against my parents. I didn't want to risk letting another woman down. Celeste was safe. But the truth is, I never would've lasted in a loveless marriage, and Celeste deserves so much more, even if she doesn't realize it.

"Celeste."

She grants me a small smile, one that most don't see. It's one that screams vulnerability. When she's unsure of how to make something right. When the situation is out of her control. The fact is she's not a bad person. She's one of my best friends. When she lets you in, she is sweet and kind and supportive. She was honest with what she wanted, and none of this is her fault.

"Don't do this, Nick. Please." A single tear escapes, rolling down her cheek. "We have a good thing going."

"This type of relationship isn't for me. And it shouldn't be for you either. We both deserve more. To be with someone who we love and who loves us back."

"So, what? You're in love with Olivia?"

"No, but I want to find out if I could be. What if she's the one?"

"You thought Fiona was the one, and she—" Before she can finish her sentence, there's a knock on the door. She walks over to it, and my parents are standing there. That's when I remember my dad had mentioned he was going to bring the papers by for me to sign.

"Celeste, what's wrong?" my mom asks.

"Nick believes he could be in love with Olivia."

"Wait, is this over the baby?" My mom gives me a confused look. "Celeste said you chose to stay home last night instead of going to the party even though she found a nanny."

"I don't want a nanny. I want to raise my son myself."

"You had a nanny," my mom points out.

"I don't want my son to have the same kind of life I had." The words are out before I can stop them, and my mom flinches as if she's been slapped.

"You had a good life."

"According to who? You? Dad?"

"You were given every damn thing you wanted," my dad says, joining the conversation. "Most would kill for your damn life. So stop acting like a spoiled brat."

"Yeah, I was given materialistic shit, but neither of you actually raised me. If it wasn't football related, you didn't even know I existed."

"Oh, Nick, stop acting like a damn little girl," my dad scoffs.

"Tell me this. Other than football, what did I participate in, in high school?" I turn to Celeste. "Don't say a word." She might sometimes be self-absorbed, but she was still my best friend growing up, and unlike my parents, she actually knows me. And even when I had no one else at my various school events, Celeste would always be there.

"Nicholas! Why are you acting like this?" my mom screeches, avoiding the question she can't answer. "Your father and I have done everything in our power to make sure you had your future paved for you. You should be thanking us, not judging us. You have no idea what the real world is like."

"What I do know is that growing up, all I wanted was to make both of you happy. I busted my ass in football to the point where I lost my love of the sport and my girlfriend left me. Did you know that when she left me, she said I put you guys first? And what sucks is that while I was putting you two before my girlfriend, you were putting yourselves first! It's the parents' job to put their child first, not the other way around."

"This is all about that flighty waitress?" my mom asks. "She was a waste of your time."

"That flighty waitress? She was in dance school. Holy shit! Can you be any more stuck up and judgmental? Do you not remember that you used to live in a trailer park?" I point to my dad. "Until he got you out! I loved her and was going to marry her. But she left me!" My voice booms. "She left me because she said it would be a goddamn nightmare to have a family with me because I put you guys first!"

"Stop!" Celeste yells, and everyone turns their attention to her. "I'm not going to let you believe that."

"Celeste, don't," my mom hisses.

"No, it's enough. Look, Nick, that woman you loved. She didn't leave you because you put your parents first. She left you because—"

"Celeste!" my mom yells.

"Your mom paid her off. She gave her five hundred thousand dollars to walk away."

My head jerks to my mom. "Is she for real?"

"I did it for you. She didn't love you! She wanted you to quit playing and start a family. And then you got injured. I knew if she had it her way, you would never play again."

"Are you out of your mind? You didn't do it for me!" I nod toward my dad. "You did it for him and for you. So he could keep making money off me and you could continue to brag about your NFL player son! That's all I am to you people!" I shake my head then turn to Celeste. "And where do you fit into all this?"

"I didn't know, Nick. I've always been upfront with you. She just told me this last night at the party."

"So, this entire time, I thought she left because she no longer loved me, but it was because she was paid off."

"You know what, Nick? Your mom might've paid her off, but Fiona took the money." Celeste puts her hand on my arm. "You chose love, and she chose money. You walked away heartbroken, and she walked away hundreds of thousands of dollars richer. I told you years ago, the world revolves around money, not love."

"Maybe so, but in my experience, money destroys the world. I'll take love over money any damn day." And that's without truly experiencing it firsthand.

"Nick, stop being dramatic," my dad says.

"Did you have anything to do with all this?" I ask him.

"No, I didn't. It was all your mother. But let's be real. Had she stayed, you wouldn't be playing. So, I have to say I think she did what was in your best interest at the time." He pulls the papers out of the envelope. "I need to get going. I need to talk to you about a possible new contract at the end of the season, but it can wait. I just need you to sign these papers." He hands me a pen, and I quickly sign them.

When I hand him back the pen and papers, he heads toward the door, my mom following on his heels. As he opens the door, I call out my mom's name. "Let me tell you something. Olivia is my son's mother, and she'll be around in some shape or form for the rest of my life. If you try to mess with her in any way, I'll make sure your status and reputation are the least of your concerns."

"Nicholas!" my mom cries, "are you threatening me?" It's the first time I've ever seen tears actually appear from her.

"No, Mom. It's a goddamn promise. Either you accept Olivia and Reed or you're dead to me."

Once my parents are out the door and it's closed, Celeste says, "I have to leave, but when I get back, I'll move my stuff out."

"You don't have to leave right away. If you need time to find a place, it's okay."

She comes over and hugs me. "I appreciate that, Nick, but it's time. You're my best friend and I'm not about to lose you because of my issues. I'm sorry for asking you to own up to that pact."

"You didn't make me do anything. But you know…" I laugh, thinking about the other half of the pact. "I really do think there's a good chance Olivia could be the one."

Celeste rolls her eyes. "Yeah, yeah."

"And I met her before I turned thirty."

"Okay…"

"So, if we end up falling in love, technically that would mean you would have to pay up."

"What are you talking about, Nick?"

"We agreed…if I found love before thirty, you would do the same."

Celeste suddenly looks crestfallen. Her eyes go glossy and she averts her gaze away from me. She clears her throat and swipes away the tears. "Sorry, there's something in my eye."

"Yeah, you've had a lot of *somethings* in your eye lately," I say. "Want to tell me what's going on?"

"Nope, it must be something in the air…pollen or dust…"

"Yeah, okay. Have it your way. But I'm not letting this pact go. You better get ready to find your true love."

"Talk to me once you're actually in love and in it for the long haul, lover boy." She pats my chests playfully, but the sadness in her features remain. "I need to catch my flight." She leans over and gives my cheek a kiss. "I'm sorry for what your mom did. Please believe me when I say I never wanted to see you hurt."

"1-right, 11 belly, pass on 2." The guys scramble, and I completely forget the play I just called. Luckily, Craig Stratum, one of the wide receivers, is open, and I throw it right into his awaiting hands.

"That wasn't the play!" Coach yells, not missing a beat. "Where's your head at? That's the fifth play you've messed up!" On any given practice, we'll go through over a hundred different plays, and I always get them right. Today, my head isn't in the game.

"All right," Coach yells. "Head on over to the weight room and give me an hour and then we're done for the day. Nick, wait back a minute." I jog over to Coach Harper, and he waits until everyone has cleared the field to speak. "You're not yourself today. How's your arm feeling?"

"It's solid," I answer truthfully.

"Good. Then what's going on?"

"Just some personal shit. I'll get my head back in the game."

"Okay," he says, not pressing me for more. "After your workout, want to get a session in?" Coach Harper has been my biggest supporter since he picked me up last year. He's stayed after everyone's left to help me more times than I can count. I've missed working out with him these last few weeks.

"I would, but I told Liv I'd pick her up for Reed's check-up." Coach nods, a hint of a smile playing on his lips.

"I heard what you did on New Year's Eve." Unsure of what he's referring to, I give him a puzzled look.

"You spent the night so Reed would be home."

"I fell asleep…"

"You didn't have to do that. You have no idea how much that meant to Olivia. I know the day will come when you'll pick up your son, and she'll have to accept that she's in a co-parenting situation, but thank you for giving her a little bit of time."

"What if it didn't have to be that way?"

"What do you mean?" He cocks his head to the side.

"What if I wanted to be more than parents with her?"

"Are you asking my permission to date my daughter? While you're engaged?" He shoots me a look of disappointment.

"I called off the engagement. Celeste is moving her stuff out when she gets back from Milan." Coach nods slowly, taking a second to think about what I've told him.

"I've never been in this situation. The first time I fell in love was with Olivia's mom, and I loved her until the day she died. The second time was with Corrine. It was a few years after Francesca died. I never imagined I would fall in love again, and at first, I felt so damn guilty for moving on. But when I called Olivia and told her, she said, 'Dad, we don't decide who we love; the world decides for us. And if Corrine is who you love, you can't turn your back on it. Nobody should be without love.'"

Coach Harper smiles in memory. "My daughter has always believed in true love, probably more than most. She believes in the happily-ever-after—the fairytales you see in the Disney movies—and it's my fault. What her mother and I had was pretty damn close to what you see in those movies, and even when times were tough, we never let her see those moments. She grew up believing that's how love should be. Now I'm afraid one day she'll wake up and lose her belief that true love exists. She's already made comments about that dumbass Victor cheating on her. And then to top it off,

she's being so hard on herself over how Reed was created."
He shakes his head, and I'm stunned by the turn this
conversation has taken. This is the same man who drills us
every day on the field, and he's talking about Disney movies
and fairytales and shit.

"I guess what I'm trying to say is before you make a
move on my daughter, you need to figure out if you believe
in love. If you're willing to give her, her happily-ever-after.
Because if you aren't, stick to co-parenting. Let her find the
guy who can give her what she deserves. My daughter
deserves her fairytale ending."

I know exactly the kind of love Olivia wants because it's
the same kind I want.

"Regardless of what happens, I'm here for you. You're
the father of my grandson. No matter where you end up at
the end of this season, or in life, I'm only a phone call away."

"Thank you, Coach."

Fifteen

OLIVIA

Because of Nick being well-known in the area—and the fact that he's three games away from bringing the team to their first Super Bowl game in well over a decade—the nurse had to rush us back to a room. I didn't even think about it when I made the appointment as I didn't plan on him attending.

"If you could please fill out this paperwork, I'll be back in a few minutes to collect it and then the doctor will be in to check out your son." The nurse hands me a clipboard of papers and walks out, closing the door behind her. Nick is standing against the counter, holding Reed in his arms, and I can't help but smile at how adorable they are. Our son looks like a tiny little peanut when he's laying against his father's muscular forearms. Nick is wearing a New York Brewers T-shirt that accentuates his muscles in all the right places, and Reed is in a matching onesie. When Nick arrived to pick us up, he handed me a small bag with the onesie inside. Since I hadn't gotten Reed dressed yet, I put it on him. We both took several pictures, and I sent one to my dad.

I get busy filling out the paperwork while Nick talks to Reed. "...so then I threw the ball to Killian for the touchdown, but the ball slipped out of his fingers like his gloves were lined with butter. He better get it under control..." I glance up, and Reed is staring at his father like he knows what he's talking about. My heart stutters and then flutters at the beautiful sight in front of me. Without Nick seeing, I pull my phone out and snap a picture of them.

Putting my phone away, I go back to filling out the paperwork, when I hear Nick say, "Whoa there, buddy. What did your mom feed you?" When I glance back up, his face is contorted into a look of disgust.

Setting down the clipboard, I reach into the diaper bag and pull out a diaper and wipes. "I can do it," Nick offers, taking the items from my hand. I'm about to argue with him but instead hand over the items.

"Thanks," I say, then go back to filling out the paperwork. A minute or so later, I hear "Holy shit! Dude, what the heck did you do? It's like a shit bomb blew up in here." I giggle softly but continue what I'm doing.

"Umm...Liv, can you get me more wipes?" His question comes out muffled, and when I look up, he appears to be paler than a few minutes ago. The bottom half of his face is hidden under the collar of his shirt, and he's making a gagging sound.

Grabbing the wipes container, I jump up to help him out and about die at the scene in front of me.

"Oh my God!" I crack up laughing. There's shit

everywhere! All over the baby, the table, Nick's hands. "What happened?" I cackle, and Nick glares.

"What the heck are you feeding this kid, Liv?" He gags again, grabbing the wipes from me.

"It's just formula." I shrug. I pull some more wipes out and start wiping up the poop, which is everywhere. I strip down Reed, who doesn't seem fazed at all by any of this. Nick grabs the diaper and gags again while wrapping it up.

"Bad gag reflex?" I joke.

"Oh, c'mon! That smell should be considered toxic. Did you see the fumes rising from his ass?" Nick says as he washes his hands in the sink. He's dead serious and that only makes me laugh harder.

We get Reed cleaned up and get a fresh diaper on him, but I don't bother dressing him, knowing the doctor will just ask to remove his clothes. Instead, I wrap him up in a blanket and hand him back to Nick so I can wash my hands and finish filling out the paperwork.

"Knock, knock." The pediatrician comes in, closing the door behind her. "My name is Dr. Fox." She shakes Nick's hand then mine. I've met her a couple times before, but this is her first time meeting Nick. She has Nick lay Reed on his back. "And how is Reed doing?" She begins to examine him, taking his temperature and checking his heartbeat. Nick stands over her the entire time while I answer the questions. We go over how much he's eating and what percentile he's in for height and weight—he's above average for both.

When she's all done, she says, "Okay, he's getting three shots today. The nurse will come in and explain what they're for. Once she's done, you can check out in the front and make his next appointment."

She shakes both of our hands one more time and then leaves.

"What does she mean three shots?" Nick looks at me horrified. It's then I remember he wasn't there at Reed's post-birth appointment a couple weeks ago.

"Babies get a lot of shots their first year." Nick picks up a now-whimpering Reed and holds him close to his chest. He's still in only his diaper.

The nurse comes in with the syringes on a tray. She explains the three shots he will be getting and gives me a pamphlet of information for each one. "Okay, Dad. You can hold him just like you're doing, and I'll get the shots in from right here." Nick's eyes shoot to mine, the first look of fear I've ever seen from the man. I haven't spent much time with him, but when I have, he's full of confidence in everything.

The nurse sticks Reed with the first shot and his whimpering turns into a high-pitched scream. Nick backs away from the nurse before she can get the second shot in. "Nope! Not happening." He backs up a little more until he's in the corner, comforting Reed.

"You're just going to let her do this to our son?" he says to me, accusingly. I let the judgment go because he's only being a protective dad.

"He needs these shots to protect him. Do you want me to hold him?" I put my hands out, and he shakes his head.

"No, forget this. He's crying." Tears are racing down Reed's face, and Nick is trying to soothe him.

"It will be over quick, I promise," the nurse says, and Nick shoots her a glare that has her flinching. If he wasn't so serious, this entire situation would almost be comical.

"Easy for you to say." Nick's hands tighten around Reed's tiny body. "You're not the one being stabbed with needles." I grab his pacifier from the diaper bag and use it to calm him down. He immediately stops crying, and the room goes quiet.

"Ready?" the nurse asks Nick, who looks like he's a wild animal trapped in the corner with nowhere to go but into a cage. He nods slowly and starts talking softly to Reed about football like he was doing earlier. The nurse pricks Reed two more times and he lets out another cry, his pacifier falling from his mouth. I catch it and push it back in while Nick continues to sway him gently in an effort to calm him.

"Surely, with all the medical advancements they've made, they can find a better way to give a baby a shot," Nick drones on over the entire shot experience that he's clearly more traumatized over than the baby who actually got the shots and is sound asleep in his car seat.

We're sitting in one of the more well-known restaurants in East Village. As we were leaving the doctor's office, Nick mentioned lunch, and I reluctantly agreed. Then Giselle called at the same time Killian did, and Nick suggested they join us. So here we are, the five of us—including Reed—eating a late lunch at the French Bistro.

Because it's January in New York and freezing, we have

to eat inside. Nick called ahead, and once we arrived we were whisked back to a private room that looks like it usually holds fifty people. He definitely gets good dad points for this one. He's sitting next to me, and while I know it's wrong, I can't help pretend that instead of us being here as just Reed's parents, we're here as a couple. I've seen a different side of Nick today. Not the same guy as the night I met him—who was straight up sexy as hell—but a softer, gentler side. The kind of guy I see in my father.

"Don't kids get like a hundred shots over their lifetime?" Killian points out, and if I knew him better, I'd kick him from under the table. Giselle, on the other hand, doesn't seem to care that she doesn't know Killian, because a couple seconds later he screeches like a little girl. "Oww!! What the hell!" His eyes dart around the table until they land on Giselle. "Did you just kick me?"

"Not helping," she hisses, and I laugh.

"So, game two of the playoffs," I say, changing the subject.

Nick grins ear-to-ear, nodding and reminding me a lot of my dad when football is mentioned. "Hell yeah. We got this!" Nick exclaims. His arm goes around the back of me, his forearm resting on the top of my chair.

"And we're going to be in Miami. We're definitely going to be getting lit after we win that game," Killian adds, raising his fist to hit Nick's, but Nick shakes his head. Killian lowers his fist and takes a sip of his drink.

Giselle shoots me a look, and I shrug.

Nick leans in close to me, his cool breath hitting my neck. "Don't listen to anything Killian says, ever." Then he leans in even closer. "I was actually thinking that maybe you and Reed could join me. Eighty degrees and sunshine." I turn my head and have to back up slightly so our faces don't bump.

Nick waggles his eyebrows, and I'm at a complete loss. I know his offer is innocent, but my body doesn't necessarily understand that.

"I—" I clear my throat. "I don't think that's a good idea. Giselle's birthday is this week, so we're going to do a girls' day." Giselle gives me a confused look but goes along with it. It really is her birthday, but we hadn't solidified any plans yet.

"Yeah, I'm turning the big two-five," she says. "We're going to spend the day at the spa."

"Okay." He nods in understanding. "Next time."

Sixteen

NICK

It's been a little over a month since my life was forever changed with the birth of my son. We've won all three of our playoff games, which means this coming weekend we'll be playing in the Super Bowl. Because the game will be in Denver, I won't be able to see Reed or Olivia this weekend. I haven't taken him for the night since New Year's Eve, and we haven't discussed it, but I make sure to see him several times a week. I usually come by every Tuesday and Thursday and one day during the weekend depending on which day we're playing or if we're out of town.

Olivia has put up an impenetrable wall when it comes to me. It's tall and concrete, and I haven't got a clue how the fuck I'm going to break it down. Sure, she'll send photos of Reed when I ask, but if I try to find a crack in her wall, try to sneak in through a crevice, she's right there, spackling the shit out of it, making sure I have no way in.

I've tried to text her several times, asking how she's doing or what she's up to, but she keeps it all about Reed. When I ask her to lunch or dinner, she comes up with some excuse as to why she can't go.

After practice, I'm planning to spend the afternoon with her and Reed, and I'm hoping maybe while he's napping, we can discuss the possibility of us. I've thought long and hard about what her dad said. And I know, had she left me her number that morning in the hotel room, I would have sought her out. That night was completely different than anything I've experienced, and I want to see if given the chance, we could work.

Since I needed clarification on what Coach meant, I made Killian watch a Disney princess movie with me. His niece owns a bunch of them, so I had him snag one and bring it over. He thought I'd lost my mind, but I needed to know what I'm working with here. Which play is going to land me the touchdown.

"Here ya go!" He flings the DVD at me. *"Planning to become one with your inner-princess self?"* He chuckles and plops his ass onto the couch.

"Fuck you. I need to see how it goes."

"How the movie goes? I can give you a play-by-play. My niece makes me watch this crap every time I babysit, so my brother and his wife can go out for some adult time. The girl seeks love, there's an evil queen who tries to fuck it up, there's a throw down of some sort, the prince saves her, and they live happily ever after. The end."

I stare at him in silence. Clearly, there's more to this shit than that. *"Let's just watch the damn movie."*

"First tell me why," Killian insists.

181

"Liv's dad said she wants the fairytale. He even compared it to a Disney movie. Usually the key to a woman's heart is through my bank account, but not when it comes to Liv. She's not letting me in. So, I'm going to figure out how to give it to her."

"The bank account?"

"No! The fairytale!"

"You're fucking nuts, man. Fairytale's aren't real. What you need to watch is Daddy's Home." He cackles, and I lift one brow, silently asking him to explain. "You know…the one where the dad and the stepdad are forced to get along. It's hilarious and more accurate in our generation."

"What happens in the movie?"

"The stepdad wants the kids to love him, but the real dad comes in and messes it up. Eventually they all co-exist."

I grab my pillow and throw it at him. "I'm not preparing for Olivia to end up with another guy!"

"You really like this woman, don't you?"

"Yeah, I do. I really liked her when I spent the night with her, but as you know, she left without leaving her number. Now I feel like I've been given a second chance, and I don't want to fuck it up. She's not like anyone I've ever met."

"Damn…going soft on me." Killian laughs.

"Shut the hell up. Now watch this fucking movie with me or leave."

"Fine…but after your fairytale shit doesn't work, we're watching Daddy's Home."

We watch the movie, and I take notes. Here's what I've learned about fairytales through Sleeping Beauty:

The princess is beautiful yet helpless—Olivia isn't helpless.

There's an evil bitch who—like Killian mentioned—fucks shit

up—kind of reminds me of my mom.

The parents send Aurora away—which is nothing like Olivia's life—unless you count her leaving to Paris after her mom died.

There's a whole lot of singing—I wonder if Olivia can sing, and I hope she doesn't want me to.

Princess Aurora sees the prince and falls in love with him after they dance together—I can handle that.

She's being forced to marry the guy she doesn't love—Olivia would never do shit she doesn't want to do.

She pricks her finger on a needle and passes out—fucking needles! Nothing good comes from those fuckers.

The prince does all the hard work, defeating the evil bitch and winning the battle—I need to convince Olivia to let me do some of the work.

The prince saves the day by kissing the princess, and they live happily-ever-after—I got this shit.

Now, I don't know anything about the other fairytales, but from what I gathered while watching that one, Olivia wants me to show her I can be her Prince Charming. The problem is, like in football, a quarterback is only as good as his receiver. I can throw perfect passes all day, but if I don't have someone there to catch the ball, it's pointless, which is why Olivia and I need to talk. I need to find out if she's going to be a team player or if I'll be throwing incomplete passes.

I'm about to head out the door when my phone rings. I see it's my attorney, Dylan Blake, calling. Dylan is Killian's brother and a sports attorney. He doesn't usually do family law, but he's familiar with it, and he's the only person I trust to handle this shit with Olivia.

"Hey, Dylan. How's it going?"

"Good. I just wanted to let you know Ms. Harper responded." Shit…I completely forgot about the petition I put in for joint custody.

"And…?"

"She countered. She wants legal custody, giving you visitation. You had requested fifty-fifty joint. This would mean sixty-forty with her legally being allowed to make all final decisions."

"What about the child support?"

"She's okay with it, but she did make a few revisions. All expenses are split down the middle including health insurance and educational expenses."

"She's something else…" I laugh to myself.

"She had to submit her bank information to the courts. Are you aware this woman could probably buy the team you're playing for?"

I chuckle. I knew she had money, but I didn't know she had that much. The brownstone she's living in has to be worth a few million, but I kind of assumed her dad might be helping her out. Apparently I was wrong. "She's definitely not the helpless princess," I say more to myself than to my attorney.

"What?"

"Nothing…go ahead and approve her request. I agree to all of the above."

After practice, I get to Olivia's place, and she lets me in. "I wasn't sure if you were still coming over."

"Why wouldn't I?" I walk in behind her.

"Well, my attorney called and said you approved the custody agreement. Today is Monday, and your days are

Tuesday and Thursday."

"I leave tomorrow to go to Denver for the Super Bowl." And then an idea forms. "Why don't you and little man join me?"

"Umm…I'm not sure that's a good idea." A beeping noise comes from the kitchen, and she runs that way, pulling a pan of brownies out of the oven. The house smells like a bakery, and my stomach rumbles.

She places the pan onto a rack of some sort, then goes about cutting up another pan of brownies into small squares and placing them on a plate. I grab one and pop it into my mouth. They're cool, so they must've been sitting there for a little bit. The brownie practically melts in my mouth. "Jesus, woman. That's some good shit." I grab one more.

"Thanks! Are you umm…are you taking…" She gulps loudly, looking everywhere but at me. "Are you taking Reed with you today?" She asks this same question every time I come over, and every time I make up some lame excuse as to why I'm just going to chill here.

"Nah…like you said, it's not my day. I'll just hang out here if it's okay with you." I move closer to her, and she backs up slightly. She has a spatula of brownie batter in her hand, and she nibbles down on the plastic nervously.

She moves the spatula from her mouth, leaving a bit of batter behind. "Yeah…that's fine. I imagine we'll have to work around your football schedule."

I close the distance between us. This is the closest we've been since New Year's Eve when we fell asleep together on the couch—the closest she's allowed me to be. We're standing only inches apart, and when I glance down, I can see her nipples are pebbling through her top. She wants me.

"What?" she asks shyly, watching me watch her.

"You have a bit of…" Without finishing my sentence, I lean down to make my move. It's risky as fuck, but I'm all about the gamble. My hands come down onto the counter, bracketing her in my arms, and I notice she stills, frozen in place. My lips brush against the corner of her mouth, my tongue darting out to swipe the bit of batter. She sucks in a harsh breath, not reacting but not pushing me away either.

Taking it a bit further, my lips move down, and I tug on her bottom lip softly with my teeth, my tongue licking across her flesh. When she doesn't move, I open my eyes and see she's staring at me, watching me with wide eyes. I move my lips up and place a gentle kiss on hers. But when my tongue seeks entrance, the trance she's in is broken.

"Stop, please." Her voice is breathy—full of want, a complete contradiction to her words. "I'm not a cheater."

I back up slightly, but my hands stay pressed against the edge of the counter, my arms caging her in. "Are you seeing someone?" Surely, I would've seen someone hanging around.

"No, but you're engaged. You might be okay with cheating, but I'm not, and I imagine your fiancée wouldn't be okay with it either. As you know, I've been cheated on and it sucks, and while it's true, I don't exactly like your fiancée, I'm not about to become the other woman." *Whoa…what?*

"What are you talking about? Celeste and I broke up weeks ago." Olivia's hand comes up to my chest and pushes me back slightly. "Don't you read the tabloids or go on social media?"

"I've been a little busy taking care of our baby. I don't stalk your social media or look at tabloids. Maybe if I did, I would have found out who you were sooner." She moves out of my hold and sticks another brownie pan into the oven. "Regardless…I can't be your rebound."

She sets the timer to forty-five minutes and makes her way out of the kitchen and down the hall to check on Reed. "Who said anything about being my rebound? In case you've forgotten, I was with you before I was with Celeste. Technically, she was the rebound." I shrug, and Olivia laughs.

"Very funny." She grabs the baby monitor and walks out onto her terrace, sitting down on the outdoor sofa set and flicking on the electric heater. I sit next to her, and she moves to the corner.

"Look," I say, my palms going up in a placating manner. "I know what it is you want."

"Oh really?" She bites her lip to hold back her smile. "Please, Nick, tell me what it is I want." She bring her legs up to her chest, and her chin rests on her knees.

"You want me to defeat the evil queen and kiss you awake."

"What?" She throws her head back in a fit of laughter, and fuck if I don't want to kiss my way down her throat.

"You know? Like in the Disney movies. You're looking for a Prince Charming, and I can be him."

Olivia's expression sobers. "Are you making fun of me?"

What? "What? No, I'm being serious. You don't want

money or materialistic shit. You don't need me to buy you anything. You're looking for your magical kiss, and I can be that guy."

"What do you know about Disney movies?" She eyes me skeptically and an idea strikes. I pull my phone out and scroll through my play list, finding the perfect song. I hit play and turn the volume up.

"Dance with me." I stand and put my hand out for Olivia to take.

Seventeen

OLIVIA

All-4-One's "I can love you like that" plays over the speaker on Nick's phone. I haven't heard this song since I was a little girl. The words hit so close to home when it comes to what I have wished for that I have to wonder if it's a coincidence or if he picked the song out on purpose after telling me he knows I'm looking for my Prince Charming.

I stare at his proffered hand, and for some reason it feels as though this moment is monumental. Like if I take his hand, I'm agreeing to so much more than just this dance. I'm agreeing to give him a chance at making my happily-ever-after fantasy come true.

He stands in front of me, his face devoid of all emotion as he waits for me to make my decision. He's allowing me to be in control. There are so many reasons why I shouldn't do this, why this can end in disaster. Each of them running through my head on repeat. But instead of listening, I push them aside, ignoring them all, and go with my heart. If it doesn't work out, at least I can say I tried. And if it does— my mind goes to our one night together, to the way he's been around Reed—there's a chance it could be amazing.

Taking Nick's hand, I rise to my feet, and he shows his first sign of emotion—a small smile ghosting upon his lips. Pulling me into his arms, his hands trail down my sides, resting on my lower back. My hands move up his chest, over his shoulders, and circle around his neck.

The music plays in the background, the guy telling the woman he will make her his world, and after a minute or so, I allow myself to relax—my head comes down and rests against Nick's chest. Our bodies sway to the music in silence, until about halfway through the song when Nick murmurs, "I can love you like that." I know it's the lyrics to the song, but he doesn't appear to be singing them, but instead telling me. I don't know what to say, so I nod into his chest. As the music continues to play, Nick's hands tighten around me, and he pulls me in closer to him, his lips brushing against my ear as he softly sings the lyrics to me. Each word shattering a piece of the wall I've been trying to build in order to keep my heart safe from this man.

The song ends and another begins. It's Imagine Dragon's "Thunder." Nick laughs as he reaches into his pocket and stops the song. "It must've switched to my pre-game music." He shrugs. "Thank you for the dance."

"What does this mean, Nick?" We're still standing in each other's arms, neither of us making the first move to separate.

"Your dad said that according to you, people don't

make the decision to love; it just happens. But I don't agree, Liv. I believe love is a decision. Who we love, how we love. It's in our hands. I grew up having no clue about the true meaning of love. When I was little, I thought it meant bicycles and PlayStations. And when I got older, I thought it meant cars and houses. To my mom, it means vacations and jewelry and status. To my dad, it means power and money. I grew up with everything a kid could ask for, yet nothing a kid really needs. It wasn't until you gave me Reed that I learned love can be more...so much more."

"What does that mean?" I rasp.

"I can't explain it." Nick shakes his head. "It's"—he backs up slightly, loosening our connection—"in here." He points to his chest. "It's not any of those things I mentioned. It's so much more powerful. When Reed cried from those shots at his check-up, my heart...fuck, it felt like my heart was going to explode. It's like nothing I've ever felt before. My parents choose to love the way they do, and I'm choosing to love my way, with my heart. And if you could give me a chance, I would love to love you the same way."

His words are so unexpected, and they frighten me because they hit all the right places. But what if this is just a phase? What if he thinks because he loves his son with everything in him that means he can love me the same way? What if he can't? A parent's love isn't the same.

Two minutes ago, I was willing to take the leap, but now listening to how strongly he feels, I'm scared. If it doesn't work, Nick just might leave me broken beyond repair. And who will be there to pick up my pieces?

"Did you love Celeste?"

Nick sighs, and taking my hand, guides us to sit. "Celeste and I have been friends since we were little. Her mom and mine are best friends who grew up next door to each other in a trailer park. Both of them dreamed of getting out, but unlike my mom who married a rich guy and created a whole new life for herself, Celeste's mom fell in love with a guy from a motorcycle club who left, promising to return, and never did. Celeste grew up poor. Her mom loved that guy, and even though she had several opportunities to be with wealthier men over the years, to provide Celeste with a better life, she chose to stay single and struggle. To this day she's never left that trailer park. She's still waiting for Celeste's dad to return. She literally chose love over money, and because of that, Celeste resents her mom for everything she didn't have growing up."

Nick takes my hand in his and massages circles into my palm with his thumb and fingers while he continues to speak. "When I was in college, we made a pact. If I didn't find love by thirty, I would marry her and give her way a chance."

"Which was?"

"A business arrangement. No love or emotions." I'm shocked at what he's telling me. You see stuff like that in books or movies but never in real life. And at thirty?

"But thirty is still so young. You were willing to give up on love at thirty?"

"I was twenty when I made the stupid pact. I was young and didn't, for a second, think I would end up thirty and alone. But over the years I allowed football and my parents to run my life, and the results were a lot of failed relationships. That morning I went to meet with Declan

Thomas, the Brewers' owner, and your dad." He laughs. "It's kind of ironic actually."

"What?" I ask.

"Your dad and Declan sat me down and told me I needed to settle down. They had a photo from an online tabloid of you and me walking into the hotel, but because I was towering over you, they couldn't see your face."

"Oh my God!" I jump to my feet and gasp in shock. "Had my face been in the image, my dad would've known we hooked up that night."

"Exactly," Nicks agrees. "But they couldn't tell who the woman was. All they knew was that my partying was a bit out of control and they needed to clean up my image so I could be the face of the team."

"So you agreed to the pact you made with Celeste."

"Yeah," Nick admits with a nod. "I guess I just needed a break from it all, and being with Celeste forced me to settle down and focus on football again…without putting my heart on the line."

"So, what's changed?" Why is he suddenly willing to put his heart back out there?

"You. Reed. I felt something for you the night we were together before I even knew we created Reed. But you left. So when I felt like my back was against the wall, I took the easy way out and agreed to give Celeste's way a chance."

"And what? You told Celeste you've changed your mind? I can't imagine that went over well."

"She's been one of my best friends for years. Yeah, she's hurt, but she understands. We've never even slept together."

Whoa! Okay, then. So it really was all business.

"I think right now she's more upset about her half of the pact." Nick smirks.

"What do you mean?"

"If I find love, she has to stop looking for a rich guy to be in a business arrangement with and try to find love as well."

"But you didn't find love. I mean, what we had…that night…"

"It was more than a one-night stand, Brown-Eyes. It might not have been love, but it was more, and if you give me a chance—*us* a chance—it can grow into love. What we have is different, and I think you feel it too." He's right. The night we spent together, the chemistry we shared. It was more, which is why I ran scared the morning after.

"I need some time to think." His face falls, and my heart cracks. "I'm not saying no. I've just…I've been hurt, Nick. I thought someone loved me and it turned out he didn't. Then to find out he cheated…it really hurt."

"I understand," he says. "I've been there, but I'm not him, Liv."

"I know you're not. But what if you're only doing this because I'm the mother of your son? Or what if I only say yes because I want the fairytale. I just need to think about everything. Had I not come back, you would still be with Celeste in a relationship of convenience. Now you're telling me you want the real deal."

"Celeste and I wouldn't have ever worked out." He stands and walks the short distance over to where I am. "It was nothing more than a temporary band-aid." His arms encircle my waist, his face nuzzling into my hair. "But I get it. You think, and I'll be waiting." He gives me a soft kiss on my cheek and then backs up slightly. "I have to get packed for Denver. We leave tomorrow. If you're willing to give me a chance—to give *us* a chance—come with me. The team charters a private plane there, so Reed won't be on a commercial flight. You can stay in the same hotel we stay in, and after the Super Bowl, we can spend some time together, the three of us."

"I don't think I can decide that quickly," I admit. "This is a big decision to make."

"If you need more time then that's fine too," Nick assures me. Then he steps back into my space once more and gives me a kiss on the corner of my mouth. "I'll be here," he murmurs, "if or when you're ready. If you don't go to Denver, I won't hold it against you. Just promise to put Reed's swing in front of the TV so he can watch his dad kick some ass." He backs up once again and shoots me a playful wink.

"Now, that I can do for sure."

Reed wakes up shortly after our conversation ends, and Nick spends the rest of the afternoon with Reed and me. While he's awake, Nick does everything for him, from changing his diaper to feeding him. He's become ten times as confident at being a dad than he was the first time he showed up on my doorstep with our son crying. It's only a matter of time until he starts taking him for the night, and I've come to accept it.

What I didn't expect was for Nick to show up here today and ask for me to give us a chance. Most women in my position would jump at the chance to date Nicholas Shaw, especially given the fact that we have a baby together. But I'm not most women. Call me crazy but I'm looking for the forever, and I'm not sure Nick can give me that. I know the man can give me the for-now. He gave that to me over and over again the night we spent together.

But I want more. I want what my parents had. I want what my dad was able to find for a second time with Corrine. Nick joked about giving me the fairytale, but does he really understand all that it entails? And then there's the fact that if we don't work out, we're stuck co-parenting together. He and Celeste might be over, and their relationship might not have been real, but if we don't work out there will be more women. Do I really want to put myself in that position? When I was in his arms, it felt so right, but once our connection was broken, my mind started to race. I wish I could be back in his arms, thinking with my heart instead of my head.

Nick leaves after giving Reed a bath and a bottle and putting him down for the night, but not before reminding me that he leaves tomorrow morning for Denver. Grabbing a glass of wine, I sit on the couch to unwind, and shortly after Giselle comes home from work.

"How was your day?"

"Amazing!" she gushes. "I am literally living out my dream. I had a meeting with Lydia, my boss, and she loves my ideas. She mentioned that she can see me one day moving into a real position there." She pours herself a glass of wine and joins me. "Of course, that won't be for a while. Most internships at Fresh Designs are for at least a year."

"I'm so happy for you. The year will fly by, you'll learn

a lot, and soon enough you'll be running the place."

Giselle laughs. "I don't know about that, but at least once I get through the internship I'll be able to finally pull my weight around here."

"Stop!" I hate when she brings up money. Money simply pays the bills. Giselle being in my life is worth more than any dime she ever pays toward the bills. Her friendship is invaluable.

"Whatever. So, how was your day?"

"Nick and Celeste broke up," I say nonchalantly.

Giselle gives me a *duh!* look. "Yeah…like weeks ago."

"And you didn't think to tell me?" I give her the side-eye as I take another sip of my wine.

"Everybody knows. It's all over the tabloids. I just assumed you knew." She shrugs.

"You came home at four in the morning to tell me Victor cheated on me when we were together, but you didn't think to mention Nick is no longer engaged?"

Giselle laughs. "I came home to comfort you because you were at one time in love with Victor. I didn't think I needed to comfort you regarding Nick. Why would you even care…" She stops speaking and tilts her head to the side, giving me a curious look. "Livi, why would you care?"

I let out a loud sigh. "He wants me to give us a chance." I throw back the rest of my wine like it's a shot.

"No way! And you said yes, right?" I avert my eyes to the picture hanging on the wall. "Livi, you said yes…"

"I said I would think about it. He wants Reed and me to go to Denver with him for the Super Bowl, but there's a lot to consider. If we don't work out, we can't simply go our separate ways. We're Reed's parents until we die. And then there's the fact he might get bored of me or meet someone else. Or he might get bored of being a dad…"

Giselle sighs and sets her glass down. "You know what I don't get…you talk all this shit about wanting your fairytale happily-ever-after, but you never let anyone in enough to actually allow it to happen. Did you see Cinderella come up with excuses? No! She wore that glass slipper like a fuckin' boss." I can't help but giggle at her words.

"And Belle… you didn't see her doubting the Beast. She went all in. Accepting him the way he was and falling in love, despite him looking like a scary monster. Oh! And Jasmine! She fought right alongside Aladdin against that asshole, Jafar. Aurora in Sleeping Beauty; she was strong until she pricked her damn finger and passed the hell out."

Giselle scoots closer to me and pats my leg. "You want this fairytale, but no one said it would be easy. You may have seen your parents in love, but you didn't see the hard work that went into their relationship. We always remember the happily-ever-after in these movies, but too often we forget the effort and struggle and heartache the characters have to endure in order to get that ending."

"When did you get so wise?" I joke, and Giselle pulls me into a hug. "I'm going to do it." I nod emphatically into her neck before pulling back. "I'm going to go all in. Consequences be damned."

"That's my girl."

I stand and grab my keys, then remember I drank some wine. "I'm going to call a Lyft. Can you watch Reed?"

"You're going to Nick's now?"

"He told me to let him know, and he leaves in the morning. I don't want to tell him over the phone. When I get back, I'll pack for Reed and me. Any chance you want to take a trip to Denver with us?"

"Oh no…you aren't using me as your buffer." Giselle shoots me a playful wink. "Besides, I love my job, and I'm pretty sure it's too soon to request time off." She laughs. "Go…go tell your baby daddy what he wants to hear."

I give her a hug then call for a Lyft. I've never been to Nick's home before, but I know what his address is from when he gave it to me. I tell the driver where I need to go, and about fifteen minutes later, I'm outside of his building. It's a nice skyrise condominium in Lower Manhattan. I walk through the marbled lobby and press the intercom for his number. Without him saying a word, I'm buzzed up.

The elevator doors open and his door is the only one on the floor. I knock once, and the door swings open. Only it's not Nick, it's Celeste.

She's standing in the doorway—all six feet of legs—in a pantsuit and heels, her makeup done to perfection and not a single hair out of place. And then I glance down at myself…I ran out the door without even thinking. I'm in sweats and a hoodie, and I'm almost positive there's some stupid logo or saying scrawled across my ass. I have zero makeup on, and my hair is up in a messy bun—and I'm not talking about those 'cute' messy buns. I'm talking the real ones that look like a rat has made his nest up in there.

"Can I help you?" She stands taller—if that's even possible—her chin jutting out.

"I was hoping to…" But I stop speaking because

suddenly it's all pointless, my reason for being here. If they're back together, I'm here for no reason. Just as I'm about to turn around, Giselle's words come back to me. *"We forget the struggle and heartbreak…"*

"I was hoping to speak to Nick," I say with more confidence than I feel. He asked me to give him a chance, and if something has changed then he can man up and tell me himself.

"I figured as much when I saw you on the camera asking to be let up. He's not here." She closes the door in my face. Okay then…

I make my way back to the elevator, shooting a text to Nick.

> **Me: Where are you?**

The bubbles appear instantly.

> **Nick: Killian's**

> **Nick: Everything okay?**

> **Me: I came by your place…**

The bubbles appear and then disappear, and a second later, my phone rings.

"Hello?"

"What did Celeste do?"

"Slammed the door in my face."

Nick sighs. "This is the part of the story where you

come across the evil witch." I can't help but laugh at his Disney story reference. "But have no fear because your prince has already taken her down."

"Are you still going on with that stupid fucking analogy?" I hear Killian yell in the background. The phone is muffled for a few seconds and then Nick comes back on the line.

"So, does you coming by my place mean you've decided?"

"Umm...can we get back to you taking down the evil witch? She's in your home..."

"She got back from Milan today. I was just kidding about taking her down. She'd probably kick my ass with those ten inch heels of hers. She's moving her stuff out, though, as we speak. Now, back to us..."

"There's a really good possibility I'm going to regret this."

"There's a really good possibility you won't."

"What if we don't work?"

"What if we do?"

"I don't remember any of the Disney movies having this plot," I joke.

We both go silent for a moment, and then Nick says, "How about instead of trying to copy stories that have already been told, we write our own?"

I take a deep breath. "I can do that."

"Good. Chapter one begins tomorrow morning. I'll pick you and Reed up at seven to catch our flight."

"I'm pretty sure chapter one was our one-night stand."

He laughs. "Fuck no, it wasn't. The was the prequel.

Our story doesn't begin until now."

We hang up, and I lean back against the wall next to the elevator, closing my eyes for a few seconds while taking several much needed calming breaths. It's really happening. I'm actually going to attempt to date the father of my son. Not so long ago I didn't think I would ever even see Nick again. He's right, though. This is our story, and therefore, we get to write the chapters. Pushing off the wall, I press the button for the elevator. I'm watching as the numbers slowly increase when Nick's door creaks open.

"So, I'm not sure what the hell Nick is talking about, but I believe he just called me an evil witch." I turn around, and Celeste is leaning against the doorframe. "Although, it might have been an evil *bitch*." She shrugs, and her head tilts to the side slightly. "I think we got off on the wrong foot." She steps out of the doorway and walks toward me. I hear the elevator open, but instead of getting in, I meet her halfway.

She extends her perfectly manicured hand. "I'm Celeste Leblanc, the *friend*."

I stare down at her proffered hand for a second before I take it in mine and shake hers. "I'm Olivia Harper, the...*baby mama*." Yep, I totally just said that.

She throws her head back in laughter. "If you ask Nick, I think he would call you more than that. Why don't we go inside? Nick called, and after yelling at me for closing the door on your face, said he'll be home soon. But I don't think he realized you were still here. Otherwise, he'd probably be hauling ass home sooner."

I take her up on her offer for no other reason than curiosity. I've never been in Nick's place before. We walk inside, and there's a woman taping up boxes and stacking them in the hallway. Celeste doesn't say a word to her, but instead grabs a bottle of wine and two glasses and nods toward the back of the room. There's a set of French doors, and when she opens them, they lead out to a terrace. It's smaller than mine, but large enough to have a table and a few chairs. We both sit, and Celeste pours us each a glass of white wine.

"I'll get straight to the point," Celeste says, handing me one of the glasses. "I don't know you, and I wouldn't know the first thing about being a mom or what you're going through. I had no right to judge you, and for that, I'm truly sorry."

"Damn it!" I take a sip of my wine.

"Excuse me?"

"I said 'Damn it.'" I shake my head. "I was prepared to hate you...hell, I did hate you. You're beautiful and elegant and successful, and you talked shit about my parenting. You were engaged to the father of my child, and did I mention you're beautiful? I was supposed to hate you. I even threw away all the makeup with your name on it." I take another sip of my wine. "And that shit isn't cheap." I raise a brow and she cracks a smile. "Then you had to go and apologize. So yes, 'damn it'."

"My makeup is worth every penny." She winks playfully. "And apologizing is a bad thing?" She laughs.

"Well, yeah...because now I'm going to have to forgive you, and since I don't have a lot of girlfriends, we're totally going to click and become besties. Then my best friend Giselle will wonder why I'm constantly ditching her for someone else and insist on meeting you, and the three of us will all have to hang out, and you're totally going to be that friend who brings us free makeup and jewelry from all your current lines and introduces us to all of the famous people you know." I shrug, and Celeste laughs harder.

"What are you? A fortune teller? Care to tell me my future while you're at it?" She smirks, taking a sip of her wine.

"Oh, that's easy!" I giggle. "Nick is going to hold you to the pact you guys made, and Giselle and I will bug the shit out of you to find a guy for you to fall in love with. You'll argue you aren't capable of falling in love, and we'll argue you are. Then one night when we're all out, you'll meet him and fall in love. You'll resist at first, but we'll be there to push you. You'll finally come to your senses, and we'll all live happily-ever-after."

"Oh my God!" Celeste cracks up. "Who is this woman?" I'm confused as to why she's referring to me in the third person until I see her eyes trained on something—or someone—behind me. I turn around to find Nick standing in the doorway, a huge grin splayed across his lips.

"She's the woman I'm going to fall in love with, and who's going to fall in love with me." He smiles warmly at me, and my heart picks up speed. Unsure of what to say, I chug down the rest of the wine in my glass, and Nick chuckles.

"How did you get here so fast?" I ask.

"Killian lives one floor below me." He shoots me a wink that has the muscles between my legs clenching. "I didn't realize when I was talking to you that you were still on my floor. I thought you had already left to go back home. Otherwise, I would've come right up."

"Told you," Celeste says as she stands. "Well, this has been fun, but I need to get going, and I'm almost afraid the love in the air might be contagious." She scrunches her nose and mock-gags.

I stand with her, and the three of us walk back into the apartment. Celeste takes my empty glass and places it on the kitchen counter next to the wine bottle and her now-empty glass. "Everything of mine should be packed. The movers will be by in the morning to pick it all up." She leans into Nick, giving him a hug and a kiss on the cheek before she turns to me.

"I'm assuming since you know about our pact, you know Nick and I have been friends our entire lives. You got one thing right. I don't have a lot of friends, so if it's possible I would like to be friends. Nick's important to me, and I know you're important to him."

"Of course, we're going to be besties." I wink. "How else am I going to make sure you find true love?" I grin, Nick laughs, and Celeste groans.

"And that's my cue to leave." She pulls her purse over her shoulder and walks toward the door. But before she opens it, she turns around and says, "By the way, when I was on my fact-finding mission to dig up dirt on you in hopes of getting you out of the picture, I read that Francesca Harper was your mom. Is that true?"

The mention of my mom has my heart tightening. "Yes, she was."

"She was my idol." Celeste smiles. "I *literally* wanted to be her when I grew up. She was walking the runway at the show I was at when I was twelve years old. Nick was there, too. Every person watching was captivated by her beauty and elegance. When I came to New York right after I graduated from high school, I was lucky enough to meet her… right before…" As Celeste's words trail off, a lump forms in my throat because I know the words she can't say: *she was diagnosed with cancer and then died.* It all happened so quickly. One day she was healthy and the next she wasn't. Less than a year after she was diagnosed, we lost her.

"I swear I cried for a week when she passed away," Celeste admits, "which says a lot since I don't cry." She sniffles and then smiles softly. "I'm sorry for your loss. I can't even imagine what it was like to have her as a mother."

"She was amazing…" I bite my lip to keep myself from crying. "But not because of how famous she was as a model, but because as a mother and a wife, she was the best. She always put me first and loved me unconditionally. She would let me play with all her makeup and clothes." I laugh, recalling all the times I would get into her stuff and she would never get upset. "Some of her model friends had kids, and they would come over to visit occasionally. The other moms were so stuck up. One time while they were having brunch we got into all of her clothes and makeup to put on a surprise fashion show." I smile at the memory. "The other kids' moms freaked out. But not mine. She pulled out her camera and took pictures, and then told the other moms to pull the stick out of their butts." Celeste laughs.

"And the love my parents had was like no other. Every Friday night was date night. Even when she was away, they would video chat and pretend to be on a date. She used to tell me that just because they were married didn't mean they stopped dating."

"She sounds like she was a truly wonderful person," Nick says.

"She was…and she was a beautiful model," I tell them, "but only because she loved with everything she had." The tears that were threatening to spill over, fall, and Nick pulls me in for a hug. When we break apart, Celeste is watching us. She doesn't comment on anything I said, but I can see it in her eyes. She's absorbing the meaning behind my words.

"I better get going," she says softly. "I'll be at the Super Bowl, but in case I don't see you before you're on the field, good luck. Let's try to do lunch soon." She looks at me. "All of us." And then she's gone.

"I thought you said she was the wicked witch." I wink at Nick.

"Good thing we're writing our own story," he volleys back.

Eighteen

NICK

We arrive in Denver, and it's as cold here as it is in New York. Reed is bundled up in his car seat, and the media is waiting to bombard us. Olivia handles it well, smiling politely while ignoring the questions that are flung at her. She covers Reed's car seat with a blanket and heads straight to the car while I stay back answering various questions. Reed's face hasn't been seen in public yet, but it's only a matter of time. I've been approached by several magazines, but it's not happening without Olivia's consent. My publicist put out one of those cookie cutter public statements to let the world know Celeste and I feel we're better as friends and our engagement has been called off. She also stated I'm Reed's dad and that I'm asking for time while I get to know my son. Obviously, based on the amount of press here throwing questions my way, they ignored my request—not that I ever really thought they would listen.

The players usually take the team bus to the hotel to check in, but today I'm going with Olivia. The car service takes us to the Four Seasons, and then I have to leave Olivia and Reed to go to the stadium for our scheduled media day. I'm glad her stepmom and stepsister are both here so she won't be alone. Not that she can't take care of herself, but it makes me feel better to know she has other people around her.

Questions about my injury, the upcoming game, and my future are tossed at me for hours by reporter after reporter. When seven o'clock rolls around, I can't get out of there fast enough. Tomorrow is the first day of practice, which means I need to rest up, but before I do, I'm going to spend some time with Olivia. The players are required to share rooms, and I always share with Killian. I was able to book Olivia a suite on another floor, and as much as I'd like to spend my free time there, I'm not going to make any assumptions. She did give me a keycard, though, so there's that.

"Brown-Eyes, I'm—" I haven't even finished my sentence when Olivia flies through the main room and covers my mouth with her hand.

"Shh...he's finally asleep. I don't know if babies can have jet lag, or if it's the time difference, but he was so cranky tonight."

She moves her hand from my mouth, and my eyes dart to her plump, pink lips. Damn, I want to taste her. Instead I give her a peck on her cheek. "Have you eaten? I was thinking we could order some room service and watch a movie or something."

"Disney?" she teases.

"Funny." I have Olivia order some food while I jump in the shower to rinse off. When I'm done, I return a call from my publicist and confirm a couple endorsement deals with my dad. He's been rather quiet lately. Now that I think about it, both my parents have been. And neither of them have once asked about meeting their grandson. Not that I should be surprised. What could he possibly do for either of them?

When I come out, Olivia is dressed in tiny cotton shorts and a long sleeve Henley—sans bra. She's closing the door and has a couple bags in her hands.

"Food's here." She places the bags on the table and grabs the boxes of food, bringing them to the coffee table so we can eat while we watch TV. I sit down before her and pull her between my legs on the couch. Her body is stiff at first, but she quickly relaxes her back into my front.

"Here." She hands me my chicken sandwich. "I got a parfait. I ate a bigger meal earlier." Grabbing the remote, she switches through the channels stopping on *That 70's show*. "I love this show!" She throws the top of her parfait onto the table and takes a bite of her yogurt.

We eat and watch the show in comfortable silence. I'm starving, so my sandwich is gone in minutes. "Want some of my parfait?" she asks. "It's the perfect sweet after your sandwich."

She turns slightly and pushes the spoon toward my lips. I open wide, and she thrusts the yogurt into my mouth, the sweetness of the strawberries and vanilla yogurt hitting my taste buds. "Good?"

"Yeah." I nod in agreement, swallowing my bite. She smiles before turning back around. We continue to watch the show, and every few minutes Olivia reaches back to give me a bite of her yogurt and fruit until it's all gone. Once she places the empty cup on the table, she settles back farther into my hold. We're in between sitting and laying down. Her head is resting on my shoulder and her ass is perfectly placed in front of my dick. My top leg parts her legs and my knee and thigh rest in between her thighs. I try to remember the last time I cuddled with a woman. Then I do remember; it was with Olivia on New Year's Eve when we fell asleep, and before that…the night we hooked up.

My right arm is situated under her—my fingers running up and down her arm. My other arm is wrapped tightly around her waist. There's no doubt about it, this woman's body was made perfectly to fit with mine.

The show ends and another episode begins. I'm not paying attention to what's happening, my focus completely on the woman lying in my arms. Her hair is up in a messy bun and her face is free of any makeup. She's the perfect mix of sexy and adorable. I lift my head slightly, and she tilts hers to give me access. My nose brushes against her exposed neck, and when she feels my skin touch hers, she releases a small shiver, reminding me how responsive she is to me.

When she doesn't stop me, I take a moment to inhale her scent. She smells sweet. It's the same perfume she was wearing during our one night together. Don't ask me how the hell I even remember that, but I do. I find myself latching on to every detail when it comes to this woman, not wanting to forget a single moment I spend with her. My nose brushes across her neck again and then my lips land on her sensitive pulse point. She lets out of a soft sigh, and my dick twitches as a result.

"If you want me to stop, tell me," I whisper into her ear.

She stills and then says, "I can't have sex…I haven't been given the okay from the doctor yet." I'm not sure how long a woman has to wait before she can be sexually active after giving birth, but for some reason this tidbit of info has me smiling. For one, I wasn't planning on having sex with her yet. Olivia needs to know I want more than just sex from her. She needs to know I'm serious about us. And two, sex is great, but the foreplay—the buildup—can be even better, and once I'm done with her, when the doctor gives the okay, she'll be begging me to make love to her.

"That just means we get to do everything but…" My lips go back to her neck as I trail open-mouthed kisses downward. My fingers brush across her taut nipples through her shirt, and Olivia's soft sighs turn into moans.

"Everything but…" She repeats my words, turning her face toward me and pressing her lips to mine.

Nineteen

OLIVIA

Nick's long fingers rub back and forth across my hardened nipples. His lips trailing kisses all over my neck. But I need more. Tilting my neck to the side, I cover his mouth with mine and kiss him eagerly. He kisses me back, his tongue passing through my lips and groping mine. And then he's moving us. His body is hovering above mine, my back now flat on the couch. Our kiss deepens, our tongues hungrily meeting thrust for thrust. We kiss passionately for God knows how long—until Nick breaks the kiss.

With one hand holding himself up, he uses his other hand to pull my shirt over my head, my heavy breasts hitting the cool air, and my nipples hardening to the point it's almost painful. Nick brushes his lips against mine once more before he trails kisses downward, stopping on my breasts. He kisses everywhere but my nipples, teasing me until I'm squirming with want. It's been almost a year since I've been with this man, since I felt his touch.

"Nick, please," I beg. He obliges, his lips parting slightly and wrapping around my nipple. He sucks on it for a few seconds before his teeth gently clamp down. My back arches and my hands go to his head. My fingers entwine in his hair. His tongue darts out and licks the areola before moving to the other breast. He sucks and bites, teasing me and turning me on. Foreplay seemed like a good idea…until now.

I can feel his bulge through his sweats rubbing against my thigh, and remembering how well-endowed he is, I raise my leg slightly, rubbing his cock through his pants. Nick lets out a moan, his teeth biting down on my nipple harder. I yelp, and he chuckles mischievously.

His lips leave my breasts and move down farther. He rains kisses on my soft belly, giving extra attention to my stretch marks. "Our son did this to you." His tone conveys pride mixed with awe.

"The downside to carrying a football player's baby. He was nearly a month early and still a solid seven pounds."

He lifts his head to lock eyes with me, laughter shining in his beautiful green irises. "I love these. They're a reminder that you carried our baby."

"I'm pretty sure the baby sleeping in the other room is reminder enough," I volley back, and Nick laughs. He kisses a couple more of the silver marks before he pulls my shorts and panties down, putting my entire lower half completely on display.

"You still have the same landing strip that you had before." His face lowers until he's face to face with my pussy. He kisses the landing strip, and I run my fingers through his soft hair, needing to touch him in some way.

His fingers part my lips, and his tongue delves into my folds, landing directly on my clitoris. My bottom bucks against the couch, and Nick's hands come down to my hips to hold me in place. His face ducks lower and then his tongue laves up the entire length of my seam before settling back on my clit. He licks and sucks and nibbles, successfully working me into a frenzy. I watch as he feasts on my pussy like it's his own personal dessert. My orgasm builds, and I'm forced to bite down on my bottom lip to keep my screams down. I can see my juices coating Nick's lips as he lavishes my pussy, working me up higher and higher. I've never felt this way with anyone I've been with. This instant connection. It's been months since we were together, and it was only that one night, yet it feels like I've been with him a million times.

His eyes lock with mine. His tongue licks. His lips kiss. He laps at my juices, and then I'm coming. My butt tries to lift off the couch, but Nick's hands grip my hips harder, his tongue and lips not slowing down at all, not letting up a single bit as my climax rips through me wave after wave. Only when I've come down from my orgasm, my lids barely able to stay open, and my head slightly fuzzy, does he remove his mouth from between my legs.

"I've been wanting to have another taste of you since the morning you left me." He gives the hood of my pussy one last soft kiss before he climbs up my body, his face intimately close to mine. He debates whether to kiss me with my juices still lingering on his mouth, but I make the decision for him when I pull his face to mine and kiss him hard. The tanginess of myself mixed with Nick's own personal taste has me wanting him something fierce.

Reaching down, I rub my hand up and down the outline of his rock-hard cock. His moan rumbles and vibrates into my mouth before he pulls back. He licks a trail back down my neck, stopping at the pulse point to suck on it. My hand makes its way to his sweatpants and boxers, and I begin to push them down. I feel Nick's hand grab mine, and what I think is him helping me is actually him stopping me.

"We were supposed to take things slow," he murmurs against my lips.

"Says who?" I ask, pulling my head back slightly.

"Me. I wanted you to see that it's not just sex I want from you," he admits sheepishly.

"Oh, okay, duly noted. Now move your hand, so I can *slowly* suck your dick." Nick laughs under his breath as he lets go of my hand, so I can finish pushing his boxers down the rest of the way. My fingers wrap around the shaft, and his dick thickens under my touch. I stroke it slowly at first, then pick up the pace. His face burrows into my neck, his breathing rapidly increasing. I love the feel of his dick in my palm, but I need to taste him. I need to feel more of him.

Pushing him back slightly, I let go of him as I slide down the couch until my head lands on the sofa pillow and my back hits the cushion. "Come here." He looks confused at first, but when my hands go to his butt and I pull him closer, he catches on quickly, all too willing to comply. He's on his knees, one leg on either side of me, his hard as steel dick bouncing in front of my face. I lift my head and take him into my mouth, circling the swollen tip with my tongue. He tastes fresh and clean—from just having showered—mixed with a tad bit of saltiness from the precum dripping out of his slit. Grabbing him from behind, I pull him closer, his dick thrusting into my mouth and down my throat as I swallow almost all of him. He's too big to fit his entire length down my throat, but it's not from lack of trying.

"Fuck, Liv. I'm never going to last…it's been…fuck, it's been too long." He groans and his words spur me on, wanting to pleasure him that much more.

I tilt my head back slightly releasing him completely. Then I lift up, inserting his entire length back into my mouth. I pull back again, and he moans in frustration. "Fuck my mouth, Nick." His eyes dart to my face, his brow raising in a silent question. "Please."

His hips begin to thrust slowly at first. My tongue swirls and licks his hard shaft. My cheeks hollow to create a suction. My fingers dig into his flesh, pulling him closer, silently telling him to give it all to me.

Nick picks up the pace. His cock driving in and out of my mouth. It hits the back of my throat over and over again, and my pussy clenches in response. I can feel it when he's about to come. His shaft begins to throb, and his thrusts become frantic. I'm ready to take it all, every ounce of his cum, when his dick leaves my mouth. Before I can protest, Nick's large hand grips his dick, and less than two strokes later, his cum shoots out and all over my breasts, warm seed coating my nipples.

"See what I mean about writing our own story?" Nick grins. His fingers come down and swirl a bit of his cum around my nipple. "This chapter never would've made the cut in those Disney books."

I come out of the shower to find Nick feeding Reed a bottle. He's sitting up against the headboard in nothing but his boxers, and I have to remind myself I can't go there, yet. After Reed finishes his bottle and Nick burps him, I take him to change his diaper. Then I rock him back to sleep before placing him back into his crib and checking to make sure the monitor is on.

I get back to my room, and Nick is still in my bed. He's reading something on his phone that has the corners of his mouth turned down into a frown. Not knowing what's wrong makes me realize how little I truly know about Nick. Sure, I know him sexually, and the night we spent together we talked for hours, but we kept it at a surface level. I know his favorite food is Chinese, his favorite color is blue, and his favorite animal is a dog—he hates cats. I know his favorite movie is The Blind Side, and he loves to go snowboarding every winter. I know his relationship with his parents is strained to say the least. But I want to know more. I want to know what makes him laugh, what makes him smile. I want to know why right now he looks so sad.

When he hears me come in, he sets his phone down on the end table to give me his attention.

"Reed asleep?"

"Yeah. Everything okay?" I nod toward his phone as I lay down in bed.

"Yeah, my mom and dad are here for the Super Bowl and want me to attend a breakfast with them and some of my dad's clients.

"And that made you frown?"

Nick scoots down the bed until he's lying on his side facing me. "My relationship with my parents is kind of tense right now."

"Because of Reed?" He hasn't once asked me if his parents could meet our son, which seems so crazy to me. My dad and Corrine can't get enough of their grandson.

He shakes his head. "It's more complicated than that."

I wait for him to elaborate, and when it's clear he's not going to, I tell him what I was thinking a moment ago. "I want to know everything about you. Talk to me. Tell me what's going on."

Nick is silent for several long seconds before he says, "You said you went to college in Paris, right? What was your major?"

"Art. I used to work at a museum over there."

"Well, my degree would've been in business."

"Would've?"

"I didn't graduate." Nick grimaces. "I wanted to major in English Literature, but my dad told me it was a waste of time, and it interfered with practice. Not that it mattered because I went into the draft at the end of my junior year, so I never graduated." I can't imagine my dad ever telling me what to major in. He's always been so supportive of whatever it is I've wanted to do in my life. Both my parents were.

"Who was he to tell you what you could or couldn't major in?"

"The school paid for my education, but my dad paid for everything else, therefore he got to have the final say in my major. I was so busy trying to make him and my mom proud, I didn't see how badly they were always trying to manipulate me."

Nick laughs softly, but it's a sad laugh. "Want to know something really fucked up? I found out recently my mom paid off my last girlfriend. Five hundred thousand dollars to leave me because she didn't want her to convince me to retire and start a family after I was injured."

My hand comes up to my mouth in shock. *What the hell!* "And she took it?"

"Yep. I came home from the hospital and found a note on the counter. Only I got there before she could leave, so she was forced to face me. We argued, and she told me that having a family with me was her idea of a nightmare."

"Oh, Nick. Is that why you didn't want to have kids? Why you didn't think you would make a good dad?" My palm rests on his cheek as my hearts break for this man. It's easy to forget that not everyone was raised in a loving home the way I was. I know Giselle's parents have issues, but she never wants to discuss them no matter how much I beg.

"I had failed my parents and team by getting injured. I failed Fiona by putting my parents and football above her." He turns his face slightly and gives the inside of my palm a kiss. "I think I was afraid of failing Reed, of failing you."

We lay here for a few minutes in silence, both of us lost in our own thoughts, when Nick says, "You know...that year after Fiona dumped me I was with a lot of women."

I groan, not wanting to know about his previous

conquests. "Do you have to remind me?"

"Let me finish," he says. "I was with a lot of women, but it wasn't until that night with you that I even considered putting myself out there to try again. I knew the moment you told me you could buy your own drink you were different."

I roll my eyes, remembering that night. "You still ended up getting your way and paying."

"That I did." He grins. "Best fifty bucks I've ever spent."

"I still can't believe I actually had sex with a guy I didn't know. I wasn't lying that night when I told you I'd never done that before."

"You were so fucking sexy." He gives me a soft kiss to my neck. "It was obvious from the get-go that hooking up with a strange guy wasn't your norm. I could see it in your eyes how nervous you were, but then when we got to your room, the way you let loose and opened up to me...fuck...I knew one night with you wouldn't be enough."

"Why didn't you say anything?" I question. We talked for hours that night and he never once mentioned wanting to see me again.

"I didn't know you were going to disappear the next morning. If I would've known I was going to wake up to an empty bed and a note, I would've tied your wrists to the headboard so you couldn't leave." He winks playfully. "I'm just glad you went to my game and spotted me." He kisses the tops of my knuckles. "Had you not been at that game who knows if we ever would've found each other." The thought of never seeing Nick again makes my heart hurt.

"Is that why your parents and you are on the outs?

Because of me?"

"I don't think it's any one thing," Nick says. "Ever since you showed back up and Reed was born, I've started to see things differently, more clearly."

"How?"

"All of the shit my parents have pulled over the years, they've always acted like it was done out of love and in my best interest. Now, though, I'm beginning to think their motives are less out of love and more out of greed. Pushing people I care about away, bribing them with money to leave, forcing me to change my major…those aren't things parents do when they love their children. I will *never* be that kind of parent to Reed."

"I think it says something about you as a person and especially as a father that you recognize that. Have they asked to meet Reed?"

"No, and that's why I was upset when you walked in. My mom implied I should show up alone, knowing you and Reed are here with me."

"I'm sorry." I scoot closer to him to give him a kiss. "I would say we don't need to go, but I'm thinking that's not exactly the point here."

"No, it's not. I wouldn't ask you to bring Reed. He's too young, and we're not showing him to the public yet. But they're acting like he doesn't exist. Other than them worrying about you distracting me from football or trying to take all my money, they haven't acknowledged Reed being my son at all."

"Well, maybe they will come around once they see I'm not going to steal all your money, and the only time I will distract you is in the bedroom." I waggle my eyebrows playfully, and Nick smiles. "Now tell me about this English Lit degree. I had no idea you liked to read."

"I do," he admits, "but lately I've been thinking about trying my hand at writing."

"Like taking a writing class?" I sit up, shocked.

"Yeah, I mean I know it's too late to get my degree, but—"

"Wait! Who says it's too late? You only had a year to go… you could easily go back and finish. And now with online classes, you could switch to English Literature like you wanted."

Nick's face lights up like a little boy who has just been told he can stay up late and eat too much candy. "You're right…I can. And I have plenty of money now, so there isn't a damn thing my dad could do to stop me."

"Of course he can't! Are you going to still major in English Lit?"

"Hell yes! And the first class I'm going to take will be the creative writing class I never got to take."

"You can totally do it!"

I lay back down and wrap my arms around him. We lay together in silence for a few minutes, and I think about Nick and me and how far we've come from being the people we were in that hotel room almost a year ago.

"Hey Nick…"

"Yeah?"

"I'm sorry I left with only a note to say goodbye." And I am sorry. If I would've known he was looking for more, I never would've left the way I did. Yes, I was only looking for a one-night stand, but once we were together, I felt something more, and the thought scared me into running, never for a second believing he felt something as well.

"It's all good, Brown-Eyes." Nick gives me a kiss on my forehead, then on my nose. "Just please...in the future, if you're going to leave a note, always tell me where you're going so I can find you."

"Deal! Now let's look up colleges. With football ending this week, you can probably take an express spring class or even take a couple summer classes."

Twenty

NICK

I've yet to take Olivia out on a date, and having her family here means we have willing babysitters. It's Thursday night and we're free for the evening after practicing all morning and going over tapes and plays this afternoon. I shoot a text to Stephen and ask if there's any way he and Corrine can watch Reed. He texts me back that they would love to.

I put a call in to a recommended restaurant to see if it's possible to have private seating. With the Super Bowl in three days, anywhere we go we'll have fans trying to get photos and autographs. The paparazzi and media are everywhere. The manager tells me they can get us into a private booth near the back at seven o'clock, so I let Stephen know to come over to Olivia's room at six.

I get back to her room—which might as well be mine since I've slept here every night—and she's on the floor with Reed singing to him about baking a cake. He's lying on a large blue blanket and his legs and hands are flailing every which way. Every day he becomes more alert...more like a real person. I can't believe I almost gave up my right to watch him grow up.

Olivia looks up when she hears the door close. "Hey you. How was practice?"

"Good." I drop onto the floor next to her and give her a quick kiss before leaning over and giving one to Reed. His face moves side to side as he makes a soft cooing sound that has me grinning. These two are quickly becoming my entire world.

"Why don't you go shower while I watch him?"

Her nose scrunches up. "Do I smell that bad? I showered this morning."

My fingers grip her nape, and I pull her into me, my mouth slanting over hers. "No, you don't smell. We're going out to dinner."

"I thought you said you didn't want Reed going out too much because of the media."

"Not Reed. Just us. I'm taking you out on a date, and before you argue, your dad and Corrine are coming down to watch Reed while we go."

"Hmm..." She taps her finger against her bottom lip. "A date, huh? Why do I feel like we've done this all wrong? Sex, pregnancy, foreplay, and now a date?" Her eyes light up telling me she's joking, but I also know deep down the way all this played out bothers her.

"We're not doing anything wrong. We're doing things our way...our story, remember? We get to write the chapters. And this is chapter two: Date night."

While she's getting ready, her dad and Corrine show up. They take over with Reed, so I can get dressed. Once I'm ready to go, I rejoin them in the living room to wait on Olivia. She comes out of the bathroom about thirty minutes later, dressed in a pair of tight—extremely tight—dark jeans. She's been working out every day—switching between yoga and Tae Bo—with Giselle in their living room, and it's showing. The woman almost looks like her pre-pregnancy self. Her hips are a bit wider now, but there's nothing wrong with giving a man something to hold onto. She's wearing a teal off-the-shoulder sweater and some fuzzy-looking boots women always wear when it's cold outside. Her hair is down in loose waves, and her makeup, like always, is the bare minimum. She looks breathtakingly beautiful except…

"Why are you wearing the other team's colors?" Stephen scowls, and Corrine laughs.

"Oh, stop! I swear, every time I go to put on an outfit, if it doesn't support New York, I never hear the end of it," Corrine says, rolling her eyes. "You look lovely, Olivia."

Olivia looks down. "Thank you. I don't own anything in that ugly grass color, so this is going to have to do." She shrugs and walks over to Reed to give him a kiss goodbye. She explains everything to her parents, and they listen even though I'm sure they've heard it all a million times.

We head downstairs to the valet, and they point us in the direction of the car service. I could rent a car, but it's easier and safer to hire someone else to drive us around.

Twenty minutes later, the car service drops us off in downtown Denver. He opens the door, and Olivia gets out first. Before I can get out, I see the lights of the cameras flash. For a second I worry how she's going to react, but she handles it like a pro. She locks her arm into my elbow and smiles softly up at me, allowing the media to snap pictures.

"I'm sorry about this. I made sure to get us a private booth," I whisper into her ear. She nods, her smile never wavering. I imagine, because her mom was one of the biggest international models of her time, and her dad was a huge college football coach, Olivia's experienced the paparazzi at some point during her life. Luckily, for the most part, they really only follow athletes during the weeks of the big games. Sure, in New York, you'll get an occasional paparazzo snapping photos, but it's not like it is when you're an actor or singer living in Los Angeles.

We start walking toward the restaurant and several fans stop us so I can sign stuff for them. Olivia offers to take pictures using their phones. We easily ignore the comments and questions about Celeste and my called-off engagement, but when a question is asked about Reed, I almost answer.

"Nick, is it true your son is the result of a one-night stand?"

Olivia's fingers dig into my arm to stop me. When I look down at her, she smiles then comes up on her tiptoes to give me a chaste kiss. "Ignore them," she murmurs against my lips before pulling back.

When we finally reach the restaurant, we're seated immediately. The waiter takes our drink order and then drops off some bread.

"Wow! Walking with you reminds me of being in high school and dating the star quarterback." She giggles, and I glare at her.

"You dated the quarterback? Who? Does he play now?" Olivia throws her head back with laughter, but I'm not laughing.

"Oh my God! Stop!" She continues to laugh. "I don't know what happened to him, but I can assure you, you're way more popular and get so many more girls than him." Her tone is playful and mocking, and it makes me crack a smile.

"Damn right I'm better, but the only woman I need to get is you. This is why you should be wearing our team colors. So everybody knows you belong to me."

"Aww…maybe you should buy me a letterman's jacket with your number on it…or better yet, I can get your number tattooed right above my ass." She laughs some more.

I, on the other hand, imagine her naked in nothing but my jersey and have to block the visual out before I'm sporting a hard-on right here at the table. Good thing the table is blocking anybody's view from seeing my crotch.

"Both those ideas sound great to me."

We spend the rest of our time at dinner getting to know more about each other. It's nice getting to know Olivia as a woman, as more than just Reed's mom. She tells me about her mom and her childhood, about her time in Paris, some more about her career in the arts. You'd never guess she's worth millions of dollars. She's down to earth and sweet, and she lets everything roll off her back. She listens to everything I say, like she's genuinely interested, asking questions and adding in her own thoughts. And with every word she speaks, and every smile she grants me, I find myself falling harder for her.

We get back to the hotel room and thank her parents for watching Reed. Olivia tells me she needs to run downstairs and grab something, so while she's gone, I jump in the shower to rinse off.

When I get out, I wrap a towel around my waist and head into the room to grab some clothes. Before I can make it out of the doorway, I'm stopped in my place. Because standing in front of me is Olivia in nothing but my jersey. I recognize them from downstairs in the hotel giftshop. They're selling them for the Super Bowl. The jersey is too big on her, exposing her bare shoulder. Her creamy legs are bare, and I wonder if she's wearing panties underneath.

Her mouth twitches into a shy smile as she waits for me to say something. "Fuck" is the only word that comes out of my mouth as I close the distance between us. My one hand cradles her face as my other one moves down the jersey and lands on her smooth thigh. My mouth crashes into hers. It's not sweet or romantic. It's raw and needy. Urgent and demanding. My tongue duals with hers, and she moans into my mouth. My fingers glide back up her thigh, under the jersey, and when I feel there's nothing underneath, I let out a low groan.

"You're killing me, woman," I murmur against her lips. My hands grip her ass cheeks, and I lift her and bring her over to the bed, laying her down under me. My mouth goes back to hers, kissing her with everything in me. Her soft, plump lips have me addicted.

We kiss until she pulls away slightly. "I feel like we really are teenagers. I'm wearing your jersey…we're making out like we're in high school." She giggles, and I shake my head at her playfulness.

"What am I going to do with you?" The question is meant to be rhetorical, but when I speak the words, Olivia's eyes widen.

Her voice is soft. "Maybe…one day love me." She shrugs her shoulders shyly.

Stick a damn fork in me because I'm fucking done. This woman is everything I need in my life, yet I had no idea I was missing.

"That's definitely a huge possibility," I say before my lips capture hers once again, and we continue to make out like horny teenagers.

Twenty-One

OLIVIA

It's Super Bowl Sunday, and I'm sitting up in the friends and family suite with Corrine and Shelby, while Nick and my dad, along with the rest of the team, are in the locker room getting ready for the biggest game the New York Brewers have faced in over a decade. The game is being played in Denver, but the team we're up against is none other than Nick's old team, North Carolina. They made it to the playoffs last year without him but lost. This year they're favored to win it all.

The last few days have been nothing short of amazing. During the day, Nick has been with the team, practicing. It's a huge game, even bigger because he's playing against his old team. They let him go, thinking he wouldn't bring them another championship, yet here he is, hopefully about to prove them all wrong.

Every evening Nick has spent his time with Reed and me. While Reed is awake, Nick's and my attention is on our son, but once he's asleep, it's a whole different ball game. I've never experienced such closeness with a man without having sex. The foreplay with Nick is out of this world, but more than that, it's the time afterward—before I fall asleep in his arms, when he talks to me.

After our conversation about Fiona and me both leaving him a note, an idea sparked. I wanted to turn something negative into a positive, so a couple nights ago I snuck out of bed, wrote him a note, and stuck it in his gym bag. Then last night I did the same thing—unsure if he even saw the first one. Only this morning, I woke up to a note as well, telling me he not only saw it, but it meant a lot to him. He promised to always leave a note, so his words are the first thing I read when I open my eyes, and in return I made the same promise.

"Excuse me." A soft voice brings me back to the now. Reed is awake in my arms, but it won't be long until he's asleep. It's 4:30 here, but he's still refusing to conform to the time zone in Denver. In New York, it's 6:30, and Reed's internal clock has him passed out by seven o'clock every night—waking up every four hours to eat and getting up for the day at six. I love that my son is already on a routine, but here in Denver that means he's up at four in the freaking morning!

"Excuse me," I hear again, and this time I look up to see if someone is speaking to me. With Corrine and Shelby to the left of me, I look to the right. It's an older woman who looks to be around the same age as my stepmom, maybe a little younger. Her hair is dyed in perfect highlights and is tied up in a tight ponytail. Her dress is Stella McCartney—a designer my mom used to love. Her lips are pursed into a half smile-half grimace, and I glance down at my son to confirm he's not crying. I learned from my stunt a few weeks ago, people don't like babies who cry in public.

When my eyes move upward, they land on her eyes—emerald green like Nick's...like Reed's. My gut tells me this woman is related to Nick, and then I recall our late-night conversations where he confided in me about his childhood and lack of relationship with his parents. How he never understood the different kinds of love until Reed was born. My initial instinct is to hate this woman, but instead I choose to pity her, because she's the one missing out on having an authentic relationship with her son.

"Can I help you?" I finally say, and her lips twitch slightly into a shell of a smile.

"I just wanted to introduce myself. I'm Victoria Shaw, Nicholas's mother." She puts her perfectly manicured hand out to shake mine, and I meet her halfway.

"I'm Olivia Harper." She obviously knows who I am or she wouldn't be standing here introducing herself to me.

Reed chooses this moment to make his presence known. He squirms slightly, his arms coming up, and when I lift and turn him around to face me, his mouth morphs into a smile—a new milestone I can't take enough pictures of. "And this is Reed," I add, my eyes staying trained on my baby boy.

Corrine reaches over and tickles his belly. "I can't get enough of those smiles," she says, joining the awkward conversation. "Every time I see him, I swear he's grown another inch." She lightly pinches Reed's cheek then glances up at Victoria. "I'm Corrine, but you know that…we've seen each other at several team functions this year. I'm also Olivia's stepmother." Corrine stands and walks around the back of the couch over to Victoria. "I've watched how you treat those around you. And I'm warning you right now, if you treat my stepdaughter with anything other than respect, I'll have you removed from the premises." She smiles saccharinely and excuses herself to the restroom with Shelby following behind.

I hold back the tears that want to break free. I miss my mom every day, but having Corrine in my life almost makes up for not having my mom here. She's everything a woman could ask for in a stepmom, and I'm so blessed to have one more person in our lives who loves Reed and me.

After a few seconds, Victoria says, "He looks just like Nicholas."

"Yeah, he does. Would you like to hold him?" I hold Reed out, but when Victoria shakes her head, I bring him back against my chest.

"I better not. This is a new dress, and I would hate to have to go back to the hotel and change if he…" She scrunches her nose up in disgust. "Well, you know." She smiles a pained smile, and it has me wanting to find Nick and hug him tightly. The stories Nick has told me about the type of relationship he has with his parents didn't fully sink in until this moment. I mean, what grandmother doesn't want to hold her own grandbaby? I can barely keep Corrine and my dad from hogging Reed when they're in the same room as him.

"Okay…" I give her a plastered-on smile and turn back

to watch the pre-game ceremony. Corrine and Shelby return a few minutes later, and we chat about the upcoming game as we wait for it to begin. Our conversation is interrupted when Nick's dad, Henry, shows up. Victoria introduces us, but just like his wife, he has no desire to hold his grandson, and they both choose to sit elsewhere instead of near us. Nick mentioned that the majority of the time they live in North Carolina, and I've never been more relieved to know they won't be around fulltime.

Just after half-time, Celeste walks in. I only know this because I hear Victoria gush over her. "Oh, Celeste! Sweetheart! I'm so glad you're here." Corrine makes eye contact with me and rolls her eyes. I roll mine back, but deep down I'm sad Nick's parents are behaving this way. I can't imagine not having the support and love I have with my family and friends. I haven't known Nick for long, but other than Killian, I haven't seen anyone else have his back. I know he and Celeste are best friends as well, but I haven't yet to witness their actual friendship.

I hear Celeste politely say hello to Nick's parents, and I hold my breath, afraid our truce was only temporary. A minute later, Celeste sits down next me and says, "About time you got control of that baby." I take a calming breath and turn to her to say something back—what, I'm not sure— but when I look at her, she's grinning ear to ear.

"Ugh…" I groan. "I'm never going to live that down, am I?"

"Probably not, but on the flipside, after hearing him cry, it cemented my decision to never have children." She laughs. "Crying babies are the perfect way to control the population if you ask me. Five minutes of hearing him cry, and I was double checking that my birth control was up to date." She shoots me a wink, and I laugh.

Celeste sits next to me for the entire game, and the more we talk, the more I find she's actually a very likable person and can see why she and Nick are such good friends. Underneath her flawless makeup and designer clothes is a sweet and funny woman. She shares hilarious stories of Nick growing up that I stow away to later rib into Nick about. Corrine and Shelby join the conversation, and we make plans for a girls' night. Corrine says she's too old to go out but would love to watch Reed. I text Giselle, and after she about dies through text over the fact I'm making plans with Nick's ex, she, of course, agrees to go out as well.

All of our talking ceases as the game winds down. New York has intercepted the ball and there's only enough time for one, maybe two plays. The next play, if done right, can mean we're Super Bowl champions.

Twenty-Two

NICK

Half the crowd erupts into an explosive roar of cheers as our defense intercepts the ball at the forty-yard line with under a minute remaining, no timeouts left. This is exactly what we needed, what we were banking on. The game has been close the entire time. If they would've scored, we would need this touchdown to stay one up on them, but because they didn't, if we score, we win. Our entire season is on the line, the entire game coming down to this next play. Everyone is counting on me. I glance up at the owner's box, not that I can see Olivia, but knowing she's up there calms my nerves.

The last time I was in this position, I was with Fiona, but she wasn't there. I know a lot of what went wrong between us had to do with my mother, but I hope what I'm building with Olivia is stronger. While I'm pissed at my mom for what she did, what Celeste said rings true. Fiona made the choice to take the money. She chose to walk away. She could've come to me and I would've given it to her, but she didn't. I'd like to believe everything happens for a reason, and Fiona and Celeste were merely stepping stones that led me to Olivia and Reed.

Offense makes their way onto the field, huddling together and waiting for me to call the play, so I jog over to join them. "All right, guys. We got this. One play…maybe two, and we'll be Super Bowl champions. We have zero timeouts, so the clock will be ticking. Here's the play: West right slot, seventy-two, z bingo U split, dummy snap count on three." The huddle breaks, and everybody lines up.

On my three-count, the center hikes the ball. Taking a three-step drop, I find an available receiver, but just as I'm about to throw the ball, he's covered by the fucking cornerback. Defense is rushing me, and I know I've got to make this throw before I'm tackled. I spot Killian sprint left. He's open—just barely. I throw the ball to him, and it's a shitty throw at best, too far to the left, just before I'm knocked to the ground. Killian catches the ball one-handed and runs. I watch with bated breath as he passes each yard line—thirty… twenty… ten… with the safety on his ass every step of the way.

A safety comes from the right, and Killian, like the crazy ass he is, leaps over the guy into the end zone.

"Touchdown!" The crowd screams, and the entire team congregates into the end zone, celebrating. Brian Peters, our kicker, makes his way out onto the field for the extra point. Then, with only twenty seconds left on the clock, the special team's unit comes onto the field for the kick off. Peters, once again kicks the ball, and the other team receives it. Their kick returner runs up the field, but he's immediately taken down by one of our players. With no time left on the clock, the game is over, and we're Super Bowl fucking champions.

Coach Harper makes his way over to me and pulls me in for a hug. "We did it!" he shouts into my ear, and I hug him back. "Hell yeah, we did." The confetti falls from the sky, and the media makes their way over to us in a frenzy, surrounding us like vultures.

Killian jumps up against me and pulls me into a hug. "Fuck yes!" We're both crying as hats are handed out. Several of my teammates come over and hug me. I place my hat on my head as one of the reporters sticks a microphone in my face. Her name is Jennifer, and she's one of the sport's channel's main reporters.

"Two years ago, you were on the other side. Now here you are with your fourth Super Bowl win; first one with New York. To get this win today, what does that mean?"

"It means everything, Jennifer. This season wasn't easy by any means. It doesn't surprise me we had to fight every step of the way through this game, until the very end." The reporter laughs. "It was a team effort. It tested every one of us, but we came through in the end."

The reporter moves on to her next question. "It's public knowledge that you're in New York on a one year contract. Can you tell us your plans for next year?" I want to say I'm not going anywhere, but the truth is contracts haven't been discussed formally yet, so I have to go with a politically correct response.

"There are definitely a lot of decisions to be made, but I have some priorities I need to get to first, starting with finding my girlfriend, Olivia, and kissing the heck out of her. Then I'm going to celebrate with my team and thank God we won so Coach Harper doesn't have a reason to ban me from family holidays. After that, I'm taking my girl and son on a much needed vacation." I glance over at Coach Harper who throws his head back in laughter, shaking his head in understanding. I just went on record, on live television, and admitted to the world that Olivia is my girlfriend.

Jennifer and I go through a few more questions and once we're done, I make my way down the field to meet up with the rest of my team, so we can celebrate our win.

Twenty-Three

OLIVIA

Nick and I are cuddling on the couch at his place, watching shit television while Reed is napping. I'm laying horizontally across the couch, my head resting in his lap, and Nick is running his fingers through my hair. The last two weeks since we've returned from the Super Bowl have been spent with Nick either at my place or Reed and me at his. The team is on break until the end of June when their training camp begins, and we have somehow created our own schedule of pure laziness. Nick and I haven't discussed his plans in regards to his contract with New York, but I think he's just basking in the glory of his win right now—he's had to make appearances on several daytime and late-night shows—and enjoying the downtime. We rarely go out in public, and if we do, it's to grab something to eat. My dad and Corrine are away in Italy. They left the day after the Super Bowl. Corrine is from there, and my dad surprised her with a romantic trip, just the two of them.

Nick pauses the show, and I turn over onto my back to look at him. "I have something I want to ask you, but I'm going to need you to be openminded."

I sit up, intrigued. "Okay."

"I want us to go away."

"Where do you want to go? Somewhere warm would be fabulous, so Reed can wear less than three layers of clothing outside."

"Actually, that's where the open-mindedness comes in. I was thinking we could go away…just the two of us."

I sit up, confused. "What would we do with Reed?"

"Giselle said she could watch him."

"You already asked her?"

"I didn't want to bring it up if she couldn't. I was going to ask Shelby if Giselle said she couldn't, but she said she can."

I stand and begin to pace the living room. Reed will be two months old this week. Am I ready to leave him for the night?

"Liv, it would only be for two nights. It's Valentine's Day weekend."

"Could we stay local?"

"Like stay at a hotel in the area?" He eyes me incredulously.

"My dad has a house in the Hamptons. It's only a couple hours' drive from here, so we wouldn't be far if something happened."

Nick chuckles. "How about I'll agree to the Hamptons, but I'm picking the place. I'm not spending the weekend under Coach's roof with his daughter."

I roll my eyes. "Deal." And then it hits me Valentine's Day is *this* week, like in two days. "Wait! We're going this weekend?"

"Yeah…we'll drive up Thursday after Giselle gets off work and stay through the weekend."

"That's hardly any time to prepare." I feel myself getting worked up.

Nick gets up off the couch and moves toward me. His arms encircle my waist, and he leans down and places a calming kiss on my lips. "Brown-Eyes," he whispers. He moves his lips to my neck and kisses the sensitive flesh just under my ear. "There's nothing to prepare for. You don't even have to pack. If I have it my way, we won't even be getting dressed." He lifts his head, and with a wide grin, waggles his brows suggestively.

"Liv, we're here." I feel Nick gently shake me, but my eyes refuse to open. "Liv, baby. You have to wake up." Reluctantly, I open my eyes and stretch my arms as I remember where I am. One minute I was talking to Nick about Reed's growth spurt and the next I'm waking up in the car. I sit up and glance around. We're in the driveway of a beautiful three-story cottage. I can't see the ocean from where we are, but I know it's back there because the home is sitting on top of a dune.

"Nick…this place is huge. Did you invite more people?"

He laughs. "Actually, I did…"

"Oh." I had assumed when he mentioned clothing was optional he was implying we would be alone. Maybe he wanted Reed home because there would be a party going on…

"Not right now. For the next two nights, it's just you and me. On Saturday, however, we'll have a full house. Giselle is going to bring Reed over, and Killian is joining us. Shelby can't make it because she has a birthday party to attend for her stepmother, but your dad and Corrine will be coming…and…" He pauses, worrying his bottom lip, nervously.

"And?"

"Well, Celeste mentioned she wanted to join, and since you guys seem to be getting along…texting and planning a night out, I said okay, and your parents said they'd have no problem watching Reed while we all go out. Is that okay?"

"Yeah! That sounds really great. How long are we here for?"

"Only five days…but then we're going away on another trip, and Giselle and Killian will be joining us for the second half of that trip."

Turning in my seat to face Nick, I place my palms on his cheeks. "You know you don't have to take us away, right? I don't need surprise trips; I just need you."

Nick frowns. "I know, but I only have so long until football starts back up again." He takes my hands in his and brings them up to his lips, kissing the inside of each of my wrists. "I want us to make the most out of it. It was only going to be us, but then Giselle mentioned she could help babysit, and once Killian caught wind of where we're going, he begged and said if I didn't let him go, I was choosing your best friend over mine."

I laugh, imagining Killian pouting like a child.

"What are you thinking in regards to your contract?"

"It's kind of out of my hands. I'm waiting to hear from my dad if New York wants to re-sign me. If they don't, I have to hope another team will pick me up. I would like to think I've proven my worth this season."

I hadn't considered New York might not re-sign him, and if they don't, he would have to move to wherever the team is that does sign him. Would he ask us to move with him? Would I be willing to move somewhere else? My thoughts go back to a year ago when Victor left me to move to Switzerland. Of course, him not asking me makes more sense now that I know he was cheating on me for a year with my so-called friend.

"Hey, I can see the cogs in your head turning. It'll all work out. We'll figure it out together. But first, let's enjoy ourselves. We have this house"—he points toward the beautiful cottage—"and it has a hot tub and a heated pool."

"Do you want me to talk to my dad? I know he's not the owner but—" Nick leans over the center console and kisses me. His tongue darts out quickly, massaging mine, but then he backs up leaving me wanting more.

"No. One, all negotiations need to be done through my agent, and two, I want to keep us separate from business. I want to have a good time this weekend. No talking shop." I nod in agreement.

After dropping our bags in the foyer, Nick and I take a tour of the cottage. It has at least seven bedrooms and even more bathrooms, a huge kitchen, and several sitting rooms. We find the bedroom we're going to be staying in, and Nick brings our bags up.

Afterward, we make our way outside. It's fifty degrees out today, so we're both dressed comfortably in jeans and a hoodie. There's a huge back patio with tons of seating and a humungous pool. Just past the pool is a wooden bridge that leads down to the beach. The sun is shining, and it helps offset the cool air.

"Let's go inside. I brought a bottle of wine, and I was thinking we could go to dinner tonight."

"Sounds good. I'm just going to go up to the room and freshen up. You pour us a glass, and I'll be right back down."

I start to walk away, but then remember something I wanted to tell him. "Oh, Nick…"

"Yeah?"

"Remember when I went to the doctor for my check-up?"

"Yeah." He nods.

"He okayed me to have sex." I shoot him an overly dramatic flirtatious wink, and Nick throws his head back with a laugh. I start to ascend the stairs when he calls out my name. I stop on the first step and turn around to find him right in front of me. He pulls me into his arms, and his lips brush mine softly before he pulls back and smiles, his green eyes shining bright. "Thank you for coming away with me. I know it was hard to leave Reed."

"Thank you for bringing me. Now let me go make

myself presentable. I feel gross from sleeping in the car."

Nick lets go of me, and I run up the stairs to our room. I jump in the shower to rinse off then brush my teeth. I'm debating whether I should go down there dressed, in a robe, naked, or in lingerie when my phone dings with a text from

Giselle: Are you busy?

Me: Nope. Everything okay?

It takes her a few seconds to respond, so I wrap the fluffy white towel around me and sit down on the bed.

Giselle: Yes…Reed took a bottle a couple hours ago, but now I think he's wanting another one. He's really fussy. I just wanted to check with you before I go off your feeding schedule.

And this is why I fell asleep in the car. My baby boy is going through a growth spurt, which means he has been getting up every few hours all night long to eat. The pediatrician said it's normal, but I was nervous about leaving Giselle to deal with it. Up until a few days ago, he's been on a great eating and sleeping schedule.

Me: Go ahead and give him half a bottle. If he doesn't take it he might just be tired. He's been up a lot throughout the night. Oh! Can you take his temperature? I just want to make sure he's not sick. Can you please text me and let me know?

I debate whether to send that entire text, but with me over two hours away I need to make sure Reed isn't catching a cold or something worse. After hitting send, I lay back in the bed to wait for her response. The pillows are comfy and the down blanket is super soft. Maybe I'll just close my eyes for a few seconds while I wait...

Twenty-Four

NICK

My phone rings, and when I look at the caller ID, I see it's my dad. Since the only time he ever calls is when it's work related, I let it go to voicemail. Right now my priority is Olivia. Speaking of which…it's been a while since she went upstairs to freshen up.

Leaving the bottle of wine, along with the glasses where they are, I run upstairs to check on her. Immediately, I spot her on the bed, passed out. When I get closer, I can see she's in a towel. Her phone dings in her hand, but she doesn't move. She's snuggled up in the sheets and snoring softly.

Taking the phone from her, I check it and see a photo of Reed sleeping with an accompanying text from Giselle saying he doesn't have a temperature and that he ate and fell asleep. I text her back a quick thank you and place her phone, as well as mine, on the nightstand. After stripping off my jeans and sweater, I climb in with Olivia—she's in the center of the bed, so I slide in behind her, my arms encircling her body. She makes a soft sighing noise as she settles into me.

Pressing a small kiss to her cheek, I lay my head down on the pillow, and for a few minutes I enjoy holding this beautiful woman. The last few days she's been supermom. Reed's been up at all hours, and while I try to help, she insists on getting up no matter what. My goal is to get her to understand I want us to be a team. She doesn't have to do this all on her own. Letting my eyes close, I drift off to sleep.

I'm not sure how long I was passed out, but what I do know is that Olivia is awake. How do I know that? Because her towel-clad ass is rubbing against my front in a way that has my dick hardening. My hands are still wrapped around her waist, and I can feel her shifting in the bed. Pressing my face into her nape, I tighten my grip on her. She sighs and moves her ass up and down my front again.

"Liv." I say her name to make sure she's awake.

"Mmhmm" is all I get.

My hand moves up the towel, and finding the knot holding it closed, I loosen it until I feel the two sides of the towel part ways. Grabbing the material separating us, I tug on it slightly until it unravels off Olivia's body. I throw it onto the floor then bring my hand back to her body. My fingers stroke and tweak her pointed nipples. My lips trail kisses down the back of her shoulder, and I feel her shiver at my touch.

"Liv, you awake, baby?"

"Yes," she breathes. I love the affect my touch has on her.

My hand glides across her smooth skin, down her hip, and around her front between her thighs. She parts her legs enough for my fingers to slip into her tight cunt. When she lifts slightly, I slide my other arm under her. Sticking one finger, then two, inside her, I fingerfuck her, getting her wetter and wetter. The room is silent, the only sounds coming from the slickness of her pussy, and from her mouth as she lets out moans of pleasure.

Using her juices, I move my fingers to her clit, circling and massaging the swollen nub. One of her hands goes to her breast, and I can see her pinching her nipple. Her moans get louder. Her other hand comes around behind her, finding my dick and stroking it. It's already hard, but with her touch, it's granite.

"Fuck me, Nick, please," she begs, turning her neck enough to lock eyes with me. Shifting her ass up slightly, I guide my hard cock into her pussy from behind. It's warm and wet and so fucking tight, and all fucking mine. Once I'm completely seated inside her, I give her neck a kiss. Then I start moving in and out of her. My fingers are digging into her side, and Olivia's meeting me thrust for thrust.

It feels so damn good from behind, but I can't kiss her or see her. Reluctantly, I slide out of her, and she lets out a disappointed whimper. She rolls to her back, and I crawl up her body, quickly pushing back into her. My hands are on either side of her face, and as I lean down to kiss her, I see her chocolate-brown eyes sparkling with pleasure. I kiss her with every ounce of want and need I have inside me as I make love to her.

Her legs part a little more, and I'm able to go deeper. I can feel my cock rubbing against her clit. Her body tightens in anticipation of her impending climax. Our kisses turn ravenous, frantic. We're all lips and tongues and teeth. My thrusts get harder, rougher. I can feel sweat beading above my brow. It's been too fucking long since I was inside her. I'm never going to last.

And then Olivia's walls tighten. I feel her pussy contract, and I know it's about to be over. She lets out a long, breathy moan into my mouth, without breaking our kiss, as she comes so damn hard around me I about lose it. My hands find their way to her head, and my fingers grip her hair as I pump into her with abandon, finding my own release. I hear myself let out a groan as my seed shoots into my woman's pussy, filling her with every fucking drop of cum I have in me.

Twenty-Five

OLIVIA

Nick's body stills, and I can feel his cum inside me. We stop kissing but Nick's lips stay pressed against mine for a few more seconds before he backs up. He pulls out of me, taking his warmth with him. When he doesn't say anything at first, I get worried. What if being with me again wasn't as good as the last time? I've had a baby, so maybe I don't feel as good to him.

"Whatever you're thinking, stop." He presses a kiss to my lips then to my cheek and last to my neck. "No, I take that back. Tell me. I can't fix it or tell you you're wrong if I don't know what it is you're thinking."

"Was—was it as good as before I had a baby?" Nick's brows pinch together. I can feel his semi-hard cock rubbing against the top of my thigh, but I block it out.

"I don't think you can compare the two. That night we spent together was incredible. Mind-blowing fucking amazing." I feel myself frown at his words, but then he continues. "But that night, it was strictly physical. You had me addicted to your body within seconds."

He holds himself up on one forearm. "Brown-Eyes," he says softly, and my stomach knots up. I love when he calls me that. "You can't compare a night of lust to what we just did. The sex that night was off the charts hot, but now so much has changed...the way you make me feel. It's what I was talking about before...so much fucking more. It's not just your body I'm addicted to. It's also your heart and your mind that's got me hooked and craving more." And in those couple of sentences, he's managed to tame down all of my fears and insecurities.

He gets off the bed and pulls me up with him, giving me a quick kiss before we go to the bathroom to clean up. Once we're done, we get dressed and head downstairs. Nick pours us each a glass of wine, and we sit down on the sofa facing each other. For a few seconds, we're both silent. Then Nick says, "Liv, I came in you...I know it's too late now, but we probably should've discussed this first." My body freezes, and I force the sip of wine down as he continues. "I don't know what happened when you got pregnant with Reed, if a condom broke, or if we didn't use one once and I didn't pull out, but—"

"I lost my luggage and my pills. I didn't take them for almost a week," I blurt out. Nick's brows raise at my admission. "I'm so sorry. The entire plane's luggage was put on the wrong plane. You can ask Giselle. I didn't do it on purpose. I wasn't trying to trap you...I mean, how could I? I didn't even have your information. And just so you know,

I'm on the pill. I promise I'll be more careful this time." I stop speaking long enough to catch my breath. "If you want to use condoms to be on the—"

"Whoa, calm down." Nick laughs. "If we would've used condoms every time, you not taking your pills wouldn't have mattered. It takes two. I don't for a second think you tried to trap me, and I don't regret whatever happened because it got us our son. And"—Nick grins wickedly—"there's no way in hell I'm using a condom with you. I've felt your pussy raw, and there's no way I'm going back to having latex between us."

His words have my cheeks heating up, and of course it only has him grinning wider.

"My baby!" I screech as I run out the door. The last couple days alone with Nick has been nothing short of amazing. The fucking and sex and lovemaking—and yes, I'm listing them separately because when Nick took me from behind in the shower, that was definitely fucking, and when he took me on top of the table, it was sex, and when he woke me up this morning, the way he languorously pumped in and out of me, well, that was most certainly making love. I feel caught up on my sleep and like a whole new person. And now I'm missing the heck out of my son.

Giselle takes his car seat out and Nick takes it from her. "I need him now," I state matter-of-factly, which makes

Nick laugh.

"Let's get him inside where it's warm and then you can have him," he says, carrying Reed inside. Killian follows Nick inside, but I hang back to help Giselle with her bags.

"How was the ride?" I take one of her bags, and she grabs the other.

"Too long."

"Oh no! Was Reed cranky?" We walk up the sidewalk and are almost to the front door when Giselle stops.

"He was a perfect angel. Killian, on the other hand, drove me nuts. I might have to drive back with your parents because another two hours in the car with that man, and I might end up in jail for murder."

"Really? He seems so nice every time we hang out with him." I shrug. "What did he do?"

"Olivia, Giselle, let me help you with those." Killian pops out from behind the door and takes the bags from both of our hands. He smiles sweetly at me, but when he smiles at Giselle, it's almost *too* sweet.

She groans and rolls her eyes, pushing past him. "I need a drink."

We head inside, and Nick already has Reed out of his car seat and is making him a bottle. Giselle grabs a bottle of wine and two glasses and brings them over to the table. "This place is unbelievable. Maybe I need to go against my rule of never dating an athlete again." She waggles her eyebrows playfully.

"You have a rule against dating athletes?" Nick asks, sitting down next to me and feeding Reed. "I thought it was only musicians."

I laugh. "Nope, she's included athletes in her ban as well."

"And why is that?" Killian asks Giselle.

"Because they think because they can throw and catch a ball, they're above God." She winks my way, telling me she's just messing with the guys. "No offense, Nick."

"No offense taken. Besides, you're not far off. Only it wasn't me throwing a ball this morning that had Olivia screaming 'Oh god' in bed."

"Nick!" I screech, and he cackles.

"Nice!" Killian reaches over and gives Nick a fist-bump.

"Pigs," Giselle huffs.

"She was just kidding!" I exclaim. "She's really just against dating in general." Giselle and I laugh.

"And what about you?" Nick asks, lifting Reed up to his shoulder to burp him. "I know you mentioned dating a quarterback, but were there any types of guys you preferred to date?"

"I'm an equal opportunist…but there is something about a tall, tan, muscular man who knows how to use his hands…to throw that gets me all hot and bothered."

Nick chuckles. "You better equally remember I'm the only one allowed to get you hot and bothered." He leans over and pulls me into a kiss before getting up with Reed. "Kill, want to grab a beer outside so the women can gossip?"

"Sure." Killian laughs then stands and follows Nick out of the room.

"Wait!" I yell, and Nick stops in his place. "Hand over my baby." He laughs as he hands Reed over to me. Then he and Killian grab a couple of beers from the fridge and head out back.

"That guy has it bad," Giselle comments once the backdoor is shut.

"It's definitely mutual. Now tell me what happened with Killian that has you drinking before noon."

She drinks her glass of wine slowly until it's completely drained. "The guy is just such an asshole," she finally says. Seeing her glass is empty, she refills it. "Now, tell me about your romantic getaway." And I know that's all I'm getting out of her right now.

A little while later, my dad and Corrine show up. Nick and Killian run to the store to buy groceries and when they return, Nick grills up some burgers and steaks while Corrine and I make several side dishes. We all congregate to the dining room to eat. The guys banter back and forth about their Super Bowl win, and the women discuss Giselle's latest job with some high-class executive who is having his entire place redecorated. It's the most content I've felt in a long time, like everything is finally falling into place.

Just as we finish cleaning up from dinner, there's a knock on the door. Since Nick is laying Reed down, I run to the door to quickly answer it, and standing there is Celeste with a single suitcase. She smiles wide at me, and I smile back.

"I'm glad you could make it."

"Thank you for having me." She leaves her luggage by the stairs, and we join everyone back in the living room. I make introductions around the room even though she knows my dad and stepmom.

"I love that everyone is here," I say. "I was so scared

when we closed up our flat to come back here, but I'm glad we did."

"I was about to drag you back myself," my dad jokes.

"Speaking of which, have you decided if you're going to sell or rent it out?" Giselle asks.

"You own a place in France?" Celeste asks, joining in the conversation.

"I lived there for six years. It made more sense to buy than rent. Giselle and I went to college there and then both got our master's. I haven't decided if I'm going to sell it, though."

Nick and Killian walk into the room as I'm finishing my sentence. "Sell what?" Nick questions as he sits down on the couch. He lifts me slightly then snuggles me into his side.

"My flat in Paris."

"You should keep it, so we can visit. I've never been. You can show me your home away from home." He presses a kiss to my neck.

"True, but we could always stay in a hotel. The market is flourishing, and I could make a decent amount on it. It's in a college district."

"Does that mean you're staying for good?" Giselle asks, and I shoot her a glare.

"What do you mean for good?" my dad jumps in, confused. I didn't want to get into this now, but it seems I don't have a choice.

"Are you planning to move back?" Nick asks, his voice devoid of all emotion.

"When I came to visit it was only for a week because I was offered a position as an Art Education Coordinator.

When we left to come here, I took a leave of absence with the Museum I was working at. You get two months of maternity leave, but I put in a request for additional time."

"How much extra?" Nick asks, his tone now ice cold.

"If I plan to keep my job, I have to return in four months."

"Olivia!" my dad exclaims. "You didn't mention this when you agreed to *move* home."

"I know. I wanted to keep my options open. I never imagined I would find Reed's dad. Obviously, a lot has changed."

Celeste's eyes are trained on me when she says, "You agreed to shared custody. You can't just leave with Nick's baby." If Nick's tone was ice cold, his friend's is equivalent to an arctic glacier, and in this moment, I can understand why they're such good friends. They might not see eye-to-eye on everything, but she one hundred percent has his back.

"I'm not going anywhere. I was just keeping my options open," I repeat. "I love my life here, and I love being near my dad."

"What happens if Nick ends up on another team? Like in Florida or Texas?" Celeste pushes, and I stop myself from telling her to mind her own business. It's clear she's only being protective of Nick.

"And this is where the conversation needs to end," my dad says. "As the coach, I can't discuss this with my player, especially with his contract up in the air."

Nick agrees, and the conversation shifts to another topic, but my mind is stuck on Celeste's question. If Nick leaves, would I go? Would he ask me to go?

He must sense my confusion because he dusts my hair over my shoulder and whispers into my ear, "I'm not going anywhere, and if I have to, we'll discuss it together. Just don't go and leave the country without me." He kisses my temple then my earlobe. "Okay?"

"Okay," I agree.

"Are you kids going out tonight?" Corrine asks, changing the subject.

"Yes!" Celeste answers before I can. "I've been wanting to check out AM Southampton!"

"Giselle?" I ask. "You down?"

"Hell yes."

"Well I'm definitely down," Killian adds.

"I guess that's a yes then," I say through a laugh.

After we spend the rest of the afternoon hanging out, Giselle, Celeste, and I go upstairs to get ready. We're all dressed in slinky, way too tight dresses, and as I stand next to Celeste in the floor length mirror, I get choked up. The woman reminds me so much of my mom. She must be almost six feet tall in heels with a slender, yet feminine body. She's tanned and...perfect. I clearly got more of my dad's genes than my mom's since I'm only five foot five and curvy.

"We look hot," Celeste winks as Giselle walks over to join us.

"You remind me of my mom when she was younger."

Celeste's face whips around to mine. "Really?"

I nod. "I used to wish I could have had her height and body."

"You might not be tall, but you're beautiful, Olivia. Trust me. You look a lot like your mom. You have her eyes and nose, and when you smile you light up the same way she used to in her photos."

"Really?" I ask as tears fill my lids. It's the first time anyone besides my dad has ever told me I look like my mom.

"Really! Now wipe those tears, and let's get this party started!"

Twenty-Six

NICK

"Holy shit, bro." Killian's eyes dart over my shoulder, and when I turn around, the women are standing at the bottom of the stairs. All of them in dresses that I'm almost positive are illegal in several countries and high heels that could kill a man—figuratively and literally. They're all wearing makeup and look beautiful in their own way. But my eyes zero in on Olivia, who looks devastatingly fucking gorgeous.

Closing the gap between us, I pull her into my arms and give her a kiss on the corner of her mouth so I don't ruin her lipstick. "You look stunning, Liv," I whisper in her ear.

"Thank you."

"All of you look beautiful," Killian adds. "Now let's go."

We pile into the SUV I ordered, and about twenty minutes later, we're at AM Southampton night club. Of course the bouncer recognizes us right away, and we're let in and brought over to the VIP section.

"Let's dance." Olivia pulls me onto the dance floor before we can even sit down. The music is thumping, and the club is crowded as hell. I pull her into my arms, and she grinds her body against mine to the music.

"It's like we've come full circle," she yells over the music, and I laugh. She's right. A year ago, we were at a club dancing just like this. I thought back then she was the one for me, but now I know she is.

We spend the next few hours drinking and dancing, and only when Olivia is so drunk and horny that I fear for the pictures that might surface, do we call for the car service to come back and pick us up.

"I need you to fuck me good and hard," Olivia slurs as we walk up the steps to our room. I chuckle at her brazen remarks. Killian, Giselle, and Celeste all laugh, and it's then Olivia remembers we aren't alone. We reach the landing, and Olivia throws her arms around Celeste.

"Thank you for not having sex with my boyfriend. If you did, we wouldn't be able to be friends and then you wouldn't be able to one day be a princess like me." Celeste shoots me a *please help me* look, but I just shake my head. My woman apparently has no filter when she's drunk.

"And don't you worry. When we get back from vacation, I'm going to find you a prince to love. I'm Princess Aurora, but you can be…" Olivia backs up, swaying slightly, and looks at Celeste for a moment. "You can be Belle." She nods, agreeing with herself. "She's not born into royalty and has no desire to marry Gaston, but when she meets the beast, she can't help but fall in love. While some would say the beast saved her, I think they actually saved each other. You're going to meet a man, and you'll both find love in each other. Yep! You're definitely Belle."

"And which one am I?" Giselle asks, of course playing along.

"You're…" Olivia taps her bottom lip in concentration. "Rapunzel."

"Rapunzel? But I have brown hair."

"It's not about how she looks. Rapunzel is strong and brave and knows how to stick up for herself." Olivia crosses the landing, and when she's only a few inches away from Giselle, she places her hand on her cheek. "And one day you're going to meet a prince you will trust with all of your secrets and he's going to save you just like Flynn Ryder saved Rapunzel."

The room goes quiet, quickly realizing Olivia's drunken silliness has turned serious. "All right, my drunken princess. Let's get you to bed before your chariot turns back into a pumpkin." I grab her hips and guide her toward our room.

"Yes!" she squeals. "But that's Cinderella! I'm Aurora!"

Twenty-Seven

OLIVIA

I wake up with the most intense, pounding headache I've ever experienced in my life. When I open my eyes, I glance next to me and see the bed is empty. Noticing a ripped piece of paper on the pillow, I snag it, and with only one eye open, read it.

Good morning Princess Aurora, I've left you a glass of water and two Advil in case you need them. I have Reed with me. Take a bath and relax. Come down when you're ready.
—Your Prince ;)

After I've taken the pain meds he left for me and soaked in a hot bubble bath, I make my way downstairs. Everybody is sitting around the table talking, and when they see me, they all go quiet and then crack up laughing.

I look down to make sure I'm dressed appropriately. No nip slips…"What?"

"Nothing, Princess Aurora." Giselle giggles, and Celeste throws her head back in laughter.

"Ha ha. Very funny," I say dryly, which only has them laughing harder. Why? I'm not sure.

Giselle's phone rings, and she stands up, excusing herself to the other room to take the call.

I walk over to Nick to sit down next to him, but before I can sit, he pulls me into his lap. "Good morning, baby," he murmurs into my neck.

"Morning. Where's Reed?"

"Taking a nap." He sniffs my hair. "You smell good. Did you take a bubble bath?"

"I did. Thank you. So, why was everyone laughing?"

"You don't remember last night?" Killian asks.

"Going to the club?" I question.

"No." He shakes his head. "When we got home."

I try to remember, but I can't. "The alcohol must've hit me hard since I haven't drank in over a year," I admit.

"Don't worry about it, babe," Nick says. "All you need to know is that you, Celeste, and Giselle are all princesses and—"

"Umm…Olivia…I need to go." Giselle comes back into the dining room, looking pale and worried. "And I don't have a car. I came here with Killian…Shit!"

"What's going on?" I ask.

"My dad left my mom. My sister just texted me that she came home for the weekend. She planned to leave this morning, but when she woke up, my dad was gone. I need to get there. You know how my mom is…"

"I know. Why don't you take Nick's car? We can ride home with Killian or my parents…"

"I'll drive you," Killian offers.

Giselle gives him a once over. "I have to go to my parents' house in Rye. It's going to be a good two-hour drive there, and another hour drive back to Brooklyn, and I don't even know how long I'll be there for. Could be a few hours… if she lets me in, that is." She cringes at her last sentence, and my heart breaks for Giselle and the rocky relationship she has with her parents.

"Then we better get moving." Killian walks back out of the room without waiting for Giselle to respond.

We spend the rest of the day out back. It's warm enough to grill outside, so my dad and Nick grill up some chicken and steak while Corrine, Celeste, and I make up some sides. We eat outside on the back patio while Reed naps. Afterward, Corrine offers to watch Reed while Nick and I go for a walk.

"I love the ocean, but I hate the sand and the salt water," I admit as I toe the sand.

Nick chuckles. "I'm pretty sure without the salt water and the sand you have a pool."

"Oh…well, whatever." I laugh.

"I looked up some schools this morning while you were asleep." Nick reaches down and picks up a stick that's washed ashore.

"And what did you find?"

"A couple schools where I can take all my classes online, but I was hoping to take the writing classes on campus. The problem is I don't know where I'll be, so I'm going to have to wait until I find out who I'm playing for next season."

"That makes sense." I sit down while Nick, using the stick he picked up, writes in the sand. "Until then you could do something you enjoy, like writing for fun."

Nick stops drawing in the sand. "What do you mean? Like write a book?"

"Sure, why not? You don't need a degree to write."

Nick comes over and sits behind me, his legs outstretched on either side of my body and his arms wrapping around me. "I also think I'm going to get more involved in the charity my mom runs for me."

"You have a charity? What is it for?"

"Promoting literacy in kids. I started it a few years ago when my publicist said it would look good. I used to go to different schools and read to classes in lower income schools."

"That's amazing, Nick! Why did you stop?"

"The short answer is I got busy, but the truth is, looking back, once it was established, my mom stopped scheduling events, and I didn't push her to do it."

"Well, if you want, I can take a look at it. I ran the youth program at the museum I worked for in Paris. I worked with several charities and organizations." And then an idea hits me. "What would you think about expanding the charity? I've always wanted to start one. What if we combine both of our passions by having one charity that helps promote the arts and literacy?"

"Absolutely. I'll text my mom and let her know you'll be contacting her. She can give you whatever information you need."

We stand, and I brush the bottom of my jeans off. When I turn around, I look at the writing in the sand.

"Umm…Nick, did you write that?" I ask dumbly as I look over my shoulder to find Nick smiling at me. I know he wrote it because I watched him.

"Yeah." He grins. "I did. I love you, Brown-Eyes. It's probably too soon to be saying those words, but they're exactly how I feel. I love you." My heart tightens and then expands. It has never felt so full in my life.

Throwing my arms around Nick's neck, I pull him down for a kiss. I'm not quite ready to say the words back yet, and he doesn't push for them. So for now, I just show him how I feel.

Twenty-Eight

NICK

"Close your eyes, Liv."

"Is this really necessary? First, you wouldn't tell me where the plane is flying us, now you're not going to let me see where the driver is taking us?"

"It's a surprise."

"Fine. I know we're in another country, though. That flight was way too long to still be in the U.S."

"I'm not telling you anything. Now shush." I put Reed's pacifier in his mouth. He's getting a bit antsy, but surprisingly he did well on the flight over here. I can't imagine having to fly commercial with a baby, though. I give major props to the moms and dads who do. It was enough work on a private plane.

Olivia rests her head on my shoulder while the car service takes us to where we'll be staying. I wanted to get away with her and Reed for a couple weeks. No media or paparazzi. Just us on a sandy white beach under the warm sunshine, where our son can—as Olivia put it—wear a single layer of clothing. She doesn't know it yet, but I've left all of our electronics at home. I gave her dad the number to the resort we're staying at in case of an emergency and gave Giselle and Killian our info for when they arrive. They'll be joining us the last half of the trip, and we'll all fly back together.

We pull up to the resort, and the driver opens Olivia's door while the valet opens mine. She steps out of the car, opens her eyes, and glances around. "I can smell"—she sniffs the air—"the beach."

A Hawaiian woman comes over and says, "Aloha" while placing a pink and yellow flowered lei over Olivia's head.

"Are we in Hawaii?" Olivia asks excitedly. She runs around the car and jumps into my arms. "I've never been here before! Oh my God! It's so warm here! Thank you!" She plants a wet kiss to my lips before dropping back onto the ground.

She fiddles through her purse then looks up with a frown. "I don't have my cell phone. I wanted to take a picture."

"No cell phones." I hand her a digital camera I picked up for the trip. "You can take photos with this."

"Where's your cell phone?" she questions.

"Back in New York. We're electronic-free for two weeks."

"A girl can get used to this kind of treatment: a week in the Hamptons, two weeks in Hawaii. Where are you taking me next?"

"Unfortunately, this is our last stop. After this trip, I have to go home and get my contract situated for the season. But once that's taken care of, we can plan another trip before the season starts."

"Are you staying with New York?" Olivia asks.

"I would like to, but you know it's not up to me. So, for now, let's enjoy ourselves."

"But what if you have to move?"

I've only known Olivia for a short time, but this is the first time I've seen any type of real insecurity shine through her tough façade. I was worried about tearing down her wall, the one she keeps erect to protect herself. But as I stare at her, I see that somewhere along the way she lowered her gate and willingly let me in.

Sliding my arm around her waist, I pull her into my embrace. Leaning down, my green eyes meet her brown. "We'll figure it out together." I place a soft kiss to her forehead and another one on her plump, pouty lips. "I promise."

We grab Reed's stroller and car seat and let the valet grab our bags. After checking in, Olivia insists we bring Reed down to the beach. I've rented a cabana on the beach and by the pool for the entire two weeks, so after getting changed into our swimsuits—thanks to the hired personal shopper who did some last-minute shopping—we make our way down to the beach.

"This place is beautiful, Nick." She plops down onto one of the lounge chairs under the cabana and lays out a blanket for Reed. I hand him over to her, and she lays him down against her stomach so he's able use her like his own personal lounge chair. The waitress comes over, and we order some drinks and food.

We drink, eat, and watch the waves hit the shoreline the entire afternoon all the way through the sunset. Reed naps occasionally on a blanket, on the lounge chair, or in one of our arms. It's relaxing and exactly what we needed. Eventually, we make our way up to the room, and after settling Reed down for bed, settle into bed ourselves. And this repeats every day for a week until Giselle and Killian arrive.

Twenty-Nine

NICK

"This is so cool!" Olivia removes her snorkel and mask from her face and finds me. "Did you see all the fish?! The one that looks like Nemo! And the shark looking one!"

Giselle and Killian are keeping an eye on Reed this morning while I take Olivia out. Last week, we stuck to the beach, the art museums, and finding the local marketplaces—all things we can enjoy with a baby in tow. We spent a lot of time talking and getting to know each other. This week, we're taking advantage of having help with Reed, and exploring the outdoors. We had surf lessons yesterday, and today we're doing some snorkeling off a private island we took a yacht over to. It's just the two of us here on this beach. Tonight, the four of us—and Reed—will be attending a dinner and show. And tomorrow, as a surprise, I've booked a day spa for Olivia and Giselle.

"It's cool as hell. I've never seen water so clear before."

We wade through the water until we're back on shore. Setting our gear down, we both grab a towel to dry off before taking a sip of our waters. There's usually staff down here to wait on people, but I requested for them to stay at the restaurant, and if we need anything we'll come up.

I sit down on the beach chair, and when I look up I see Olivia is right above me. She straddles my lap, a sexy leg on either side of me, and her hands come up to my cheeks. "I love when you don't shave," she says with a smile.

"Oh yeah, and why is that? Because when I don't shave I look closer to your age?" I joke, and she shakes her head.

"No." Her hands move up and down the sides of my face along my stubble. "Because when you go down on me your hair tickles the insides of my thighs." She blushes pink, and I laugh. Then I imagine my face buried between her thighs, and I groan, my dick enjoying the visual as well.

Her eyes widen slightly when she feels my bulge pushing through my board shorts. "Are we...completely alone here?" She glances around. Even if we weren't alone, the cabana we're in blocks anyone from seeing inside unless they're standing directly in front of us.

"Yep."

"So if I wanted to pull your shorts down right here and ride you, I could?" Her eyes are hooded with lust.

"Fuck yes, you could, and I fully encourage it."

Olivia backs up slightly, her ass coming off me long enough so I can pull my shorts down. My dick bobs between us, but I'm only semi-hard. When she looks down at it, she frowns for a second before she gets a mischievous glint in her eyes. She lifts each of her legs up as she pushes her bikini bottoms off her, exposing her delicious cunt. Then she pushes the triangles, which cover her tits, to the side.

My dick is getting harder by the second. My mouth goes to her perky tit, and my lips wrap around her pert pink nipple. My hand goes to her other tit as I massage it. Olivia lets out a moan, the outside of her pussy grinding against my shaft. Her back arches slightly as I suck on each of her nipples.

"Jesus, Nick. I want you inside of me," she groans. My lips move upward as I trail kisses along her breasts and neck. She grinds harder, and I can feel the wetness from her pussy against my dick.

"Are you wet enough?" I ask. She nods, but I don't take her word for it. Instead, I push two fingers into her. She wiggles her ass, needing more, and lets out a growl when it's not enough.

I swallow her frustration with a kiss to her lips. It's filled with lust and want. She quickly attacks my mouth with fervor I've yet to see. Her thighs clench on either side of me as I continue to fingerfuck her, her pussy grinding down on my fingers.

"Please," she begs. I pull my fingers out of her wet and ready cunt, and within seconds she's guiding herself onto my dick. When I'm all the way inside her, my head goes back, hitting the back of the chair. It's never felt as good with any other woman as it does with Olivia. I know that sounds fuckin' nuts. Like she has some special pussy that's unlike any other woman's. But it's the truth. Every time I'm with her, I feel it. I don't think it's her pussy per se—although, it really is a great fucking pussy. It's the connection we share.

When I'm with her, it's more than just sex. It's every-fucking-thing.

She begins to move up and down—her arms wrapping around my neck, her fingers threading through my hair. She pushes her tits into my face as she comes almost completely off my dick before grinding back down and taking me all the way back inside her.

"Suck on my tits," she moans, and I about come right here on the spot. I love when Olivia lets loose, when she turns into a sex-crazed wanton woman. My lips suck on her nipple, and I bite down hard. She moans loudly, picking up speed. My fingers make their way between us, landing on her soaked pussy. I gather up her juices then circle my arm around her back side, pushing a finger into her tight hole.

"Oh my God," she screams as she picks up the pace, her ass bouncing up and down on my dick, her juices dripping down my balls. I'm mesmerized by the way she moves on top of me. Rolling and shifting her hips in such a way that has me ready to come. I continue to suck her nipple and finger her tight hole as she rides me harder and faster. When I feel her getting close, her walls tightening like a goddamn vice grip around my shaft, I glide my lips to her neck, sucking on the sensitive flesh. Olivia moves forward slightly, her pussy grinding me, her clit getting the friction it needs to get her off.

"Nick…holy shit…I'm. Going. To. Come." I push my finger a bit farther into her ass, and she loses it. Her movements turn desperate, her clit grinds harder, her cunt begins to pulse around my dick, and then she's coming all over my dick and balls. I pull my finger out and grip her hips, taking over. Her head is thrown back in pure ecstasy as I push her down, bottoming the fuck out in her tightness as I come inside her.

We both come down from our highs, and she looks at me with tears in her eyes. "What's wrong? Did I hurt you?" I've used my finger in her ass before, so I can't imagine it hurt, but you never know...

"Nothing's wrong." She begins to sob. "Everything is perfect. I-I love you, Nick."

"I love you too, Brown-Eyes, so goddamn much."

Thirty

NICK

It's the last day of our trip, and we're packing to go home. It's an eleven-hour flight, so we're getting everything ready to take on the plane for Reed so it goes as smoothly on the way back as it did coming here. The bellman knocks on the door, and we head out. We stack all of our luggage on the cart then make our way down to the valet.

Once we're seated on the plane, and Reed is sleeping in his portable crib, Olivia comes over and sits next to me. "Thank you for this, Nick." She gives me a kiss on my cheek. "I had a really good time." She wraps her arms around my neck. "I love you."

"I love you, too."

I don't think I'll ever get tired of hearing those words from her. The night we got back to the hotel, after she told me she loved me, I made love to her several times, demanding each time she tell me again. She thought I was joking at first, but once she realized I was serious, she complied, screaming and moaning the words every time I made her come.

We have less than an hour left of our flight, and Olivia is playing with Reed on a blanket she has spread out on the floor. Killian and Giselle are sitting next to each other, looking at Killian's iPad. I told them no cell phones allowed on the trip, so of course he found a loophole and brought his iPad.

"Everything okay?" I ask when I notice they're talking in a hushed whisper. Just the fact they're sitting next to each other without killing one another should be a red flag. Giselle looks up at me and glares, and Killian gives me a wounded look.

"Damn, man…you could've at least told me," Killian says, and I'm confused as hell.

"Told you what?"

He throws the iPad into my lap, and when I read the headline, my heart stops.

Nick Shaw signs five-year contract with Los Angeles

I scroll down and read the story. It says I signed the contract a couple weeks ago and will be their starting QB.

"This doesn't make any sense." I click out of the article and google my name. Article after article all say the same thing.

"You're saying you didn't sign with LA?" Killian asks, and I see Olivia's head pop up out of the corner of my eye.

"You signed with LA?" she asks, hurt evident in every word.

"No." I shake my head. "This doesn't make sense."

"They can't just print something like that if it's not true, Nick," Giselle points out. And she's right. There's no way LA would announce something false, nor would ESPN.

I go to call my dad but remember I don't have my cell phone and we're thousands of feet in the air. "I didn't sign with them," I state again. Olivia gives me a sad look but doesn't argue.

We land and head to our vehicles. After we get all the luggage put into our trunks, Killian comes over to me and says, "Listen, if going to LA is what's best for your career…"

"I didn't sign with them," I say. "And if I had, I would've told you."

He sighs but nods his head in acceptance. "Okay, let me know if you need anything." We bump fists and take off in our own vehicles.

The entire drive to Olivia and Giselle's place is done in silence. I don't know what to say or do, and I know I need to first figure out what the hell happened before I attempt to say anything. When we arrive at their place, I help the women get all their luggage and Reed's stuff inside. "I need to go speak to my dad," I tell Olivia. "I'll call you as soon as I know what's going on." She nods, and I give her a kiss. "I love you." She nods again, and it doesn't go unnoticed that she doesn't say it back.

I get back to my place and grab my cell phone, powering it on. A million texts and missed calls come through. I ignore them all and call my *agent*.

"Son," my dad says when he answers on the first ring.

"Don't fucking 'Son' me," I growl. "What the fuck did you do?"

"Why don't we meet to discuss this in person?"

"Are you in town?" Because his cliental has increased in New York, he's expanded his company here and has purchased some office space in the Financial District. He said he's only planning to stay here long enough to make sure everything is in order, then he and my mom will be going back to North Carolina. That day can't come soon enough.

"Yes, I'm at my office. They completed the renovations last week."

Twenty minutes later, I'm standing in his office. "I didn't sign a contract with Los Angeles" are the first words out of my mouth. My dad is sitting in his chair, typing away on his laptop. He takes his time before looking up at me.

"Actually, you did." He pushes some paperwork at me, and I grab them off his desk. My eyes scan the documents. It's a contract between LA and me, and sure enough, on several of the pages is my signature.

"What the fuck did you do?" I throw the papers back at him.

"I did what was in your best interest."

"When the fuck did I sign these? You never said a word to me!" I boom.

"Right before your trip to Hawaii."

My mind goes back to our brief visit before I left.

"Any news about New York?" I ask, sitting down on the couch with Reed in my arms. Olivia had a doctor's appointment, so I offered to keep Reed with me so she could go by herself.

"That's not why I'm here. I need your signature on a couple of papers…endorsement contracts and such. I'll make it quick so you can get back to your son." My dad hands me the documents as Reed starts squirming and getting fussy. He's due to be fed, so he's cranky. I grab the pen and flip through each page quickly, signing and initialing where the yellow arrow sticky notes point to sign.

Once I'm done, he snatches the papers off the coffee table. "Enjoy your trip. We'll discuss your contract when you get back."

"Holy shit, you had me sign a fucking contract with LA without my knowledge. You realize I'm going to fight you on this, right? And after I win, I'm going to destroy any credibility you have. Fuck, if I have to, I'll go after your license."

"Did you not read the contract? Five years, one hundred and sixty million dollars. As your agent, and your father, I did what was best for you. I wasn't going to let you throw away your future for that woman!"

"I don't give a fuck how much it's for! You went behind my back! You didn't do what was best for me. You did what was best for you." I slam my fist down on the desk. Then it hits me. "Did New York not want to re-sign me?"

"Not for what you're worth."

"But they would've signed me," I clarify.

"For fucking pennies!"

"You're going to fix this, or I'm going to sue you."

My dad stands. "You're thinking like a pussy-whipped

285

fool!" He leans over his desk, challenging me. "If Olivia wants to be with you, she'll move to California. You're not going to stay in New York to make her dad happy and get paid half. That's ludicrous!"

"It's my choice to make!"

"You're making the wrong choice. Choosing love over money will get you nowhere fast."

Realizing nothing I say to this man will change his money-hungry mindset, I stalk toward the door. "I'm giving you an hour to fix this shit and then I'm coming after you." I slam the door behind me and head to the elevator. Once I'm to my car, I call Olivia, but her phone goes to voicemail. I try again, but it does it again.

Next, I try her dad.

"Nick," he says when he answers.

"I need to talk to you about my contract."

"Son, you know we can't discuss this." *Fuck!*

"Okay, can you at least tell me if you've spoken to Olivia? I can't get a hold of her."

He's silent for a second, and my heart starts racing, the hand holding my cell phone getting sweaty. "Stephen, where is she?" There's no way she would've taken our son away from me. "She didn't go to Paris, did she?"

"No! No," he says, finally speaking. "I think she's headed to our place in the Hamptons. She said she needs some time."

Fuck that! She's not getting any time. "Stephen, in those fairytales, I highly doubt when the princess runs, the prince sits back and gives her time."

Stephen chuckles softly. "That's probably true." Just as

I'm about to say goodbye, he adds, "Like I told you before, Nick, regardless of what happens in this business, you're part of our family. That will never change. I don't know what happened, but I'm always here if you need a friend...or some fatherly advice."

"Thank you."

I hang up and turn my car toward 27-W toward the Hamptons when my phone rings. Olivia's name pops up on Bluetooth.

"Liv," I answer.

"Hey, can you come over? We need to talk."

Thirty-One

OLIVIA

One hour ago

Nick drops me off and the first thing I do is call my father. When he answers, I breakdown. "Is it true? Did he sign with Los Angeles?"

"He did, sweetheart. He didn't tell you?"

"No! He didn't say a word." I start to gather Reed's clothes, throwing them into a small suitcase. "I asked him so many times and he said we would figure it out together." I shove diapers and a container of wipes into a bag.

"We just don't have the money they have. We offered what we could, but it was still only half of what LA could offer him."

My body freezes in place. "This is about money? Are you serious?" A lump lodges in my throat. "One of his biggest concerns was that everyone around him was money hungry, and in the end, he chose money over his son and me?"

"You don't know that. He could want you to join him." My dad, always the optimist, always seeing the best in everybody.

"Then he should've asked before he signed the contract."

"Do you want me to come over?" my dad asks, concerned.

"No, I'm leaving." There's silence over the phone.

"You're not going back to Paris, are you? Because I would really miss you and my grandson. I feel like I just got you back."

"No, I'm not going to Paris. Probably just to the Hamptons. I'll call you once I'm on the road."

"Okay, sweetie. I love you."

"Love you too, Dad."

Just as I'm ending the phone call, Giselle comes down the hall. "Reed's asleep." She assesses the situation in front of her. "Where are you going?"

"To our place in the Hamptons."

"Wow! You're running again?" She snatches the luggage and throws it to the side. It hits the floor with a thud. Giselle has never been mad at me before, never raised her voice with me, so her actions have me frozen in place.

"What do you mean, *again*?"

Giselle scoffs. "You ran to Paris when your mom died. Then you ran home when Victor dumped you. *Then*, you ran home again when you found out you were pregnant. And two out of three of those times I ran with you. Well, I can't run, Livi." Tears threaten to spill from her lids, but Giselle is too strong to let that happen.

"I can't run anymore. It's not that I don't want to…but I *can't*. And if you stop for one damn second and think about this, you don't really want to run either. It's just what you're used to doing, and up until now, you've never had a good enough reason to stay because everything you were running from you had already lost. Your mom died. Victor broke things off. We graduated. But now—"

"Now I have Nick," I finish her sentence for me. She's right. I always run. I want the fairytale, but I never fight for it. I want the happily-ever-after without wanting to work for it. I don't know what is going to happen with Nick or what's going through his head, but instead of running, I need to face this head on because he's worth fighting for. I ran when I felt like my life was out of my control, but now it's time to stay and fight. Then it hits me…

"Giselle…what if in order to be with him, it means having to move to California?" She knows what I'm asking. *Does this mean I'll be living across the country from my best friend?*

Fresh tears brim over as she opens her mouth to speak, but no words come out. Then she closes her eyes for several beats before opening them back up. "Then I'll come and visit you and Reed every chance I get." My heart tightens. I can't imagine my life without Giselle in it. I shake my head, not liking her answer.

"Livi…" Her tears fall like a waterfall down her cheeks. "My mom…she's not doing so well, and I don't know how to help her. And now with my dad gone and my sister away at college, I have to stay here."

I hug my best friend. "I'm so sorry. I completely

understand."

"Thank you. I probably shouldn't have left to Hawaii, but I just needed a breather from it all, to escape from reality for a few days, and since my sister was off of school for spring break, she offered to keep an eye on our mom, so I could go."

"I hate that you're going through this. What can I do?"

"You can go figure out what's going on with you and Nick. One of us deserves a goddamned fairytale ending." She laughs softly, trying to play off the seriousness of what she just told me about her mom. "Go! Go call him." She stands and grabs her keys. "I have a couple errands to run, but I'll be back later."

Before she makes it out the door, she says, "Oh! By the way, this came for you." She hands me a large envelope.

"Thanks." I open it and inside is all the information I requested from the accountant who handles Nick's charity, Touchdown for Reading. Apparently, the original accountant retired, and Nick recently hired someone new. When we spoke, I asked him to go through and let me know how active the charity has been these last few years, so I know where to begin. I pull the papers out of the envelope and a note falls out.

You might want to check the charges I highlighted.

I flip through until I find the highlighted amounts. I read over them several times. This can't be right. There's no way...

My intercom buzzes, so I put the papers down. "Hello."

"It's Victoria."

"Okay, I'll buzz you up."

Knowing it will take a minute for the elevator to make its way up to my floor, I call Nick.

"Liv," he says when he picks up.

"Hey, can you come over? We need to talk."

"I'm on my way now. I should be there in two hours."

Two hours?

"Where are you?"

He pauses for a second. "Where are you?"

"Home...where else would I be?"

"Your dad said you were going to the Hamptons. I was on my way there." *Oh no!*

"I was going to, but Giselle talked some sense into me."

"I'll be there in a few minutes."

"Okay, good, because your mom is on her way up."

I end the call just as Victoria knocks on my door.

"Victoria, come in."

"Thank you." She steps into my home, and I close the door behind us. "Well, this is a beautiful home you have here," she says, her gaze darting around my living room.

"Thank you. Would you like something to drink?" I ask, trying to be polite, but also wanting to stall so Nick has time to get here.

"No, thank you. I won't be here long."

"Well, I'm thirsty," I tell her. "Feel free to get comfortable while I grab a drink. You sure you don't want anything?"

"I'm sure," she snaps, losing a bit of her patience.

While in the kitchen, I read through the documents

once more just to make sure what I'm looking at is correct. Unfortunately, it is.

After grabbing a bottle of water, I head back out to the living room to find Victoria is still standing where I left her, texting on her cell phone. When she hears me enter, she puts her phone away and looks up.

"So, to what do I owe this pleasure?" I ask.

"I'll cut right to the chase," she says. "Convince Nicholas to keep his contract with LA, and I will make sure you're taken care of."

"Excuse me?"

"This home you're living in runs roughly three million dollars. If you want to continue to live a life of luxury, convince Nicholas to keep the contract with LA. I'll make sure your home is paid off, and on top of whatever child support he's agreed to pay, I'll double it so you're living more than comfortably."

I stare at this woman for several seconds. I can't believe she raised Nick. But then I remember, she didn't. His nanny did.

"You are really something else—" But before I can say anything more, there's a knock on my door. I open it, and Nick saunters in.

"You're just in time. Your mom was just offering to pay off my home." I laugh humorlessly. "Which by the way"—I turn back toward Victoria—"is actually worth four-point-two million. You underpriced it. If you're going to be so generous and offer to pay off someone's loan, you should at least look it up, so you know how much to offer."

Her eyes are wide as saucers as she looks between Nick

and me, knowing she's been caught.

"You know how I know that? I own it," I tell her. "And if you did your research, you would know that too."

"You offered to pay her off like you did to Fiona?" Nick eyes his mother incredulously. "What the hell is wrong with you? First of all, Olivia is worth millions more than I am!" His mom gasps in shock. "And second of all, didn't you learn your lesson from paying off Fiona?"

"Oh, it gets better...or I should say worse." I grab the papers from the table and hand them to Nick. "Your mom not only used your charity to pay off Fiona, but she's been siphoning money from the account to pay your parents' bills."

"I was going to put it all back!" she screeches. "Mind your own business!"

"What the fuck." Nick takes the papers from me and scans through them.

"I contacted the accountant directly when Victoria refused to let me have access to anything. I thought something might be up when you mentioned she pushed you away from being actively involved. Since you gave him the go ahead, he sent these over to me. She paid off Fiona through the charity funds, and she's been using the funds to pay several of their bills, including their mortgage and car payments, claiming them as business expenses directly related to your charity."

"Nicholas," his mom pleads. "A few of the investments your father made didn't pan out. We were upside down and just needed a little bit of help to get through. With your new contract, we'll be able to pay you back."

"I'm done." Nick throws the papers onto the table. "You and dad are dead to me. I've already told him he's going to fix my contract or I'll sue him. Get out of this house and out of my life."

"You don't mean that!" Victoria cries.

"Yeah, I do. You are so far gone, there's no saving you. You aren't my family, and you have no idea what it means to love someone. Now get out." He swings the door open.

With tears streaming down her face, Victoria walks out. Once she's gone, Nick closes the door and comes over to me. He pulls me into him, his arms enveloping me. "Thank you for not running, Liv," he murmurs into my ear.

We have a seat on the sofa, and Nick takes my hands in his. "Remember when Celeste was at my place and I told you that was the part of the book where the evil witch had to be beaten?"

I try to hide my smile, but I can't contain it. He's just too fucking adorable. "Yes."

"I guess it was actually my mom who was the evil witch. Talk about a plot twist."

"I'm sorry, Nick." I know he's trying to turn this into a joke, but it's only because he's attempting to cover his hurt.

"It's her loss. I never really had a mom to begin with. Unfortunately, though, this part of the story isn't over yet. We still need to defeat the villain…like in Sleeping Beauty."

"What happened?"

"Apparently, my mom wasn't the only one fucking me over. My dad came by to see me before we took off on vacation and had me sign some papers. I didn't look at them. I was busy with Reed, and I trusted him. Turns out he was having me sign a contract to play for Los Angeles for five years."

My hands come up to my mouth. "Oh my God. You didn't know?" That's what his mom meant by convincing Nick to keep the contract as-is.

"Nope." He shakes his head. "New York could only offer me half of what LA was offering, and my dad knew I would choose New York, which would mean less money in his pocket. He's so money hungry, Liv. It's insane. He can't see anything besides the potential dollar bills in his pockets. But now it makes sense. If they spent too much money, they needed the percentage my contract would bring in to pull them back up."

"How much was the offer for?"

"One hundred and sixty million."

"Damn, that's a lot of money."

"I don't give a fuck about the money. I meant it when I said we're in this together. I'm not going anywhere without you." His lips meet mine for a kiss, but before it can go any further, his cell phone rings. "Speak of the villain." He answers the phone. I try to move off him, but his fingers grip my hips, silently telling me not to go anywhere.

"Dad, I'm assuming you're calling to tell me you fixed the mix-up." He pauses for a long moment while he listens to whatever his dad is saying. "That's good for you, since you're going to need to keep your license to make more money to get yourself out of the hole you created. All the money Mom stole from me, you two will be repaying."

I don't hear what his dad says on the other line, but Nick shakes his head. "You know, Dad, you spent so much time chasing all the wrong things in life: money, respect, success. And while you were so busy chasing those things, you didn't even realize you were leaving your son behind. I kept chasing you, trying to catch up, but you never once stopped for me. So, now you have not only lost all of your money, but you've lost me, and let's be real, you barely even have mom now that you're broke. I hope it was all worth it. The one thing I've learned is all of those things you were chasing aren't worth a damn if you don't have anyone to share them with. Good luck in life, *Dad*."

He ends the phone call and drops it onto the couch cushion, his head falling against my chest. My fingers run through his hair while I wait for him to gather himself together. I can't even imagine what's going through his head right now. He's disowned both of his parents in a matter of minutes.

"He got me out of the contract. I'm a free agent. LA said the offer is still on the table, though, if I want it. I have twenty-four hours to decide what I want to do, but there are a few other teams who have made offers as well."

"And what is it you want to do?"

"I need to know something…before we go any further." He moves me off his lap and sets me on the sofa next to him. Then he pulls something out of his pocket…a box…a ring box! He kneels in front of me on the floor, his bright green eyes sparkling as he smiles nervously up at me. "If I have to move, whether it's to California or Texas or…I don't know…Florida. Will you go with me? Will you continue writing this book with me as my wife? Because Liv, I'm not ready for our story to end yet. Olivia Harper, will you marry me and keep our story going no matter where it takes us?"

He opens the box, which holds a beautiful diamond ring, and his eyes lock with mine as he waits for my answer. My brain tries to think logically—rationally—weighing the pros and cons to determine the right decision. But my heart speaks louder, winning over. The fact is I would follow this man anywhere he goes because I love him. He's buried himself deep into the valves of my heart, and it can't beat without him. He makes me want to fight.

"My happily-ever-after is wherever you are. If it means we move then Reed and I will be right there beside you. Yes, I'll marry you." I throw myself into his arms, and he kisses me hard.

Then he pulls back and puts the ring on my finger. "Good because we're moving to Montana."

"Montana?" I question. "They don't even have a football team."

Nick's shoulders shake with laughter. "I'm glad you know your football. I'm just kidding. We're staying right here in New York. But I should warn you…money is going to be a bit tight. New York could only do a five year, eighty-million-dollar contract."

I sigh. "However will we live off that? It's a good thing your soon-to-be wife is loaded. Don't worry, baby, I'll be your sugar mama." I give him an over exaggerated wink, and he throws his head back in laughter.

"I've never had a sugar mama before. What do I have to do in return?" Nick pulls me down onto the floor with him, my legs straddling his lap.

"In return?"

"You know…in exchange for you taking care of me. What do you want?" His lips move to my neck, and I tilt my head slightly to give him access.

"Hmm…sex. Whenever I want."

"Mmm…I like the sound of that." He continues kissing upward, landing on the sensitive flesh behind my ear. "What else?"

"I want a house. A big one with at least five bedrooms."

"Oh, really? Do we get to fill this bigger house with more babies?"

"Umm…" I try to focus, but his lips wrap around my earlobe, and it's hard to think. "Yes," I moan out. "Yes, more babies."

"What else?" he asks, his tongue circling the inner part of my ear, eliciting a chill down my spine. "What else do you want, Liv?"

"I want to get married soon and for the three of us to have the same last name." Nick stops his assault on my body momentarily and looks at me.

"That can definitely be arranged." His lips touch mine, and his tongue sweeps into my mouth before he pulls back. "What else?"

"I don't know. I can't think with your mouth all over me." He chuckles. "Let's just start with number one. Sex now."

"Sounds good to me." Nick picks me up and carries me to the bedroom where he proceeds to make good on my first demand of being his sugar mama.

Epilogue

NICK

One Year Later

"Do you realize how this looks?" Olivia laughs as we look down at the home pregnancy test.

I know where she's going with this, but it's her own fault. I've brought up getting married several times, but she keeps saying, "Soon." Right after I proposed, she accepted a job at the local art museum as an Art Educator Coordinator. She organizes and teaches art classes to children a couple days a week. Between her working part-time, my playing football, and us raising our now one-year-old son, we haven't done anything we said we were going to do…well, except for the have sex part. So now here we are. Expecting our second baby and still not husband and wife, and still living in separate places.

"Like there are two lines indicating I got my fiancée pregnant?" I answer her question jokingly, earning me a slap to my chest.

"No! Like you keep knocking me up out of wedlock!" She giggles and throws the test into the trash.

"It's not my fault my super sperm overpowers any birth control."

She snorts, rolling her eyes. "Now we really do need to get married…and buy a house!"

I chuckle because she's said this too many times to count. I've finally gotten her to agree on a date to get married. Now we just need to buy a home. "Whatever you want, my beautiful brown-eyed girl." I pull her into my embrace. We're standing in the bathroom, and Reed is sleeping. "But right now, I think we need to shower together." She nods emphatically, liking my idea, so I turn the water on to hot.

We both undress at the same time, our clothes flying to the floor. I open the shower door then shut it behind us. We're at her place, and the shower has an extremely convenient bench running along the back. Sitting down on the bench, Olivia straddles my lap, her warm cunt rubbing friction against my semi-hard cock. Her lips press against mine and her tongue pushes through. Her hands entwine in my hair as she moans into my mouth.

"I need you inside me," she pleads. She rains kisses all over my face then moves to my neck, sucking on my flesh. She lifts slightly, and I guide my dick into her until she's filled completely.

"Oh God, Nick." She doesn't move for a second, her body adjusting to my size. Then slowly, she begins to rock her hips up and down and side to side. The feeling of being inside my woman, this closeness we share, is fucking unbelievable. Her ass moves as she rides me faster and faster, taking what she wants—what she needs—from me.

I bend my head to snag a nipple between my teeth, and she thrashes against me. "Oh shit! They're so sensitive." I still, afraid I've hurt her. "Don't stop!" she commands, her voice wild, out of control. I bring her nipple back up to my lips, licking and sucking on it before giving the other one equal attention.

My other hand rests on her ass, making sure she doesn't fall as she continues to ride me, bouncing up and down on my cock. Her clit is rubbing against my front. I feel her muscles tighten and know she's close but not quite there.

Lifting her off me, I turn us around. "Hands against the wall, now," I demand. Her delicate hands slap the wall and her ass juts out on display. I separate her thighs and watch the water drip down her perfect round ass. I give it a good slap, and she lets out a soft moan, her ass squirming with need. She turns her head slightly, about to say something, but before she can say a word, I grip her hips and thrust into her from behind.

She lets out a loud groan as her head falls forward. Gripping her hip with one hand, I pump into her over and over again. My other hand skirting around to her clit, massaging the swollen nub as Olivia meets me thrust for thrust.

"Oh God! Harder, please." I've never seen her this starved for sex, this needy, but her every wish is my command. My fingers dig harder, holding onto her tighter as I move in and out of her tight pussy—my fingers stroking her clit simultaneously. She's so close I can feel her tight cunt squeezing around my cock.

"Come on, baby. Come for me."

She's panting and moaning. I press my thumb down harder on her clit as I push into her from behind, hitting her G-spot over and over again, building her up until she can't take it anymore. And then she's falling. Her body trembles. Her legs shake. She whimpers loudly as she comes all over my cock. My orgasm follows right behind. I pull out of her, and she releases a shiver.

"Come here." I pull her into me, so she's under the hot water. "What was that?"

She smiles sheepishly. "I think that was a very horny pregnant woman."

Extended Epilogue

OLIVIA

I'm sitting at the table feeding Reed some sweet potatoes and fish when Giselle makes her presence known, slamming the door behind her. She's been acting strange lately, and she won't talk to me about anything. I know she has a lot going on, but she won't let me in, and as her best friend, it hurts my heart.

"That motherfucker!"

"Who?" I ask, feeding Reed another bite.

She notices Reed is now staring at her. "Shit...I mean, shoot! I didn't mean to curse." She gives Reed a kiss on the top of his head. "Hey, handsome."

"Who were you cursing about?" I ask again.

"It doesn't even matter. I was just having a bad moment." She shrugs. Her phone dings, and she glances down at it. "I need to get going. I just came home to change."

"Another date?" I ask, concerned. Ever since Giselle found out Christian cheated on her and broke things off with him, she's gone from zero to one hundred. Whereas before Christian, she rarely dated at all, post-Christian, she's going on dates several nights a week, none of which she ever brings home or introduces me to. And the weirdest date of all was when she showed up with Killian to our charity fundraiser we hosted to announce the expansion of Touchdown for Reading, which is now Touchdown for Reading and the Arts.

"Yep!" She doesn't say anything else before she disappears into her room.

Reed slams his hand down wanting another bite, and I turn my attention back to him. A few minutes later, I hear Nick come in from outside on the terrace. "Hey, babe." He presses a kiss to my temple. "There's something you need to know about Giselle."

My hand freezes in place. "Okay."

"Killian said he paid—"

"Don't you dare finish that sentence!" Giselle yells, cutting him off just as Killian walks through the front door. "This is none of your business." She glares from Nick to Killian.

"Somebody tell me what's going on, please," I demand.

"Either you tell her, or I will," Killian threatens.

"I hate you!" Giselle shouts, and I notice tears are now streaming down her face.

"No, you don't, but if you continue this you're going to hate yourself," Killian says to her.

305

"I already do," she whispers before she runs out, slamming the door behind her.

Other Books by Nikki Ash

The Fighting Series
Fighting for a Second Chance
Fighting with Faith
Fighting for Your Touch
Fighting for Your Love
Fighting 'round the Christmas Tree: A Fighting Series
Novella

Fighting Love novels
Tapping Out
Clinched
Takedown

Imperfect Love series
The Pickup

Stand-alone Novels
Bordello
Knocked Down
Unbroken Promises
Heath

Acknowledgements

First and foremost, I want to thank my readers! It's been two years since I've released my first book and if it wasn't for your reading and loving my books, I wouldn't be writing this acknowledgment. It's because of you I can continue to create and write stories for you to read. So, thank you! To the bloggers who sign up and share my covers, sales, teasers, and releases. Thank you! It means so much to me. To my beta readers, editors, proofreaders, and book friends, thank you! Stacy, Nicole, Brittany, Andrea, Ashley, Tabitha, Lisa, Kristi, and anyone else I forgot. You guys make a lonely job less lonely. Thank you for welcoming me into your lives and reading and loving my books like they're your own. Juliana, every cover, if possible, gets even more beautiful. Thank you for treating my book babies like they're your own. Fight Club members, you guys are everything! Every post, comment, like, and share. You guys are amazing. Ena and Amanda with Enticing Journey, thank you for keeping everything organized so I can simply focusing on writing. To my children, I love you both so much. You are my inspiration in everything I do.

About the Author

Nikki Ash resides in South Florida where she is an English teacher and writer by day and a writer by night. When she's not writing, you can find her with a book in her hand. From the Boxcar Children to Wuthering Heights to latest single parent romance, she has lived and breathed every type of book. While reading and writing are her passions, her two children are her entire world. You can probably find them at a Disney park before you would find them at home on the weekends!

Reading is like breathing in, writing is like breathing out.– Pam Allyn

To stay in touch, join The Fight Club:
www.facebook.com/groups/BooksByNikkiAsh

Printed in Great Britain
by Amazon

79087700R00180